T0065253

Also by Jon Howard Hall

Noccalula: Cherokee Princess of Alabama
A Short Story (available only as an eBook)

Kyzer's Destiny

Kyzer's Promise

Corporal Archer and the Siege of Vicksburg

A PLACE CALLED
WINSTON

A NOVEL OF HISTORICAL FICTION

Jon Howard Hall

A PLACE CALLED WINSTON
A NOVEL OF HISTORICAL FICTION

iUniverse books may be ordered through booksellers or by contacting:

iUniverse
1663 Liberty Drive
Bloomington, IN 47403
www.iuniverse.com
844-349-9409

ISBN: 978-1-6632-2715-7 (sc)
ISBN: 978-1-6632-2714-0 (hc)
ISBN: 978-1-6632-2738-6 (e)

Library of Congress Control Number: 2021916413

Print information available on the last page.

iUniverse rev. date: 08/19/2021

For the grandchildren
Trey, Braxton, Lydia, Austin, Anna

A PLACE CALLED
WINSTON

Fade in …

Winston County, Alabama
Looney's Tavern
4 July 1861

"Ho! Ho! Winston secedes – the free state of Winston," yelled Richard "Uncle Dick" Payne to the nearly two thousand Alabamians who were gathered in and around the overflowing local tavern that day. Bill Looney, the proprietor, was speechless.

Heads were shaking, fists were pounding, arms were waving, and tempers flaring while the widely controversial meeting was drawing to a close. Several southern states had already seceded from the Union over the main issue of slavery. Many people were saying that if a state had the audacity to do this, why couldn't a county secede from the state?

Two opposing men stood at the bar in a face-off as the outraged gentleman's wife pulled and tugged at his sleeve to leave while the equally upset young Confederate clenched his fist in anger.

"Each and every citizen of this state has a right to his opinion about the issue of slavery while we forge ahead into a civil war," said the Union sympathizer.

"Yes they do, sir, and I whole heartedly agree, but opinions are like arseholes. Everybody's got one!"

"So, you don't believe a state has that right?"

"What do you think?"

Fade out …

CHAPTER 1

Lightning flashed the midnight sky with a burst of white-hot color while its overall effect lit up the night like last year's 4th of July fireworks. A severe thunderstorm continued to pour down after bedtime while heavy rain and wind gusts pelted relentlessly upon the little cabin in Double Springs, located in Winston County, Alabama.

Libby could hardly stand it any longer when that last thunderbolt shook the room and suddenly awakened her in the dead of night. Boom! She immediately sat upright in their warm cozy feather bed. Her sleeping husband Cole, married to her almost six months now, never stirred, never moved. She listened with a hushed stillness for a moment in the darkness while she detected the sound of water dripping through the tin roof of their little cabin. *Drip...drip... drip...*

After lighting the kerosene lamp on the night stand, she reached for the lamp and tumbled out of bed. Her feet immediately felt the coldness from the bare heart pine floor after she neglected to put on her slippers. Libby, stumbling slightly in the dark, made her way to the center of the room and held the lamp outstretched as high as she could reach. Looking upward, she saw the two places on the ceiling where the water was now pouring down as it splattered onto the floor. She grabbed a pail and the slop jar, and positioned them on the wet floor to catch the water. This would have to do until morning.

Libby settled back into bed while she snuggled against her husband's warm body. The sensuous touch from her cold hand as it pressed upon his belly instantly sprung new life into his waking manhood. Her fear of the storm subsided momentarily while Cole's sudden reaction eased her anxiety with his firm and reliable gentle thrust.

Elizabeth Anne, affectionately called "Libby," was the beautiful twenty-year old, dark-haired daughter of farmer James Samuel Parker and his wife Amelia. The Parker family roots went as far back as the Revolutionary War when they left Virginia and settled in Winston County. James Parker ran a small dairy farm in Double Springs.

The summer Libby returned home from boarding school in Florence, her father had hired her future husband to work on the farm. It didn't take long for the handsome young man to discover this most enchanting farmer's daughter.

Cole Alexander "Mule" McTavish, after the first sighting of her, knew that Miss Libby Parker would one day become his wife. Libby would later admit that at the time, she felt the same. Cole was a strapping young lad of twenty-four, tanned and muscular, over six feet tall. He had medium length brown hair and blue eyes. His cheek would produce a tiny dimple on the left side whenever he broke into a full smile. Those penetrating blue eyes were like sapphires and were at first thought by Libby to be his best feature. After her wedding night, the new Mrs. Cole Alexander McTavish would definitely have to change her mind. According to her best friend, Greta Hassendorfer relished any opportunity to spread the least bit of gossip to many of the ladies in town.

It seems one evening after a few too many brandy cordials at a party, Libby had confessed to Greta, in the strictness of confidence, that in fact, her husband Cole was "hung like a mule" and had caused her tremendous pain on their wedding night. Besides that, it nearly "scared me to death," she admitted after the sight of seeing a man's naked body for the first time. However, it only took a few more times and Libby eagerly looked forward to their frequent times of intimacy. At last, she knew why Cole's buddies always called him "Mule."

Cole's family ancestry was originally from Dumfrieshire, Scotland, the home of his paternal grandparents. His parents had immigrated to America after the birth of his sister Rosie and settled in North Carolina in 1830. Later on, the McTavish Clan moved to Winston County where his father, Malcolm, found work as a bricklayer. Three months later, following hours of intense labor by his mother, Colleen, Cole was born in the little town of Lynn in 1837.

Cole grew into his teens almost like an only child since his sister Rosie had married at sixteen and moved with her husband, Frank Reynolds, to Kentucky. He was almost thirteen when he said goodbye to Rosie on her wedding day. Over the next few years, Cole would often spend a week in the summer with Rosie and Frank in Lexington. At seventeen, he dropped out of school to assume almost full responsibility of their farm. With his father Malcolm, hired for numerous brick laying jobs in and around the county, Cole and his mother took care of all the chores at home. Beside plowing and working in the garden, Cole and Mama Colleen fed and milked three cows, fed the chickens, gathered the eggs, and slopped the hogs. On the days when Malcolm was home, their work days were much easier. Life was good for the McTavish family in Lynn, Alabama.

The summer that Cole turned twenty-three, his father retired from his job and settled back to life on the farm. With his meager savings, Cole bought five acres and built a small log cabin in Double Springs, and moved there to start work at Parker Dairy. On the first day of his new job, he met Miss Libby Parker, and as they say, "the rest is history."

Cole McTavish married Miss Libby Parker on 20 May, 1860 in Double Springs.

"Cole, get up! I'm not going to call you again. Breakfast is almost ready, and it's finally stopped raining," Libby said while she finished setting the table.

"Where's the slop jar," he bellowed as he rolled to the edge of the bed and used his long arm to feel the floor underneath for the chamber pot.

"You'll have to get up, honey. I had to move it during the night to catch the water from your leaking roof. In case you didn't know, we had a tremendous thunderstorm during the night."

"I thought I heard something and wasn't just dreaming," Cole replied as he threw the covers back. "Dang, it's cold in here!"

"Put some clothes on silly, and help me by getting a fire started in the fireplace. It serves you right for sleeping without your nightshirt."

"Yes, darling. Your wish is my command." Cole dressed himself hurriedly and started through the back door toward the outhouse.

"Now, where are you going?"

"Be back in a few minutes," he said as he brushed against Libby and kissed her on the cheek. Ten minutes later, Cole was back inside with an armload of wood for the fire. As he knelt onto the hearth, he positioned the logs and lit the kerosene soaked kindling. In a few minutes, the fire began to crackle while the smell of hickory soon filled the room.

"Your breakfast is on the table," Libby said while she took her seat. Cole quickly joined her and they shared a delicious breakfast of ham, eggs, grits, and Libby's special biscuits. "I'll be going to mother's house today. Just stop by there after work." She poured his coffee.

"What's going on?" he asked.

"I told her yesterday that I could help. She's got a piece ready to quilt."

"That's good, honey. You need something to do. Remember, I've got a meeting tonight in town, so I doubt that I'll be able to go to your mother's. Forgive me?"

"That's all right, but you'll have to fix supper for yourself."

4

"Thank you for the breakfast. Now, I need to get to work. Your father is supposed to be buying several new heifers today."

Cole rose from the table, walked around to where Libby was seated, and put his hands on her shoulders. He bent down across her right shoulder as she turned ever so slightly to receive his goodbye kiss. Cole disappeared through the front door while Libby stood to clear the table. Her news would have to wait a bit longer.

Winston County is rectangular in shape with a total area of 630 square miles. It is located in the northwest section of the State of Alabama. Winston is bounded on the north by Franklin and Lawrence counties, on the south by Walker, on the east by Cullman, and on the west by Marion. Its topography ranges from rolling hills to rough and mountainous areas throughout the county. Water resources are provided by its many creeks and rivers, including the Sipsey River, which flows into the much larger Black Warrior River.

Following the many Indian trails, the first white men came to this area of the state during the Revolutionary War. After making peace negotiations with the Cherokees, Creeks, and Chickasaws, they each claimed indefinite parts of this territory while using it as a shared and common hunting ground. In 1814, the first permanent settlers came from North Carolina and established their homes in the area. Soon after, they were joined by families from Georgia, Tennessee, South Carolina, Kentucky, and Virginia. The main attraction was coal mining since the area was rich in its mineral deposits as well as the plentiful farmlands.

On 22 January 1858, with its designated name in honor of former governor, John Anthony Winston, the new county was created with the town of Houston becoming its first county seat. At the time, Winston County had only fourteen slave holders with a recorded 122 known slaves in 1860. The records indicated that less than five percent were actually slave owners. Many Southern Democrats in the county were against the Democratic nominee, Stephen A. Douglas because he did not agree to permit the slave owners to carry their slaves into free territory where the people had earlier voted it out. During the election of 1860, the majority of the voters in Winston County supported Douglas; however, the opposition wanted to nominate as their choice, a slave owner and sympathizer, John C. Breckinridge, originally from Kentucky.

Upon his arrival at the town hall, Cole was met outside in the yard by his closest friend, Nathaniel Overstreet. Nate was also a newlywed, having married his beloved Marcie in March just a few months before his boyhood friend, Cole. The two of them had shared many adventures together throughout their young lives while hunting, fishing, gambling, and drinking. Nate was a robust young man of the same age, with long dark brown hair and eyes. He was broad through the shoulders and stood barefoot at an even six foot. His voice had a distinctive characteristic that was always pleasant, deep, and mellow. Both men spotted each other about the same time as Cole approached his friend. They shook hands and moved closer to the front door of the meeting hall.

"Hello, Nate, how are you?"

"Just fine, I guess. What about you?"

"I've had a busy day at the dairy. Mr. Parker bought a dozen head of milk cows and we had to get them settled into the barn. By the time we got them fed and milked, it was already late afternoon. I barely found the time to get home and clean up in order to come to the meeting."

"I went hunting today. Shot a couple of quail that Marcie dressed out and fixed for our supper. My wife is a wonderful cook, I do believe."

"Yes, I know. Whenever we come for dinner, I really like her fried chicken. Libby is away at her mother's today, so I didn't get my usual good meal late this afternoon."

"Listen, it's still a few minutes until the meeting is set to begin, and I wanted to ask you about this Breckinridge fellow. What do you know about him?"

"Don't know all that much, but I've heard that he was a lawyer, politician, and a soldier. They are supposed to have some information about him at the meeting, I believe."

"All I know about Breckinridge is that he is from somewhere in Kentucky, served in both houses of Congress, and became the fourteenth and youngest-ever Vice-President of the United States in 1857."

"Looks like the meeting is about to get started. Let's go inside and try to find a seat." Cole said.

In haste, Cole and Nate found two seats together near the back of the hall. The place was packed to almost full capacity and nearing standing room only. While they were both outside talking, neither of them paid attention to the gathering crowd who was now assembled in the hall. The smoke-filled room was alive with endless chatter and the noise of shuffling feet while benches and chairs scraped against the heart pine floor.

"Raise the damn windows!" yelled a voice down front, "Let's get some air circulating in here."

The moderator stood at the podium and pounded his gavel loudly to quiet the crowded room and call the meeting to order.

"Gentlemen, this meeting will come to order! We are here to discuss the qualifications of Senator John C. Breckinridge for consideration as a presidential candidate for the Democratic Party. If I could get a couple of you gentlemen to pass out these pamphlets, you will be able to read for yourself about him. Thank you, sirs."

Four men on the front row volunteered and moved quickly down the aisle while they passed the information sheets down each row. As soon as Cole received his copy, he began to read.

John Cabell Breckinridge was born on 16 January, 1821 near Lexington, Kentucky. He is presently 39 years old. Breckinridge attended Centre College, College of New Jersey, and Transylvania University where he studied to become a lawyer by profession. He was married to Mary Burch, and his children were named Joseph

Cabell, Clifton Rhoads, Frances, John Milton, John Witherspoon, David R. Witherspoon, and Mary Desha.

Following non-combat service with the Union Army during the Mexican-American War, he was elected as a Democrat in the Kentucky House of Representatives in 1849. Once seated, he took a state's rights position against interference with slavery. In 1850, he was elected to the U.S. House of Representatives where he allied with Stephen A. Douglas in support of the Kansas-Nebraska Act. Reapportionment in 1854 made his re-election unlikely, and he declined to run for another term. At the 1856 Democratic National Convention, Breckinridge was nominated as vice-president to share the ballot with James Buchanan. Although the Democrats won the election, Breckinridge lost his influence with Buchanan since he was a presiding officer of the Senate and could not express his opinion in debates. As the vice-president, Breckinridge later joined President Buchanan in his support of the pro-slavery Lecompton Constitution of Kansas. This action led to a split in the Democratic Party.

As the moderator stood once again behind the podium, he hit the gavel three times. "The chair will now receive any questions from the floor."

The heated meeting, comprised of dozens of questions and comments, continued for nearly three hours until the final tally was taken by a standing vote. In the end, the majority decided that Winston County would support the regular Democratic nominee, Mr. Douglas.

"That was some meeting," Nate said. "I'm not so sure that we've made the right decision."

"Neither, am I. The vote was so close. We're talking about our livelihood in the south and any future little Overstreet and McTavish babies we may have. What are we going to leave for them?"

"I've got to do some more thinking. It scares the hell out of me with this upcoming presidential election," said Nate.

"Nate, I hate to cut this short, but I need to get home and see that Libby made it back all right. I'll see you Sunday at church."

"All right, Mule. See you then. Maybe you and Libby can come for Sunday dinner. I'll ask Marcie." Nate said while he placed a friendly hit onto Cole's left arm. The two men shook hands and walked away into the darkness of the night.

By the time Cole reached home that night, he found Libby already in bed. "What's the matter, darling, don't you feel well?" Cole said as he stood at her bedside.

"I'm really tired. Hurry to bed and just hold me, please. Let me tell you about the day's events in the morning," she replied in a whisper.

Cole stripped off completely on the spot while rapidly removing his boots and clothing while dropping everything onto the floor. He quickly slid under the covers and came to rest against Libby. He drew her close to his side while she lay her head on his shoulder with her hand resting across his hairy chest. Her eyes closed drowsily as she drifted into sleep.

The next morning, daylight was peering through the open window curtains while its rays shone brightest along the foot of their bed. Cole and Libby were waking up.

"Don't get up, don't you dare leave me," she said while sliding herself in position against the oak headboard. "I want to tell you what happened yesterday."

Cole, not fully awake, attempted his response while he re-positioned the pillow behind his back and sat up beside her in bed. "I'm listening," he said.

"When I arrived, Mama was extremely upset. I could tell she had been crying and her hands were trembling when she hugged me at the door. I asked her immediately what was wrong while she pulled me across the parlor toward the sofa. We sat down while she lifted the corner of her apron to wipe her reddened face. Needless to say, I knew then we wouldn't be quilting."

"What about you, honey? Are you all right? You look worried yourself."

"Still a bit shaken, and I'm also upset."

9

"Then, pray tell me. Get on with it! For God sake's, what has happened?"

"It's about her neighbor's little boy, Seth. He has been missing for the last three days, and early the day before yesterday, a hunter found his decomposing little body in the north woods. He was partially hidden there in some thick underbrush."

"What neighbors, you say? You don't mean the Carter's?"

"Yes, I'm afraid so. I can hardly believe it! It is John and Sarah's baby son. He's only five years old."

"What do they think happened to him?"

"According to what Mama told me, she couldn't help but notice all the commotion happening over at the Carter house. She was aware that Seth was missing because Sarah, who was in great distress, had shared the news with her on that first day. Mother had already been questioned by Sheriff Kincaid, also that same day. In fact, the last time she remembered seeing little Seth was at church on the previous Sunday morning."

"What about John, his father?"

"Mama told me he was just pitiful, and Sarah as well. They had both been questioned at length until they were both exhausted. This was immediately after news of the disappearance first surfaced. Many of their neighbors and friends joined together with the law officers while they began to search everywhere in the area."

"What woods? Does the sheriff know the name of the hunter?"

"In the dense forest near Pebble. You may know the hunter, Randall Fraser. He had a witness with him on the day of the gruesome discovery. Burt Allison happened to be hunting with him at the time."

"I know both those boys, even hunted with Fraser myself. Don't recall any dealings with Mr. Allison."

"Anyway, I can tell you that Mama is clearly upset while she has been trying to bring comfort to John and Sarah."

"What about the other children? I believe they have some other children, don't they?"

"Yes, there's four of them. Supposedly, all were asleep in their rooms on the night in question. Seth still slept by himself in the former nursery while Willie and James slept together in their room. Daughter Janet, the oldest, was away at the time in boarding school in Florence."

"Any speculation into what actually happened?"

"Nothing right now, the sheriff is keeping a lid on it. All anyone seems to know is that on Tuesday morning when Sarah went to check on Seth, he was missing from his bed. There were no signs of a struggle or any other type of disturbances observed in the room. Along with his little teddy bear, Seth had simply vanished."

"Libby, is there anything I can do for you, my darling?"

"No, I believe you have already accomplished that!" Libby took her husband's right hand and placed it onto her little bump. "I'm in the family way now. We're going to have a baby in June."

Cole was so caught up with this joyous news, he could hardly control himself. Suddenly, he jumped out of bed, naked as the day he was born, while he leaped and danced his way through the little cabin. What a surprise to see his awaking mother-in-law in a state of shock as he passed close by the sofa where she had spent the night.

With her jaw dropped, she simply said, "I guess Libby forgot to tell you that I was staying overnight!"

11

CHAPTER 2

T he talk in Winston County continued long after the town hall meeting was history. Many citizens remained upset about the politics in the country and hearing rumors about the possibility of yet another war on American soil. Then came news about the presidential election that shocked most of the South. Some of it still involved Senator Breckinridge.

When the Southern Democrats walked out of the 1860 Democratic National Convention, rival conventions were held in Baltimore to nominate Douglas and Breckinridge for president, respectively. Also, a third party calling themselves the Constitutional Union Party nominated John Bell. With that in play, these three men split the southern vote. The anti-slavery Republican candidate, Abraham Lincoln, won all but three electoral votes in the North while he won the election. Senator Breckinridge continued to urge a compromise to preserve the Union while Unionists were in control of the state legislature. He finally gained more support when the Confederate forces moved into Kentucky. With that, Breckinridge flipped and fled behind Confederate lines where he became commissioned as a brigadier general in the CSA Army. Needless to say, he was immediately expelled from the U.S. Senate when this news found its way to his fellow senators.

"Such constant turmoil and people everywhere getting their feathers all ruffled," Libby said while she sat with Cole at their breakfast. "I saw Greta Hassendorfer yesterday at Shaw's Mercantile. She told me that her husband Jacob believed we were heading straight to war."

"Reckon so, I guess. There's no telling what is going to happen if Lincoln frees the slaves," Cole replied.

"Slaves! I'm the only slave around here," she laughed. "We should be so fortunate. Maybe in my next life, I will become a rich slave owner."

"Yeah, me too! Just like Washington, Jefferson, and half of Congress."

"Then tell me, Cole McTavish, what's going to happen to people who depend on slave labor to run their plantations in the South?"

"If it were to become law, then we would have two choices in my estimation. We would be forced to comply or simply rebel. I hear now that there's talk of secession."

"My father, just like us, supported the Democrats, but since Douglas failed to get elected, it seems as though Winston County remains split over the politics of this new administration."

"I agree, but we don't have that much concern in the matter since we do not own any slaves."

"Anyone can see that we don't have that problem in Double Springs and the county; however, I'm certain that it is a major concern for many others."

"The states of Louisiana, Georgia, and the Carolinas will no doubt suffer more than Alabama, I believe."

"We'll see about that, if and when that problem happens. This morning, I'm going back to spend the day with my mother. At last word, there seems to be no more news since the initial report of the Carter tragedy."

"How is your mother?"

"The last time I saw her, she appeared to be all right. She has been spending a lot of time with Sarah. The Carter family is suffering greatly through this ordeal."

"I can only imagine. I'm seeing everything in a whole new light, especially now since I am going to be a father myself."

"I believe you will be a wonderful father, Cole. With your strong moral character and determination to overcome any obstacles along the way, plus my beauty, charm, and wit, our child will be amazing."

"Speaking of our child and everything that concerns us, how are you doing?"

"Just a few weeks along, I am still experiencing a little morning sickness. Right now, the month of June seems so far away. Mother says that I need to see Dr. Blake next week."

"Want me to go with you?"

"No, darling, I'm sure that Mother is already planning to accompany me. She has been taking me to see Dr. Blake since I was six years old."

"Oh, I see. It's a woman thing."

"That's right! Birthing babies is definitely a woman thing, as you say. I remember when Greta's husband passed out cold onto their bedroom floor when little Natasha was coming out. Cracked his head wide open just like a Georgia pecan."

"I'll be around, count on me; however, I may choose to wait it out at Looney's Tavern," he laughed.

"We'll see about that when the time comes. Speaking of time, look at the time, Mister. You need to go milk some cows. Daddy is probably already up and waiting on you."

As the brisk autumn days slowly faded, much colder weather continued while month's end changed to December. It seems everyone in town was praying for a mild winter this year while others looked forward to a white Christmas. Hopefully, the current temperature during the next few weeks would remain about the same, thus eliminating the possibility of sleet or snow. It wasn't uncommon for Winston County to get snow anytime between December and February; however, most of the time it was only snow flurries with little or no accumulation.

Cole would always remember the winter he turned seventeen when snow fell for three days and set a record with eight inches in his hometown of Lynn. It happened at that same time when he lost his boyhood pal, John Walter McDaniel, in a tragic accident. When his parents had not returned from a shopping trip to town, sixteen year old J.W. left home to go looking for them. Being an only child at home alone, the late afternoon was beginning to grow dark and Mr. and Mrs. McDaniel were long overdue to arrive back home. Concerned and worried, J.W. made his decision to go look for them. In preparation, he bundled himself with boots, heavy coat, hat, and gloves while remembering to grab a lantern from the mantelpiece. It was almost dark when he closed the front door to begin his journey into town on foot. Hours passed as Walt and Mary McDaniel finally returned to their empty home. *Where was John Walter?*

Cole still kept the old newspaper clipping in his Bible at the place marking the page of the Twenty-Third Psalm. It served as a reminder in memory of his first best friend.

Sunday   16 December 1854

Early yesterday morning at daybreak, Sheriff Thomas Kincaid, along with Deputy Joe Williams, discovered the body of missing sixteen year old, John Walter McDaniel. Located at the scene, the victim appeared to be partially submerged in the icy water at the edge of Miller Pond in Winston County. The Lynn resident, identified as the son of Walt and Mary McDaniel, had been reported missing by his parents late Friday night when they returned to find their son absent from their home. Sheriff Kincaid, leading a small search party of volunteers, tracked a single set of footprints to the area around Miller Pond. The tracks in the snow were found to be leading in close proximity along the southern banks and ending at the edge of the partially frozen pond.

"There is no reason to suspect foul play. The report by the coroner, following an autopsy, has been ruled as 'death by severe head trauma

followed by hypothermia.' With deepest sympathy to the McDaniel Family." Quote by Sheriff Thomas Kincaid.

Cole and his family, along with the entire community of Lynn, grieved for many days following this tragic accident. It was later determined that J.W. in his haste to take a shortcut to town, took the path around Miller Pond and accidently ventured onto the frozen pond where he fell through the ice in the dark. An extinguished broken lantern was discovered nearby at the scene. The gash on the back of his skull indicated that the fall had caused him to hit his head on a log which lay just underneath the water's surface in the ice. The blow had rendered him unconscious as his heavily-clad body sank halfway down into the icy water while he froze to death. The irony of this tragedy was that J.W.'s parents reportedly arrived back home less than ten minutes after he set out to find them. Cole missed his friend for months afterward until he eventually met his current best friend in the person of Nate Overstreet. Nate always said, "A true friend is someone who knows everything about you, but still likes you just the same."

"It's cold outside, Libby, and you what? Surely, you don't want me to go right now into the freezing cold and cut down a Christmas tree," Cole said while he tried to avoid eye contact with his wife. When he turned his head, he could see out of the corner of his eye that she hadn't moved, not an inch.

Libby repeated herself once again. "Cole, darling, I need you to go into the woods and cut down a tree for me to decorate for Christmas. I have been making some of the ornaments for the past two weeks. Don't make me have to do it myself."

"What size?" he muttered.

"About six feet tall should be fine. It doesn't have to be a large tree, but its branches should be suitable for hanging about fifteen ornaments. Do I need to come with you?"

"No, honey, I think I know what you have in mind."

"A nice, full scotch pine or cedar would be just fine. I love the fresh smell of either one."

"One special Christmas tree coming right up for you, Mrs. McTavish, this very afternoon on 21 December, 1860. I would love a cup of hot apple cider when I return."

"You got it, Mister! Dress warmly, and don't forget your hat and gloves."

"Yes ma'am," Cole said while he threw on his heavy woolen coat and headed out the back door to the woodshed where he would pick up his ax. "Glad Christmas comes only once a year," he mumbled to himself.

Christmas Day was spent at the home of Libby's parents. Cole's folks had also been invited to join them for the meal to be served at noon. The house was warm and cozy with a roaring fire in the parlor while outside on the lawn, there was a light dusting of snow beginning to fall.

"James Parker, please try to be extra nice to Malcolm and Colleen when they arrive," said Amelia while she finished setting the dining room table. "It doesn't matter to me if they're Scottish or Mexican." She paused, giving him the *look*. "For goodness sakes, they are your daughter's in-laws."

James Parker didn't have anything to say while he left the room.

"*Men,*" Amelia thought to herself. "So, Malcolm didn't finish out our fireplace exactly like my dear husband wanted it, *get over it!*"

"Mama, want me to check on the ham? It should be done by now. The apple pie you made looks delicious," said Libby. "I believe I hear Mr. and Mrs. McTavish at the door. Cole is supposed to be bringing them."

"I'm letting your father get the door. Hopefully, he'll be in a better mood after he eats," Amelia said while she stirred the lima beans on the stove top."

"Somebody's at the door," yelled James from the parlor.

"Get it yourself, James! The door won't open itself," Amelia yelled back.

17

Momentarily, James Parker opened the front door only to have his right hand immediately grabbed by Malcolm McTavish in one fell swoop. The handshaking motion was so rapid and unexpected, Mr. Parker felt that a jolt of electricity was now running through his arm. He was near speechless while he recovered enough to see Colleen holding a pot of steamed vegetables at her husband's side. Behind them, Cole was coming up the steps.

"Merry Christmas," said James while he motioned everyone into the house. "Hope you're all doing well. We're about ready to sit down for Christmas dinner."

Cole and his father joined Mr. Parker in the parlor, while Colleen made her way past them where she found Amelia and Libby busy at work in the kitchen. The three women worked well together, while they finished the final preparations for the dinner.

The men folk had no longer settled in the parlor to relax when Amelia appeared in the doorway and called them to the table in the dining room. Cole and Libby took their seats on the far side in front of the window, while Malcolm and Colleen sat facing directly across in position nearest the doorway. James took his usual seat at the head of the table while he slid his chair closer, causing the table to wobble a bit as the chair bumped into it. Amelia remained standing at the opposite end until she took a quick glance to insure that everything on the table was as it should be. Satisfied, she sat as elegantly before her guests as she appeared those years ago following graduation from Miss Habersham's School for Young Women in Florence.

"Why all the silence?" Amelia asked while she gave a nod across the table to her husband. "James, you may say Grace."

"Let us pray," he said while everyone bowed their head.

"Our Father, we pause to give thanks for the many blessings you have provided for our family. We are grateful for our health and the wonderful bounty you have bestowed upon us. We ask that you bless this food we are about to receive to nourish our bodies, and our bodies in service to you.

As we celebrate this day, remembering the birth of our Lord and Savior, Jesus Christ, we pray for all those less fortunate and for all those who remain unsaved. We remember the Carter family, John and Sarah, especially during this time of their bereavement. Watch over our family and the distress facing our nation while we pray that we will not have to go to war. In Jesus' name, we pray. Amen."

"Parker, do you think we're headed to war?" asked Malcolm McTavish.

"I don't really see how it can be avoided. It's probably just a matter of time until something is going to happen to trigger it. Our country is on the brink of racial tension as the issue of slavery is foremost on everyone's mind," he replied.

"Please, gentlemen, let's not talk war and politics at the dinner table. We're here to celebrate Christmas and enjoy this delicious meal together," Amelia spoke up. "There will be plenty of time for you men to discuss that topic after dinner. Would someone start and pass the ham platter?"

General conversation continued at the table, while everyone enjoyed the delicious meal. At the conclusion, the women began to clear the table while the men returned to the parlor.

"Have a seat," James said while he walked over to his chair. Malcolm moved to the sofa while Cole sat in the chair usually occupied by Amelia. James Parker lit his pipe while he began the conversation. "What about the hanging up in Lawrence County? The local newspaper is just breaking that particular story."

"Haven't heard anything about it," replied Malcolm. "You hear anything, Cole?"

"No sir, I reckon not. What happened, Mr. Parker?"

"The way I hear tell of it was like this," he said while puffing away on his pipe. "Judge Roy Harry Jessup, also known as *Hangin' Harry*, had this fine looking daughter named Wanda. Now, Miss Wanda, being the only daughter of the wealthy circuit court judge, didn't have to want for much, particularly whenever it had to do with her own desire or pleasure. After all, she was quite beautiful, they say. A full-figured gal of twenty-three, not ever been married, long blonde hair with big blue eyes, she had lots of men just begging for a chance to be with her. In and around Jessup Plantation, she was known as *Miss Wanda;* however, in shantytown, they called her *Wicked Wanda.* The talk was that she could put a spell on you really bad; so bad, in fact, just like a witch, that's how she gained her reputation locally as *Wicked Wanda."*

"What about her mother?" Malcolm interrupted while he blew a smoke ring from his cigar.

"I was told that Nancy Jessup died when Wanda was almost nineteen. As a young, single woman, with her father away from home and in court most days, Wanda had full reign over a household of servants and stable boys. What she didn't have was her mother's love anymore. Her father didn't seem to care much about Wanda, what she did, and who she was with in town."

"That's really a shame," said Cole. "Please, get on with your story. I really would like to know what happened. What caused a hanging?"

"It was reported in the article I read in the paper about the little known facts. However, this latest development was things I had already suspected. Anyway, the report stated that a few weeks back, Judge Jessup arrived home unexpectedly and caught Wanda and a stable boy named Ben together upstairs in her bedroom. Black as night, there he was in heated passion, doing the deed. Clearly outraged and mad as a hornet in a disturbed nest, the judge ordered young Ben off the bed and up against the wall. Ben's hands were shaking as he reached down in an effort to try to cover himself. Harry Jessup ordered the young man downstairs, across the yard, and toward the barn. Giving Ben a nudge in the small of his back with the pistol, he pushed his victim inside the barn and closed the door.

"Get your sorry self over there and up that ladder. Remember, I'll be right behind you with this pistol pointed in your back."

Ben froze in sudden desperation like a rabbit caught in a trap. "Please, Mister Jessup, let me explain," he begged.

"Get on up, boy! I seen what you did to my daughter. I don't need your explanation, do I?"

Ben held his fixed gaze upward while he slowly ascended the seventeen foot ladder leading to the hayloft. Jessup was right behind him as he stashed the pistol under his belt.

"Don't go any further, you trash," Jessup instructed while he walked a short distance to retrieve a piece of rope lying on top of a hay bale. "Put your hands behind your back. I don't know why in the hell that I don't just shoot you here and now."

Jessup whacked Ben across the cheek with his powerful clenched fist while the blow turned Ben's head sideways. Recovering from the hit, Ben steadied himself before the judge while he cast his eyes toward the floor. Jessup came up behind Ben, grabbed his hands, and tied them securely behind his back.

"Sit down! Don't you dare move, you hear me boy? I said to sit your black arse down."

Ben went to the floor in a cross-legged position while he watched the enraged man who was attempting to take his life. Jessup pulled a coil of rope from a nearby hook and ran it through his long fingers until he found the end. After completing a large knot, he threw the rope upward and watched it as it fell from the rafter above his head. Standing alongside the edge of the loft, he reached for the noose while he leaned out to catch it, while nearly losing his balance. After placing the rope onto his captive, he tightened the noose around Ben's neck and secured the other end to the nearby support beam.

Without another word spoken, Jessup came up quickly behind the frightened young man. He drew in a deep breath, and with one swift kick, the force sent Ben over the edge. His trembling body fell down while his weight broke the fall and snapped his neck. His legs flew out with a kicking motion while his dangling body twitched for only a brief moment before it came to its final rest.

Benjamin Washington was dead.

Hangin' Harry, both judge and executioner, had passed his sentence. In his mind, he had done the right thing. Judge Roy Harry Jessup moved slowly toward the ladder to make his exit. While he turned to secure his footing on the first rung of the ladder, a loud shotgun blast suddenly penetrated his back. In a flash, he fell from the hayloft while his body hit below with a thud. The newspaper reported it was Wanda who discovered the bodies. Later, that same day, she was taken into custody.

"Did she do it?" Cole asked.

"Don't know," replied his father-in-law. "The trial is set to begin next month when a new judge will be appointed."

The menfolk were about to discuss politics when Amelia, Colleen, and Libby appeared together at the doorway.

"Cole, I'm not feeling well," said Libby. "Would you please take me home?"

"Yes, we should be getting home ourselves," Malcolm chimed in.

"Thank you for having us," Colleen added. "The meal was delicious, Amelia, and it was good to see you both once again. Merry Christmas!"

"Merry Christmas, everyone," Amelia said. "Your coats and wraps are in the front bedroom where you left them. You'll have to bundle yourselves quite well. The snow is falling more heavily now, so be extremely careful on your way home. Libby, darling, I hope you will soon feel much better. We all pray for the same, I'm sure."

"Thank you, Mama, I just need to rest," Libby said while the McTavish clan moved onto the porch.

"I'll bring the buggy around," said Cole. "Wait here!"

Amelia turned toward James as she gently closed the front door. "Libby looked so pale, didn't she? I pray that her baby is going to be all right."

James and Amelia Parker sat by their fireside in the parlor while a white Christmas settled over Double Springs. The last week of the year passed while the townspeople patiently withstood the unsuspecting blizzard that had blanketed many parts of Winston County.

Happy New Year 1861!

CHAPTER 3

S heriff Kincaid never attempted to track or locate any other suspects while Wanda Jessup's trial was set to begin 28 January, 1861.

The scene of the crime committed at Jessup Plantation had been cleared, the bodies had both received a Christian burial, and the only murder suspect sat alone in her cell at the county jail in Houston. Since her arrest, Wanda's only visitor had been her Aunt Minnie, her father's older sister. Minnie Jessup had been faithful to visit as often as she could over the past few weeks while Wanda had been locked up in the jailhouse. She, along with Wanda, proclaimed her complete innocence. There was no way this loving daughter could deliberately shoot her father in the back with a shotgun in such a cold and heartless way.

The anxious crowd began to gather on the courthouse lawn while they waited for the doors to open precisely at 9:00 a.m. Endless chatter prevailed at the scene and continued when the bailiff finally opened the double doors. Immediately, the crowd pushed its way toward the court room in search of a good seat. The show was about to begin.

The accused walked into the courtroom with her jailer and found her seat at the long oak table beside her attorney, Mr. J. Silas Martin. Wanda appeared to remain calm and to portray herself as the innocent young lady she previously claimed in her written

24

statement. She was dressed in a plain blue muslin gown with a simple white bow in her long blonde hair which flowed down her back. For her first court appearance, she wore no makeup or jewelry. Following closely to her attorney's advice, she now looked sixteen.

A hush fell over the courtroom while the bailiff stood to make his announcement.

"Please stand! The First District Circuit Court of Winston County is hereby in session. The Honorable Judge Thomas K. Winslow, presiding."

The judge, dressed in a long black robe, entered from the right and took his seat on the bench.

"Be seated, ladies and gentlemen."

Heads were turning and necks were craning around the packed courtroom while everyone was trying to get a good look at the new circuit court judge, formerly from Mobile County. The jury box was empty, indicating this would not be a trial by jury. Certainly, no one had a clue as to how this judge ruled or passed sentences. Judge Winslow was a young man, age 42, with dark brown hair and eyes. He wore a thin moustache underneath his aquiline nose. Judging from the faces of several young ladies present in the courtroom, this new judge was an extremely handsome man. No one yet knew if there was a *Mrs.* Winslow. Somehow, that would never matter to Miss Amy Lynn Crutchfield who immediately brought out her fan to cool herself after the first glimpse of Judge Winslow.

The judge slowly looked up from the papers before him, cleared his throat, and began his opening remarks. The courtroom drew still and quiet in anticipation.

"Ladies and gentlemen of the court. I, Thomas K. Winslow, am here to pass judgment on Case No. 114, the People vs. Wanda D. Jessup. Miss Jessup stands accused of the murder of her father, Judge Roy Harry Jessup." The judge looked down from his position, across the courtroom, toward the table where Wanda sat with her attorney.

"Miss Jessup, how do you plead?"

"Not guilty, your honor."

"The clerk will record that the defendant has indicated a plea of 'not guilty.' Mr. Martin, you may call your first witness for the defense."

"Very well, your honor. I call Miss Jessup to take the stand." All eyes followed Wanda while she stood and took her walk down front to the witness box.

Calvin McCluskey received a sharp elbow to the ribs from his wife after he leaned out into the aisle to catch a glimpse. Other wives in the courtroom began to give their husbands the *eye* while they took notice of the lead from Maybelle McCluskey. Judge Winslow also took notice of all the unnecessary movement in the room.

"Settle down, everyone."

The bailiff approached Wanda and stopped to face her directly. He drew a Bible from his side.

"Place your left hand on the Bible and raise your right hand. Do you swear to speak the truth, the whole truth, and nothing but the truth, so help you, God?"

"I do."

"State your full name and present age for the record."

"Wanda Dawn Jessup, age 23."

"Be seated," said the bailiff while he returned to his station outside the chamber door.

"Mr. Martin, you may begin," Judge Winslow announced.

Silas Martin took the floor as he rose from his seat and proceeded to walk toward the witness box. He stopped to the right where Wanda was seated. She had both feet placed on the floor and hands folded together resting upon her lap.

"Now, Miss Jessup, for the record, would you please share with the court once again the time and date of the incident as you recall. I'm referring to the time when you left your room and walked out to the barn?"

"I would have to say the time was a quarter past four on Tuesday afternoon. I believe the date was the 3rd of December, as I recall."

"When you arrived at the barn, was the door open or closed?"

"The big doors were closed, but the side door we use most of the time was partially opened."

"So, assuming that you walked in through this side door, what did you see?"

"Well, sir, I saw my father. He was laying at the base of the ladder that goes up to the hayloft. I called out to him while I ran over to where he lay in a pool of blood. He wasn't moving."

"What did you do then?"

"I screamed. I cried. I fell to the floor beside him. That's when I could see his back ripped open and oozing blood. I was trembling. It was such a shock for me."

"Do you need a moment?"

"No, I'm all right."

"Let's continue. Would you please try to describe the position of your father's body at that time? Could you do that for us, Miss Jessup?"

"The best I can remember was…..my poor Pa, God rest his soul. He was laying on his side with one arm concealed underneath him. His other arm was bent above his head, palm resting up with his fingers somewhat closed in a fist. One leg was folded back under the other and his head lay on the floor. I think it was his left cheek; it was flat against the dirt floor."

"What happened next, Miss Jessup?"

"I tried to feel a pulse and felt nothing. I leaned close to his face and he wasn't breathing. I knew he was dead. I stood to my feet and happened to look up and that's when I saw him. I saw Ben hanging from the rafter above. I guess that's when I must have fainted. I don't remember anything else, I'm sorry."

"Miss Jessup, tell the court Ben's full identity, would you please?"

"I call him, Ben. His name is Benjamin Washington. He is one of my father's stable boys. Ben has been with us for as long as I can remember."

"What is your relationship with Benjamin Washington?"

27

"Ben is in charge of our livery and whatever it takes in and around the barn and horse pens. He was really good with all the animals. Ben would usually saddle *Princess* for me, she's my mare, whenever I wanted to go riding."

"Miss Jessup, following the discovery of the bodies of your father and Ben, you stated that you fainted. Where were you when you regained consciousness?"

"In my bedroom. Callie, one of the house servants told me that she found me in the barn and got me back to the house and into bed. She sent her son, Jacob, to fetch the sheriff."

"No more questions. Thank you, Miss Jessup."

Wanda started to stand and leave the box, but the judge quickly called out to her.

"Hold it right there, young lady. Mr. Lawrence, do you wish to cross-examine?"

"Yes, your honor," replied Matthew Lawrence, the prosecuting attorney.

"Miss Jessup, kindly return to your seat. Mr. Lawrence may also have a few questions. Remember, you are still under oath. You may proceed, Mr. Lawrence."

Unlike the much older, grey-haired, and well-groomed senior district attorney, Matthew Lawrence appeared to be closer in age actually to the new judge himself. There was seemingly no comparison between the well-dressed, John Silas Martin, and the more casual look that Lawrence was wearing in the courtroom today. Matthew Lawrence wasn't considered handsome, but his curly red hair and bright blue eyes complemented the muscular body now bulging underneath his dark blue trousers and long grey waistcoat. On his feet, he wore a pair of shiny black boots. Matt Lawrence had been a prosecuting attorney for the county seat at Houston since moving there three years ago from Dalton, Georgia, with his wife Deborah and three children. He usually won most of his cases. On this particular day, he was beginning to feel that this one was going to be an open and shut case. He stood tall at the table while he began his questioning. His gaze fell upon Wanda.

"Miss Jessup, how long have you been screwing your stable boy?"

"Pardon?"

"You heard me! Let me re-phrase the question for you. How long have you been having intimate relations, copulating, or if you prefer the biblical connotation 'to lie with.' How long, Miss Jessup? This is not a complicated question."

Wanda's hands began to tremble while she tried her best to conceal them within the folds of her dress. "A few times," she uttered in a whispered voice.

"Speak up, Miss, we can't hear you!"

"A few times," she answered louder.

"Few as in one, two, three, or more? What constitutes a few?"

"I believe it would be five, sir."

"Five, you say. Miss Jessup, let's not beat around the bush. I already have the goods on many of your prior personal encounters with several different men, understand? I can produce quite a number who would be willing to testify about their intimate encounters with you."

"Objection, your honor! Counsel is badgering the witness," Silas Martin shouted.

"Objection, sustained. Mr. Lawrence, let's move along. I believe you have already established the character of the defendant."

"All right, your honor. I want to present to the court this original written statement of Miss Jessup as she related to Sheriff Kincaid on the evening of her arrest and interrogation. May I ask if you are familiar with this document?"

"I am, sir. I have already read it several times. I will enter this document to be recorded as Exhibit A in the court record," replied the judge.

"Thank you, your honor. Since you are already aware of all the findings related to the scene of the crime, I have no further questions for the defendant."

"Very well, you may step down, Miss Jessup. Mr. Martin, you may call your next witness."

"I would like to call Callie Johnson, your honor."

Nervously, Callie rose from her seat in the back and slowly made her way down the aisle to the front. After being sworn in by the bailiff, she took her seat in the witness box. Callie gave her age as thirty-three while sweat beads formed on her forehead. She pulled a handkerchief from her pocket and blotted her face and neck. There wasn't a person in court that would deny that Callie was as nervous as a cat in a room full of rocking chairs or another one equally as familiar, nervous as seeing a bull in a china shop. Already, the loyal mulatto house servant was almost in tears. Callie slumped in her chair while she awaited her first question from Attorney Martin. Her moist, reddened eyes grew large while she dabbed at them with her damp handkerchief. Dressed in a worn calico shift with a brown shawl draped around her shoulders, she jumped when she heard her name called. *Callie!*

"Callie, it's all right. Just try to relax. I only have a few questions for you. Here's the first one. What time was it when you went to the barn and found Miss Jessup?"

"Reckon it was about half past five in the evenin'. We's eat 'round six, so it before then."

"What did you see when you first walked into the barn?"

"I seen Miss Wanda passed out by the side of her daddy and Ben hangin' down from the hayloft. His hands, they was tied behind his back and he didn't have on any clothes."

"What did you do then, Callie?"

"I's went over to Miss Wanda, and I see she done fainted. She breathin', but not movin'. I look at Mister Jessup, he dead. I run back to the house to try to find my son. He on the back porch. I gets Jacob to go back to the barn with me. I tells him to pick up Miss Wanda and take her to the house. He carry her upstairs to her room and puts her on the bed for me."

"One more question, Callie, and I promise we're through. Did you see anyone else inside the barn or outside near the house?"

"No, sir, I don't see nobody."

"I have no more questions for Callie, your honor."

"Mr. Lawrence, your witness."

"No questions at this time, your honor."

"The witness may stand down."

"Callie…..Callie, that's all. Go back to your seat."

"Yes suh," she replied gladly.

"I have no more witnesses at this time. The defense will rest."

"Very well, we will take a recess until 11:00 a.m. when I will hear all the witnesses for the prosecution. Court now stands in recess."

For a brief time, the courtroom was all in a buzz while many on the hard benches vacated their seats to go outside to use the facilities. At a quarter until eleven, most all of the spectators had returned inside to find their seats. Several people were angry when they discovered they had lost their seats. The bailiff had to escort a very angry Slim McCreless outside after he began using foul and abusive language while nearly striking the elderly gentleman who had taken his former seat. At 11:05 a.m. Judge Winslow was back on the bench. He hit his gavel three times.

"Court is now back in session. Mr. Lawrence, are you ready with your first witness?"

"Yes, your honor. We call Sheriff Kincaid to the stand."

The sheriff walked to the front, took the oath, and settled into the witness chair. He provided his introduction as Sheriff Thomas Milton Kincaid, age 53.

"Sheriff Kincaid, may we assume that you were the first on the scene at Jessup Plantation on December 3, 1860?"

"I was, that is correct. My deputy had already left for the evening. I was still on duty."

"What time did you arrive at the scene?"

31

"Well, let's see. It would have to be around six o'clock or just a bit later. I do remember it was still daylight. By the time I finished up out there, it was night."

"Sheriff, would you tell the court everything you did or observed during that entire evening until the end of your investigation?"

"First, I checked Judge Jessup and determined that he was deceased. With most of his back blown away, he had to have been killed instantly, and that's not including the fall from a seventeen foot ladder. I could see from where I stood below, the second victim, a young, naked black man. He was hanging from the highest rafter and he was definitely deceased. There was a lot of blood splatter at the top of the ladder. I saw this when I climbed up to the hayloft. Also, there was some more blood sprayed along the edge of the loft nearby. It was relatively easy to spot the areas where the scattered straw now lay saturated in red. So, I determined the fatal shot was fired as soon as the judge first turned his back to descend the ladder. After viewing the body of the stable boy whose name I later learned was Benjamin Washington, I determined that it was the judge who had hung him there. Young Ben could not have tied his hands behind him with that particular knot, struck a blow to the left side of his face that produced a deep cut, and also, I can't see him stripping off his clothes on a cold afternoon to kill himself."

"By this time, I knew that I was going to need help, no doubt. I walked up to the house to get Jacob, Callie's son, to stand guard over the barn because I didn't want anyone else going in there. Once Jacob was in place at the barn door, I left on my horse for town to round up the coroner and my other deputy. Within the hour, we were back on site, just before the evening settled into the darkness of night. I dismissed Jacob, and as he was leaving, I told him to tell his mother that I needed to talk to her mistress, Miss Jessup, whenever I finished in the barn. He said he would tell her right away."

"The three of us entered the barn by the side door and went to work immediately. I told the coroner that we needed to work fast because daylight would soon be gone. I told my deputy, Sam, to find as many lanterns as he could, and go on and get them lit. While he was doing that, Blackburn, the coroner, helped me move Jessup's body and lay him out in a lighted area where he would be able to examine him. I looked up at the hayloft. How are we going to get this boy down? There was no way we could take him down without just cutting the rope and letting him fall. So, I had to do it. I climbed back up the ladder with the axe I found, walked to the support beam where the rope was tied, and swiftly chopped the rope with a single blow from the axe. The body fell with a sudden thud. It sounded like someone had dropped a big watermelon from twenty feet above to watch it fall and splatter onto the hard surface as it landed. By the time I had climbed back down the ladder, Sam had already removed the rope from the victim's neck. Working together, we picked up the body and moved him next to Jessup."

"While Sam and Blackburn remained in the barn, I went to the house to see Miss Jessup. She received me in the parlor after I had to wait several minutes after Callie had first announced my entrance into the foyer. Callie told me to wait in the parlor. When Wanda walked into the room, she appeared to be upset and a little discomforted, maybe in slight pain, I observed. She moved slowly past the sofa where she pointed for me to sit while she made her way toward her chair. She wore a white dressing gown that reached to the floor, and I couldn't help notice how she kept pulling at the top to insure keeping the front of the gown closed. We talked briefly, but long enough for me to determine that I had heard quite enough from her. I put her under arrest and ordered her to get dressed immediately. She would be accompanying me to jail for further questioning. Wanda excused herself to return upstairs to get dressed. When she turned to leave, I could see a patch of blood that stained the back of her gown. 'Wait a minute, Miss Jessup. You're hurt and bleeding. I can see the blood on the back of your gown. What happened?' With absolutely no hesitation, she made her quick reply, 'Oh, that's where my father whipped me!' I have to admit that I wasn't surprised. I knew then, I know now, that girl just killed her father!"

"Objection, your honor," shouted her attorney. "Hearsay! I move that last remark be struck from the record."

"Sustained," said the judge. "The clerk will strike that last statement from the record. Sheriff, you may continue with your testimony."

"When I started down the front steps with Wanda, we were met by Sam, who was holding a twelve-gauge shotgun. He told me that he found it behind a barrel near the barn door. I asked Wanda if she had ever seen this gun before, and she said 'yes, I have. That's my father's shotgun.' Grabbing it from my deputy, I took a quick look while I held what I believed to be the murder weapon. With the shotgun in hand, I escorted Wanda to the horse pen where our horses were tied to the fence. I put Wanda on my deputy's horse while I mounted up on mine and we both rode off toward the Houston jailhouse. I kept thinking, all that was left to do that night was to send a wagon back for the bodies, along with Sam's horse. Coroner Blackburn already had his mount tied just outside the barn. This would allow him to leave as soon as he saw that the bodies were loaded onto the wagon to be transported into town to the morgue. It was probably around 9:30 p.m. when I got Wanda settled in her cell. That's about all I can remember right now, sir."

"Thank you, Sheriff. I have no more questions," said Mr. Lawrence.

"Mr. Martin, do you wish to cross-examine?"

"Yes, your honor, I have one question for the sheriff." He paused long enough to rise and stand in front of his table. "Did Miss Jessup ever tell you why she decided to go out to the barn that afternoon?"

"Why yes, she did indeed. That was one of the first questions I asked her. Her response was that she knew her father was taking Ben to the barn at gunpoint. She was afraid of what she thought he was planning to do to him. She was trying to finish up cleaning herself from the beating she had just undergone from her father, when she heard a shotgun fired from the vicinity of the barn. Hurriedly, she threw on a dress and ran barefoot toward the barn, only to find her father laying at the bottom of the ladder and Ben hanging from the hayloft. That's the account she gave me, anyway."

"No more questions," said the prosecuting attorney.

"Sheriff Kincaid, you may step down," said the judge. "Mr. Lawrence, call your next witness."

"There are no more witnesses, your honor, the prosecution will rest."

"We will take a recess for lunch until 1:00 p.m. when I will hear closing arguments. Court stands adjourned until that time." The handsome Judge Winslow stood from the bench and exited the courtroom through the chamber door, followed by the bailiff.

Several spectators at this time chose to remain in their seats, in fear of losing their places, should they decide to leave the courtroom. However, the majority rushed out to use the facilities once again, and find something to eat for lunch. Still, others lingered in the hallway or sat in various places outside on the lawn where they huddled in groups to talk, drink, smoke, or chew. The scene at the Houston court house was bursting alive with the abundance of varied noise levels and fast paced movement from the people scattered everywhere on the property. Other than regular court days, this venue was usually as quiet as a church mouse. However, today was not one of those days.

It was nearing 1:00 p.m. as the people started filing back inside the courtroom, while trying to re-locate their seats. Judge Winslow returned to the bench to signal the beginning of the closing arguments between Silas Martin and Matthew Lawrence.

"Mr. Martin, the court will now hear your final statements from the defense table. You may choose to stand or remain seated."

Producing a calm and confident appearance before the judge, Attorney J. Silas Martin stood at his table to deliver his closing argument. A hush fell over the courtroom while he began his speech.

35

"May it please the court, your honor, let us start with the *time* factor. Time can be a valuable asset in many situations; it can be critical in others. We look forward to the time we get to share each day. Sometimes, we feel saddened by the time we've lost. Most all our lives, including everything we do, these activities are all centered primarily during the time we have to spend in doing them. In this instance, how much time do you think Miss Jessup had from the moment her father left her bedroom with young Ben until she had to make some quick decisions? First, is she going to take the time to clean her wounds and try to stop the bleeding? Second, is she perhaps going to blot and dry herself off? Third, will she fully dress herself, with the exception of the time it could take to lace or button her shoes? We know already from previous testimony that she was barefoot, so she should be able to gain a little extra time for this. Now, all she has to do is leave her bedroom, go downstairs, run across the yard, make it to the barn, open the door, and locate her father to see what he is doing with the stable boy without them seeing her. After this, she has to run back to the house, go into her father's study, unlock his gun cabinet, pull out the shotgun, find the shells, load the weapon, and immediately head back to the barn just in time to shoot him in the back at the precise moment he turns around to start down the hayloft ladder. Did she have enough time to do all these things before she had to return even once again to discover both bodies? Were there any witnesses? How did she get rid of the shotgun? Did her clothes smell of gunpowder?"

"Your honor, the investigation into these homicides were botched from the start. There was never an attempt to try to find the real murderer of Judge Jessup, other than the blatant accusations against my client. All over this town, the gossips were having a field day. 'It had to be the daughter, the tramp, she killed her own father, so there is no need to look for anyone else.' I submit, your honor, that there is not one shred of evidence that links Miss Jessup to this tragic murder. We contend that Judge Jessup was indeed responsible for the hanging and ultimate death of Benjamin Washington; however, the murder of Harry Jessup was committed by someone other than his daughter. The killer is still out there and needs to be apprehended. I am asking you to take into consideration everything you have heard in direct testimony that contradicts time, place, and motive in this case, and find my client 'not guilty.' Thank you, your honor."

"We will now take a ten minute recess, after which time I will hear a closing argument by the prosecution," said the judge. With time elapsed, Judge Winslow returned to the bench in five minutes, and gave the nod for Matt Lawrence to begin his summation.

"Judge Winslow, have you ever been mad at someone, I mean really mad, mad enough to kill? Probably not, sir, because most people aren't usually that way; however, in fact, there are many disturbed individuals who fit this category. In countless, similar cases that I have tried since becoming a prosecutor, anger is right up there at the top of the list. Believe it or not, I have convicted at least nine individuals during the course of my career so far where anger was the motive for murder. Allow me to continue."

"With no witnesses, and two dead bodies, we have based our case findings upon the present circumstances, circumstantial evidence, if you choose to call it that. If you will think about the lifestyle that Miss Jessup has chosen for herself, we already have a number of witnesses, which you will note that we did not call, that could have readily testified about the defendant's moral character. Furthermore, it is our belief that this incident may not have been the first that Judge Jessup had witnessed or even heard about. We suspect that he may have punished his daughter any number of times before, being either physically or verbally abusive to her person. This was most likely the last straw for Wanda Jessup. No longer was she going to take a beating from her father, especially since he had just put to death one of her lovers by hanging his nude body from the rafters in the barn. The boy was only seventeen years old, only eight when he first came to live at Jessup Plantation. Later, I found out that was also the same year when Callie and Jacob arrived from the Belmont Plantation in Marion County."

"So, let's take a closer look, shall we? Wanda is a strong woman; everyone can see that as she sits at the table over there in this courtroom. Wanda is a good shot. One of the other boys told me that although she didn't have a shotgun herself, she would sometimes use her father's gun whenever she went hunting with him on different occasions. This same boy also saw her one day when she was target shooting with this same gun. She never seemed to have a problem loading or firing the weapon. Lastly, she had ample time to dress in a hurry and follow her father to the barn. I believe she heard her father say what he intended to do to Ben when he first ordered him out of the house at gunpoint. She followed, but now she already had a loaded shotgun with her as she left the house; however, she was too late. By the time she actually arrived at the barn, Harry Jessup had already hung Ben. He had started down the ladder when Wanda Jessup took aim with that 12 gauge and riveted his back with a round of buckshot. If that didn't kill him, the fall most certainly did. Your honor, we ask that you will find the defendant guilty of murder in the first degree while she deliberately set out to kill her own father in cold blood."

"The court will stand adjourned until 10:00 a.m. in the morning when I will deliver the verdict," said the judge while he slipped out into his chambers. The jailer was present to escort the defendant back to the jail, the place where she would spend yet another night.

"I'm innocent, I'm innocent," pleaded Wanda just before he shut the door and locked her cell.

The next morning, the courtroom was equally packed once more as excitement filled the room while Judge Winslow entered and took his seat. He gazed around the room, looked at the notes before him, and raising his head, he began to share his remarks, along with the final verdict.

"Ladies and gentlemen, you may rest assured that I have spent a most disturbing night while I have diligently sought judgment as what to render before God and man, a just ruling in this case. In all fairness, I complement both of these fine lawyers, Mr. Martin and

Mr. Lawrence, as they have presented their findings to the best of their ability with the evidence that was presented yesterday in court. It is my judgment in Case #114, the People vs. Wanda D. Jessup, as to the count of murder in the first degree. I find that the defendant is 'not guilty!' Miss Jessup, I did not find enough evidence presented beforehand for a conviction; however, I am in hopes that you will see this tragedy as an important lesson in your life, and will use it to make better choices and decisions while you get on with your life. Do you want to make a statement? He paused. Seeing no response, Miss Jessup, you are free to go. This court stands adjourned."

Two weeks later, Jacob sat with his mother, Callie, in the sheriff's office. Her body was literally shaking while the tears fell as she tried to utter her confession. At last, Callie was able to unleash the burden she had carried for weeks. As she began to unravel her story, the sheriff could hardly believe what he was hearing now. After all that had happened before and during the trial, the true identity of the shooter was finally revealed. Acting alone, it was she who broke into her master's study, stole the shotgun, loaded it, and went to the barn that afternoon. There was only one thing on her mind after witnessing the aftermath of Judge Jessup's rage. Now, her sole purpose was to put an end to the life of the angry man who was in the process of killing her other son, Ben. Only Harry Jessup knew about this secret, not even Wanda herself, since Ben's deceased father had been a former slave named Daniel Washington.

After much thought, remembering how he was so bent on seeing Wanda Jessup finally punished for the murder, he made his decision to release poor Callie. Sheriff Kincaid felt that she had already suffered enough and would have to live with what she did for the rest of her life. He felt justice was served when Callie took upon herself to become the executioner of the villain who took the life of her younger son. In the end, most people would never know about this surprising turn of events.

CHAPTER 4

March of 1861 came in like a lion. It seemed to Libby that the howling winds were never going to let up anytime soon. By late afternoon, she halfway got her wish. The winds had stopped, but a heavy line of thunderstorms prevailed until bedtime. She was waiting on her husband to arrive, so she settled in the rocker and picked up her needlepoint. Cole had been out hunting, and was drenched to the skin when he arrived home at supper time. Libby was doing well at six months pregnant, and Dr. Blake reassured her last week that she should be delivering a strong, healthy baby by the middle of June.

"Did you or Randall Fraser kill anything today?" she asked.

"Fraser got him a buck. We dressed it out in the woods and he offered me some of the meat. I'll tend to whatever I brought home when this rain lets up. It's on the back porch. Randall kept the rack, but I took the hide. Maybe I can get it dried and tanned for you, and it will make a nice rug to have in front of the fireplace."

"You had better get out of those wet clothes. I don't need you to get sick," she said.

"I had a chance to talk to Randall about the Carter boy," Cole said while he undressed.

"Oh, you did. What did he have to say?"

"He's not all that familiar with the woods around Pebble, but that's where his friend, Burt Allison, lives. His place is about a mile before you head into the dense forest. This is what he told me. On that fateful day this past winter, he met Burt at his house at daybreak to go hunting. His pal, Allison, says that he has hunted these woods all his life, so he knows the area pretty well. So, they stay relatively close to each other for most of the morning. Not having much luck in tracking any deer together, they decide to separate. Hey, Libby, want to hand me some clean drawers? I've got my naked butt hanging out over here," he chuckled.

"I see that mister, and I like what I see," she replied.

"You, go on girl! Please get me some dry clothes. No time for love right now," he laughed.

"I'm still listening," Libby said while she pulled Cole's shirt, pants, and long-johns from the bureau next to the bed.

"Where was I? Oh yeah… they both took off in opposite directions. He went east, and Allison went west while they agreed to meet back up in an hour or two."

"Here's your clothes. I guess you left your boots out on the porch."

"Yes, don't worry about them. I'll bring them in to dry when we finish talking."

"I can put some coffee on. Would you like a cup?"

"That would be nice, darling. I'm almost through dressing, and I'll just come to the table when I'm finished." Cole took a seat at the table while he waited for his coffee. "That's when Randall said he nearly lost it."

"Lost what?" Libby asked.

"In the woods, when he saw it, you know. It was a shock for Randall when he first discovered what he later learned was the remains of little Seth Carter. It struck him hard because Fraser has a five year old himself. Of course, at first he didn't hardly know what he was looking at, he told me."

"Oh, Cole, how awful! I just can't imagine," Libby said while her eyes began to fill with tears.

"I know this is extremely upsetting to everyone. Just to think how Randall felt at the time, but more than that, how John and Sarah felt also, and what they continue to go through each day. Fraser said that if he hadn't decided to go over to that particular spot to relieve himself, he more than likely would have never found the little boy."

"It's so sad," she said. "The Carter's will never be the same, even my mother is still upset over it. Absolutely, no peace until they will be able to have complete solace."

"Anyway, Randall went on to say that he fired off a round in hope that it would bring his friend Allison to him. He waited for five minutes and got off another shot. So, he sat on a nearby log and waited. Almost an hour had passed until he could hear Burt coming through the woods. When he finally got there, Randal led him to what he had found in the underbrush. They marked the spot and left immediately to go get Sheriff Kincaid. The rest of the story, you already know."

"As far as I know, they don't seem to be any closer to finding out what actually happened," she said. "You haven't heard anything more, have you?"

"No, but those working on the case probably know a lot more than you think. It's just not spread out there for everyone to know right now, only speculation. There's plenty of that, I'm sure. The true facts will come out one of these days."

"You're right, everyone I know still wonders about it. I'm afraid I still do," Libby said.

"That's just it. We all feel so helpless when we realize that there's nothing really any of us can do about this situation other than pray for the family."

Cole put his hand upon Libby's as she placed the coffee cup before him. She bent down and gave him a passionate kiss on his lips. He stood up, took her in his arms, and drew her rather large mid-section as close as he could to his. They held each other for the longest time.

At this same time, taking place just below Winston County, the suspect of a recent botched child-abduction case was being questioned at the Walker County jail. Taken into custody the day before by Sheriff Lonnie Hardeman, the alleged assailant had been held at gunpoint by the intended victim's father until the sheriff could arrive at the residence and make the arrest. Joseph Lee Doberman, a drifter who listed his residence as Lawrence County, was charged with the attempted abduction of six year old, John Michael McShan on March 3, 1861. Doberman, age 37, was taken down and held by the child's father, Mr. John M. McShan Sr., until proper authorities could arrive on the scene.

Mr. and Mrs. McShan were awakened around 10 p.m. on Thursday night when the intruder had broken into their house on Mulberry Street. Caught by surprise in their son's room, Doberman already had the boy in his arms in an attempt to flee when the child cried out. Due to his quick response, Mr. McShan was able to save his son from the apparent abduction.

Joseph Doberman, who listed his occupation as a gravedigger, was a single, rough-looking character having scraggly, long black hair and beard with dark bloodshot eyes. He had a reddish complexion, pock-marked face, and the remaining teeth he had were yellow-looking and tobacco stained. When he opened his mouth, his foul breath smelled of hard liquor. He wore a pair of filthy overalls with no shirt and mud-covered brown boots that laced.

Fortunately, Sheriff Hardeman had a few relatives in Winston County, and was familiar with the unsolved Carter case. He had been grilling Doberman for hours, trying to see if there was going to be a connection between the two cases. Now, time was going to be the main factor after the news started to spread that a person of interest was in custody. It was going to take a little more time for a conviction and to bring the alleged suspect to justice.

Three more weeks passed, and now they finally had him. Joseph Lee Doberman, after an intense interrogation by Sheriff Hardeman, broke down and gave his full confession. He admitted guilt in trying to abduct the McShan boy for his own out of control sexual gratification. He had escaped from Halcyon, the mental institution, located in Lawrence County just days before the abduction of Seth Carter. He also confessed to first seeing the young boy playing in his yard, and his desire to seize and take him. He watched the house for hours until he was able to find a place to hide while the family had been away. He further admitted talking to Seth earlier in the day while he was playing outside alone and promising to show him a big surprise. He lured the Carter boy from his home, taking him into the woods miles away in Pebble, and once there in a remote area, assaulted and strangled him to death. He tried to conceal his crime by taking the body and hiding it in a thicket of underbrush. When he realized that the boy had brought along his teddy bear, he tucked it under Seth's little arm while he prepared to leave. Doberman fastened his overalls and walked away.

Labeling Doberman a "perverted monster," the townspeople angrily cried out for the death penalty. Joseph Doberman was spat upon by the crowd while obscenities filled the air as he was led away from the Walker County jailhouse. He was taken back to Winston County to stand trial where he was found guilty in a trial by jury. Judge Thomas K. Winslow sentenced him to death by hanging.

John and Sarah Carter made only one brief statement following the trial where they were able to see the accused murderer, face to face. John addressed the court while Sarah stood with her head leaning against her husband.

"Though our hearts are broken today, no one is the victor in this judgment. We forgive Mr. Doberman who will lose his life; however, we realize that this will never bring our son back to us. God is the ultimate judge, and it is through forgiveness and our trust in Him that we have that blessed assurance. One day, we will see our Seth in Heaven once again."

Judge Winslow set the execution date for Joseph Lee Doberman on 23 April, 1861.

Shocking news as South Carolina is shattered by a mortar hitting Fort Sumter in Charleston Harbor on 12 April 1861. President Abraham Lincoln responds to the Confederate challenge by the issue of three proclamations. In the first, he calls up the militia from several states. In the second, he orders that all southern ports will be blockaded. Thirdly, coming two weeks later, he calls for three year volunteers for the regular army. With the arrival of summer, both the North and South had raised enough troops to begin the war.

A new day was dawning while the sun continued rising on the breath of the morning dew. Birds were chirping while chipmunks and squirrels busied themselves digging in the earth all over the place. Cole was first up this morning and noticed already that today was going to be a bright, sunny day. He whistled joyfully as he returned to the cabin from the outhouse. Libby hadn't yet stirred, so he left her sleeping while he attempted to put on the coffee. Most mornings, it was she who usually woke up first and had the coffee perking. How he loved to wake up to the smell of freshly brewed coffee. While he waited, he picked up the broom beside the fireplace and began sweeping off the hearth. By the looks of it, with scattered fragments of bark and soot, he knew that Libby would have to sweep if he didn't. She kept gaining weight and was quite large now, so Cole thought his meager effort would be somewhat of a help to her. He loved her so much. About the time he finished, he could hear her stirring in the bed. The coffee was ready, so he poured a cup for himself and sat down at the table while he waited on her to awake.

"Good morning, darling," she said as she walked in and threw her loving arms around him. She tried to bend down to kiss his cheek while he was seated at the table, but couldn't quite make it happen.

"Hey, little Mama, you're not so little anymore," he laughed. "Let's see you bend down and touch your toes."

"You go to the dickens, Cole McTavish! I'd like to see you at nearly seven months even trying to get up out of your chair."

"Only kidding, darling. Forgive me?"

"Well, maybe I'll think about it. I see that you swept off the hearth. Thank you for your help. That's just something else that I won't have to do today. What do you want for breakfast?"

"Just coffee is fine this morning. I see that there are two biscuits left over from supper last night setting on the stove. I'll just have them to eat and get on to work. What are you going to do today?"

"We still have that quilt we're working on, so I may go over to Mother's in just a while."

"I assume she's doing a lot better now that the Carter tragedy is somewhat behind us," he said.

"Yes, she is, I'm pretty sure, but John and Sarah aren't. Mama told me that Sarah has almost lost her mind, and she only eats enough to barely remain alive. I worry about both of them and the other children. What must they all be feeling?"

"I saw John Carter at the general store last week, and he hardly spoke two words to me. He looked really bad. I noticed they've also quit coming to church."

"I'll try to get over there to visit them later this afternoon," she said.

"Speaking of the afternoon, when I leave work today, I'm meeting up with Nate and we're going to Looney's Tavern. I'll have something to eat while I'm there, so don't plan to have any supper for me tonight."

"That's fine. I'll eat with Mama. She always has something going on the stove or in the oven. If she feels like baking, we may just make you an apple cobbler."

"That would be great!" he replied.

"By the way, how is Nate and Marcie? I haven't seen her in quite some time."

"The last time we talked, Nate told me that they were trying to get pregnant, but so far, no luck. Marcie was beginning to worry about whether they were going to be able to have children or not. He said she really wanted a baby, and was working him nearly to death," he laughed.

"Cole, tell him for me when you see Nate this afternoon, let's all get together for dinner."

"I will, but now I need to go, right away. See you tonight. Love you, girl!" Cole said while he headed out the door.

"Love you, more," she said.

"Running a little late this morning, as usual. Sorry for the delay, Mr. Parker," Cole said as he found his father-in-law already at work in the barn.

"That's all right, son, I'm about finished in here. We've got a wagon of supplies that needs to be unloaded. Other than that, Cole, just get on with your regular work. How's Libby?"

"She's doing well this morning. She should be coming here after a while. Maybe you will have a chance to see her later in the day."

"I'll make it a point to try my best to do that," Mr. Parker said.

"I wanted to ask you, sir, if I finish with my work, do you mind letting me off a little early? I am planning to meet Nate Overstreet later this afternoon at Looney's Tavern."

"Why certainly, son, I have no problem with that. I may slip over there myself, but you know I have to tread softly. Amelia watches me like a hawk." They both shared a hearty laugh. "Where would we be without our womenfolk trying to keep us in line?"

When Cole arrived around 5:30 p.m. at the tavern, Nate was already there and seated at the bar. With a couple of drinks already under his belt, Nate threw up his hand to signal his buddy Mule as he walked through the crowded joint to join him.

"Hey, Bill, what about a whiskey for my friend?" yelled Nate to the barkeeper.

"Thanks Nate, but just one shot, and I'm done. You know how too much alcohol affects me. How long have you been here?" Cole asked.

"I've been here about an hour, I guess," replied Nate.

"A whiskey comin' right up," said Bill Looney, the barkeeper and proprietor of the tavern.

Nate moved in closer to Cole, almost in his face. "See that high-falutin' bunch of big-wigs over there at the table by the window? Bill tells me that's Chris Sheats, newly elected to the U.S. House of Representatives, sitting with his entourage."

"Wonder what they're doing here?" asked Cole.

"I dunno. I'll ask Bill when he brings your drink."

"Who wanted this?" Bill asked while he pushed the shot glass toward Nate.

"Oh, that's for my buddy, Mule. Here man, drink up!" Nate placed the glass within his reach. "Hey, Bill, what's Sheats doing in here?"

"Well, Nate, it's like this. You know every year on the 4th of July, we always have a big celebration here at the tavern with fireworks and a barbeque. Remember?"

"Yeah, I know, I hardly ever miss it."

"Well, my friend, on that date we will be hosting a political meeting here to discuss the possibility of secession, and Mr. Sheats, sitting over there, will be the main speaker. His office has just paid me for that venue set for July. That's all I know right now."

"I need to find out more about him before then. All I know is that I didn't vote for the man in this last election," said Nate.

"Me, either," replied Cole.

Within the hour, Chris Sheats and his party left the tavern while Nate and Cole wasted no time in pressing Bill Looney for any information he knew about the man. They caught up with Looney at the bar while they settled for another round of drinks before they left for home.

At the time when South Carolina, Virginia, and the other states seceded from the Union, support for the Confederacy was far from being a done deal. Charles Christopher Sheats, deemed a *scalawag* by many, ultimately vowed that he would never support secession. His stand on this current issue made him an enemy of the Confederacy, but politically brought him support from the Union while this conflict continued to heat up all over the nation.

Christopher Sheats was born on 10 April, 1839 in Walker County, Alabama, the son of a planter. He attended public schools there during the years of his early education, and later finished at Somerville Academy in Morgan County. At age eighteen, he became a schoolteacher in Walker County. With a keen interest in politics, at age twenty-one, he was elected to the Alabama House of Representatives in 1861.

In each of the adjoining counties, especially Winston, so many of the people were not wealthy enough to own slaves since they hacked out their meager living as honest farmers. To many of them, the idea of secession or breaking away from the United States was completely unheard. Why would any existing state in the Union want to do that?

Sheats attended a convention in Montgomery where the first vote taken was 53-46 against immediate secession. He took sides with a group calling themselves the "cooperationists." Their argument was that secession should not be allowed to happen without first giving President Lincoln's policies a try. Furthermore, in the event secession did occur, it should be approved by a popular vote of the people. With the increasing tensions, and the secession of several more southern states, the Alabama Convention took another vote. On 11 January, 1861, the vote was 61-39 in favor of secession. As a result, Sheats, who was opposed to secession was quoted as saying, "Not now, not ever!" He quickly refused to sign the ordinance that was adopted at the convention. For this reason, it was primarily his decision to lead an anti-secession rally to be held at Looney's Tavern.

During this time, Winston County residents who sided with the Confederacy angrily called for all the Unionists, like Sheats, to be jailed. After Christopher Sheats was elected to the House, he remained a popular figure for a time; however, he never attended another session of the legislature. There was a requirement that every representative had to sign an oath of allegiance to the Confederacy to serve, so Sheats chose to remain at home, rather than pledge his support to a cause he didn't believe would benefit his county or state.

What has been recorded as the incident at Looney's Tavern actually took place there on 4 July 1861, with an estimated crowd between 2,500 and 3,000 in attendance from several neighboring counties. The main agenda was to discuss and pass a resolution on that date, following an address by House Representative, Chris Sheats. At the conclusion of his formal address, the secretary recorded three resolutions as follows:

1. *"We commend the Honorable Charles Christopher Sheats and the other representatives who stood with him for their loyalty and fidelity to the people whom they represented in voting against secession of Alabama from the Union first, last, and all time."*[1]

2. *"We agree with Jackson that no state can legally get out of the Union, but if we are mistaken in this, and a state can lawfully and legally secede or withdraw, being a part of the State, by the same process of reasoning, a county could cease to be a part of the State."*[2]

3. *"We think our neighbors in the South made a mistake when they bolted the convention and the Democratic Party, resulting in the election of Mr. Lincoln, and that they made a greater mistake when they attempted to secede and set up a new government. We, however, do not desire to see our neighbors in the South suffer wrong, and therefore, we are not going to take up arms against them; but on the other hand, we are not going to shoot at the flag of our fathers, Old Glory, the flag*

of Washington, Jefferson, and Jackson. Therefore, we ask the Confederacy on the one hand and the Union on the other, to leave us alone, unmolested, that we may work out our own political and financial destiny here in the hills and mountains of North Alabama."3

1.2.3. Wording of the resolution as originally phrased in the book, The Free State of Winston by Wesley S. Thompson

Did Winston County actually secede from the State of Alabama?

No, not exactly, Winston did not officially secede from the state. The term "Free State of Winston" is credited from a sarcastic remark made by Richard "Uncle Dick" Payne at the conclusion of the meeting at Looney's Tavern. He allegedly stood and shouted:

"Ho! Ho! Winston secedes – the Free State of Winston!"

History records from that date until the present, there has been an untold number of references made about the little county in northwest Alabama simply known as "The Free State of Winston."

CHAPTER 5

A newborn baby's cry suddenly filled the air while James Parker, Greta Hassendorfer, Marcie and Nate Overstreet, and Malcolm and Colleen McTavish patiently waited outside on the porch of the little cabin. Dr. Blake, Amelia, and Cole were present inside where Libby had just given birth to a beautiful baby boy on this hot and humid Sunday afternoon, following a hard labor of three hours. Two weeks after an expected due date of June 27, Alexander Malcolm McTavish was born 15 July 1861 at 3:29 p.m. Mother and baby were doing fine.

"Thank you, Dr. Blake, for arriving on time. Don't think I could have handled this on my own," said Cole. "In fact, I know I couldn't."

"But you had Mrs. Parker here with you to help," said the doctor.

"Yes, but still I'm glad you were here," Cole said while he looked down on the bed at Libby. "Darling, he's beautiful! He's, well…he is just perfect is all I can say."

"Glad to know that you think so," Libby answered. "Guess he's a keeper, huh?"

"Yes, most definitely. I love you both so much." He leaned down to kiss her.

"Mama, may I hold him?"

"Why certainly, dear. Just a minute more and I'll have him all cleaned up," said Amelia as she finished and wrapped the baby in a light blanket. "Here he is."

Libby took her son and held him close to her bosom. "Guess he'll be wanting to eat before long. What about everyone on the porch? Give me a minute and then invite everyone inside. It's sweet of them to have waited all this time."

Malcolm and Colleen were the first to enter, followed by Greta, James, Marcie, and Nate. They all stood around Libby's bedside while enjoying their visit in getting to see the baby minutes after his birth.

"Oh, how sweet! He's precious," said Colleen. "Reminds me of how Cole looked when he was born."

"A fine boy," Malcolm said.

"We're naming him after you," said Libby. "Alexander Malcolm will be his Christian name, but we'll call him Alex."

"Libby, is there anything you need?" Greta asked. "He's just wonderful, a big boy, I might add. Looks at least seven pounds, I'm guessing."

"He felt like a ten pounder coming out," she laughed. "No, Greta, I don't need anything."

"Cole, you may have tomorrow off, son. You just help and take good care of my fine grandson," said James Parker.

"Such a head full of hair and those bright eyes looking all around," Marcie commented.

"Hey Mule, you've got fine looking boy there," said his buddy Nate. "Haven't seen it yet, but do you think we might have us a Mule Jr.?"

"Oh yes, I think so, most definitely!" laughed Cole.

"I guess I'll be going," said Dr. Blake as he picked up his bag. "Libby, bring the baby to my office in another week and we'll do a check-up and circumcision, if you decide to do that."

"All right," she answered. "Thank you, Dr. Blake. We'll settle our bill with you at that time. Goodbye for now."

"We appreciate your service, doctor," Cole added.

"That Dr. Blake is a fine doctor," said Libby after he left the cabin.

"He delivered two of my sister's children," said Marcie.

"Everyone's welcome to stay as long as you want, but right now would you give me and Cole a little time together? Alex is getting a little fretful as you can probably see. I think it's time for him to nurse."

A week later, Cole and Libby took Alex to see Dr. Blake at his office in Double Springs.

"Let's weigh the little man, shall we?" The doctor said as he placed the baby on the scales.

"Looks like exactly eight and three quarter pounds. He's doing well, I'd say. Any problem nursing, Mrs. McTavish?"

"No, doctor, I believe he does that just fine."

"Did you and Cole decide if you wanted to have him circumcised?"

"Yes, I do, but Cole is having second thoughts, I'm afraid."

"Well, it's all right, I guess," Cole said. "I just find it difficult in knowing that I'm doing to my son what was never done to me. It's got to hurt like hell!" He paused. "Ah, go ahead with it, but I'll wait outside until you're done."

"He didn't hardly whimper or cry," Libby said as she met her husband outside. "Here, take him."

Cole cradled baby Alex in his strong arms, and with Libby at his side, the McTavish family loaded into the buggy and headed home.

Over the next few weeks, Cole and Libby settled into their newly established routine that now included a baby to look after, 24 hours a day and 7 days a week. Where did all their extra time go? Cole usually went to work at the dairy every day, but helped out as much as possible when he got home. Libby had to find time to balance out her time with the baby, changing and feeding him, along with regular housework, cleaning, and cooking. Now would be a good time to have a slave to serve as a house servant or maid. Their child was only one. How did parents care for seven or eight?

As Alex continued to grow over the next few weeks, Libby brought up to Cole that she needed more space. She felt that the little cabin was getting a bit crowded.

"More space? You would like, what?" Cole asked.

"Build me a new house, darling."

"A new house! That's near impossible right now. Where am I going to get all the money to do that? Extra work is scarce and there's a war going on. You have heard about Bull Run, haven't you?"

"Why, of course, I have. I've already talked to my father and he promised to loan us some of the money. I figure that we could go up the hill, just beyond the cabin near that old oak tree, and lay a foundation. Then, later, frame in the structure according to the plans I have in mind. We can continue to live in the cabin until the new house is finished, however long it may take. How does that sound, darling?"

"Sounds like you already decided. That's crazy!" Libby batted her eyes at him while quickly adjusting her dress to show a little cleavage. "Well, give me some time," he said. "You know I'm always open to your suggestions."

A week later, and Cole was all in it, hook, line, and sinker. He promised he would build his bride the house she wanted, but there was something far greater pressing on his mind. He prayed that he was making the right decision and would find the right time to talk to Libby about it. His very life was going to depend on it this time.

In the meantime, Cole put his personal agenda on hold, never mentioning it to Libby or anyone, even his closest buddy, Nate. Instead, he jumped wholeheartedly into the construction plans of the new house. When Cole and Libby had finished their discussion on the logistics concerning everything that she wanted in the house, the planning part was over, and the dream became a reality. With the money he received from his father-in-law, and the loan secured from the bank, Cole hired an architect. It would be his job to draw up the plans and build the house in accordance to the orders given him as directed by Mrs. Libby McTavish. Of course, Cole would be able to make suggestions, changes, and whatever else was necessary in order to build his wife's dream home. It was understood that this would be a joint undertaking between both of them and that there would be no arguments.

One month later, the location was chosen about 500 yards above the present site of the little cabin where ground was broken, and the foundation was laid. Local architect and builder, William J. Ledbetter provided slave labor at all his construction sites, and this project would require the services of at least twenty-eight men for approximately eighteen months for completion. Every slave was the property of Mr. Ledbetter with the exception of the brick mason. Cole's own father, Malcolm McTavish, would oversee and help when necessary with any or all of the brick work.

"That woman is driving me crazy," complained Bill Ledbetter to Cole on the first day of construction. "She's out here with the baby hanging onto her hip while her free hand is directing the changes to the plans. My original drawings are so marked up that I'm going to have to re-calculate several of the measurements. I can't work like this."

"Sorry, Bill, I'll have a word with Libby tonight at supper," replied Cole.

"I don't have to tell you that with each change there will be additional costs. Is that what you want?"

"Not hardly! What are some of the changes that she wants?"

"Mrs. McTavish is a fine woman who definitely knows what she wants, but we are going to have to stick closer to the original plans if you want to stay within your budget."

"I completely understand and agree with you, Bill. Tell me about the changes."

"Well, the first structural change is to the front portico. Mrs. McTavish wants to add two additional Corinthian columns to the porch foundation, six instead of four. That can be done, but it will take a re-configuration on my part with additional costs for materials and millwork. Presently, I have only four on order."

"Four, you say?"

"Yes, each column will be constructed from six sections after they arrive on site. The pieces will be stacked and positioned into place after which the former supports are taken out and removed. After sanding and whitewashing, each column will appear uniquely as a fifteen foot structure. The overall effect will be quite impressive, I believe."

"Tell you what, Bill, let's go ahead with the four original columns. If you will properly space them, later on we can always add the two additional ones. How's that?"

"I can do that with no problem."

"What else?"

"She wants running water added to the kitchen basin, and also to the tub in the wash room. I'll have to order the white porcelain commode she wants from a supplier in Atlanta."

"How much extra will that cost for everything?"

"Nearly five hundred dollars, I'm guessing."

"Let's do it, Bill. It will be worth it not to have to go outside anymore to pee."

"One more thing she wants is the installation of gaslights in nearly every room."

"Let me think about that. We can discuss this next week. Right now, I need to get back to work." That night Cole had his talk with Libby to help her understand the situation and clear up the problem she was causing for the builder.

While the summer months rolled along, the new house on the hill began to take shape. Although it was never intended by either Cole or Libby, the skeletal structure was turning into what the townspeople would eventually call a mansion. With the framework almost completed, construction suddenly came to a halt.

"We're out of money," Cole said. "The columns are on back order and the price of lumber has skyrocketed."

"What do you mean?" Libby asked while she placed Cole's plate before him and joined him at the supper table.

"Where's Alex?" he asked.

"I left him with Mother for his first overnight stay. She is making a new outfit for him, and also, I wanted to see how he would react if we ever had to leave him with her for whatever reason."

"I miss the little fellow being with us tonight," Cole responded.

"Darling, you didn't answer my question. What do you mean we're out of money?"

"I meant to say things are beginning to tighten while the war continues. It's difficult nowadays to get the necessary supplies delivered, and besides that, our cash flow is almost gone. What I'm trying to say, Libby, is we're going to have to hold up construction for a while."

"I understand, darling. At least, we have it framed. We're at a good stopping point."

"We may have enough bricks already on hand for my father to get started on the front portico."

"That's good, I'm not complaining. We have each other, the cabin, and a roof over our heads, that's all that matters to me right now."

"I'm afraid that's not all that really matters. Darling, we need to talk about something that I can't get off my mind," Cole said while he drew Libby close to his side.

"What's that, my love?"

"Darling, it's like this. Ever since the meeting at Looney's Tavern this past July, I can't shake what I feel inside. I'm seriously thinking about joining up with the Union forces. What do you think about that?"

"What will our Confederate friends say?"

"Let the truth be known, dang it! This is what we all must face. Our nation, our state, even our county is tearing itself apart. Right now, I give no thought as to what my friends think of me. Looks as if everyone is going to have to choose a side and fight."

"Surely, you're not serious!"

"I am, my darling. My only regret will be having to leave you and Alex."

"When is this to happen?"

"Not right away. I'm going to have to talk with Nate. We may be going together."

"I can tell you that Marcie is not going to like this."

"Not surprising, no one likes this."

"I can tell you for a fact, Cole McTavish, that I don't like it!"

"I know, darling, me either. All I'm asking is to let me check things out. I hear that there is a new cavalry unit forming in Huntsville."

"Confederate or Union?"

"It's Union, of course."

"What's your father going to say?"

"What can he say to his grown son? If he were younger, he'd probably be enlisting with me."

"I find that hard to believe."

"Do you now, Missy? Then you don't know Malcolm McTavish very well."

"Well, maybe I don't, but what I do know is I'm tired hearing about all this talk of war. Greta told me last week that her husband, Jacob, up and joined the Confederate Army a month ago. That poor girl is crying her eyes out."

"Well, that tells me now about the mindset of that idiot, Jacob Hassendorfer. I should have known his scrawny butt was for the Confederacy."

"That's enough, no more of this talk! I've got to go to Mother's and get Alex. Want to come with me?"

"Sure, darling, why not?"

Needless to say, there was no more talk of war for the rest of the evening.

Late the next afternoon, Cole sat alone at the bar in Looney's Tavern while he waited on his buddy Nate to arrive. He slowly nursed a whiskey sour while his attention suddenly shifted to the loud voices at the table in the corner. He glanced up to see Jonah Leviston pounding his fist on the table while he shouted obscenities toward any patrons in the tavern who sided with the Union.

Cole had known Jonah since grade school when they had been boyhood rivals at anything involving physical competition. It had been quite a number of years both men had seen each other after Jonah left Winston County. Spotting his former nemesis across the room, Jonah stumbled from his chair and staggered slowly toward the bar area. He gave Cole an exaggerated slap across his back while he made his presence known behind him.

"Well, I'll be damned if it ain't my old buddy Mule McTavish! How the hell are you?"

Cole turned himself on the barstool well enough to look into the face of the man who now demanded his full attention.

"Hello, Jonah, I'm doing well. It's been quite a while since I last saw you. What brings you back to these parts?"

"I'm seeing Wanda Jessup. She's a mighty fine woman. Thinking 'bout askin' her to marry me, I reckon."

"I thought you married Amy Stevenson after we got out of school."

"I did. We were only married less than a year when she ran off with that bastard Matthew Lonergan. Served her right when old Matt simply vanished two years later while he was out deer hunting."

"I'm sorry to hear all that, Jonah. I really mean it."

"No bother, I've long been over her and ready now to move on. Had my eye on that Jessup gal for quite some time now. Would you believe she won't let me.....you know.....? I know she wants it bad, but keeps on telling me 'not until we are properly wed.' No wonder I've heard her called Wicked Wanda!" Jonah let out a few more expletives. What brings you to Looney's, Mule?"

"I'm waiting on Nate Overstreet to get here. We're thinking about joining up with the 1ˢᵗ Cavalry Unit in Huntsville."

"That's Union, ain't it? Hell, you aren't planning to side with the Yanks, are you?"

"Seriously thinking about it, I reckon."

"Winston County is full of too many damned pathetic Yankee sympathizers. Do you really want to side with them, Mule?"

"I believe every man in the county has a right to his own mind and everything he believes. It's a matter of a man being able to make his own choice, I might add."

"Why you're just a nigger lover?"

"No, Jonah, I'm not! I own no slaves nor do I intend to. This is not a black or white issue for me, and I'm sorry if you don't see it exactly like I do."

"Well, go on to Huntsville then, you slimy bastard! Git yore damn ass out of Winston County and take that sorry ass friend with you. You're both just two more turncoat traitors, and you'll be sorry when you realize what you're doing."

"Sorry about what, Jonah? Sorry that I stand for what I believe in!"

Jonah shuffled his feet as he leaned heavily against the bar for support. "My daddy has owned several slaves over the years. He doesn't mistreat them as some masters do, but they are his property. Hell, he bought and paid for every one of their black asses. Doesn't make him a bad man, a tyrant, does it?"

"No, it doesn't. Mr. Leviston is ultimately responsible and should be able to make his own decision. Lincoln's Emancipation Proclamation declares that all slaves should now go free, and your father will have to contend with that."

"Papa Leviston won't be letting his slaves go. That will never happen while he's still breathing."

"So, you're joining the Confederacy real soon, I'm assuming to fight for your Papa?"

"I haven't fully decided right now. I really want me and Wanda to get married."

"Well, Jonah, just let me say this. I hope that I never have to face you on the battlefield in the future. God of Mercy, I pray for the both of us that we will never have that to encounter."

"You think you could kill me, Mule?"

"I don't want to ever have that sudden decision to have to make. Listen, Jonah, it's been good to see you and talk again after so long, but I see that Nate has just walked in and he's looking for me. Maybe we can talk some more before we decide to leave."

"I can take a hint, my friend, I'm not that drunk," Jonah said while he turned and staggered back to his table.

"Who was that?" Nate said while he joined Cole and took a seat beside him.

"You remember Jonah Leviston, don't you? Don't even look over that way. He's probably staring at us right now. What a pathetic asshole!"

"Why do you say that?"

"You don't want to know, believe me. He's just been ranting and cursing us for being traitors to the Confederacy. He's drunk, don't give him a second thought." Cole held up his glass for a refill.

"Just like me, I guess you've had enough time now to make up your mind. What do you think about joining the cavalry?" Nate asked while he gave a slight smile.

"Libby finally agreed with me and said I should do what I am already determined to do anyway. What about you?"

"Marcie keeps on crying her eyes out, pleading with me not to go. Cole, I don't think I can do it. At least, not right now, please understand."

"That's all right, my friend. Perhaps it will benefit us both in the days to come. If you were to remain here at home, you and Marcie could also look out for Libby and little Alex. I'd be mighty obliged to you for that!"

"I hadn't even thought about that, Cole. You know I would gladly do anything for you, my friend."

"I'm counting on you to save me from that worry."

"When do you think you will leave for Huntsville?"

"We've put construction on the house on hold for now, so it will probably be in the next couple of days. I think I have almost everything in order. I've already spoken with my father-in-law and he has a new hire ready to take my place at the dairy when I finally decide to leave."

"So, that's it! You've made up your mind, so I wish you Godspeed and prayers for your safe return when all this is finally over," Nate said while he stood to hug his friend goodbye as they sadly left Looney's Tavern.

CHAPTER 6

Cole thought he had everything in order when he went to bed that night. He would be leaving for Huntsville in two days. Wishing that his buddy Nate could go with him, he had to resign himself to the fact that this was never going to happen. Nevertheless, he would feel relieved knowing that Nate would remain at home with Marcie to keep a check on Libby and Alex.

Libby rose from the rocker while she held her sleeping baby cradled in her arms. Slowly, she walked over to the crib where she put Alex to bed for the night. After she tucked him in, Libby extinguished the lamp on the nightstand, and slid into bed beside her anxiously awaiting husband. As her warm hand slid underneath the cover across his belly, Cole's passion suddenly ignited. It was like a blazing brush fire raging out of control on a most powerful windy day. While her intense movement continued downward, ever so slightly, across his naked body, he was now fully aroused. Knowing that this could possibly be their last opportunity for sex in quite some time, the two young lovers took full advantage of the situation. Breathlessly, bewitched, bothered, and bewildered, the feeling was like two runaway locomotives, traveling nonstop at the highest rate of speed, racing toward each other on the same track. Climaxing in an unavoidable collision as shattering iron and flying steel erupted out of the spewing steam bursting out in all directions. The shrill screaming of the two derailed locomotives as they overturned, crashed, and burned while at the same time, both engines lost their load. Afterward, Cole rolled over and quickly fell asleep while Libby's body grew still in the dark as a tear rolled down her cheek. She could hardly bear the thought that her man would be leaving home in one more day and night.

The sun was nearly up around 5:30 a.m. when Libby and Cole were suddenly awakened by a loud rapping at the door of their little cabin.

"Who could be at the door this early in the morning?" Libby mumbled while she rolled over to shake her waking husband.

"I dunno. I'll go see," Cole said while he rolled out of bed and hurriedly grabbed for his pants. Stumbling across the floor while trying to get his left foot down the pant leg, he pulled on his trousers until he had them up enough to cover his naked butt. Not taking time to button the fly, he held the pants together at the waist while he made it to the door. "Who's there?"

"It's me, James."

Cole opened the door to see his frantic-looking father-in-law standing there in an apparent shaken state. He appeared to be in total shock. Cole fumbled to get his pants fastened while he grabbed James Parker's arms. He led him to a chair and seated him at the table. By this time, Libby had pulled on her robe and was quickly moving toward her father.

"What's wrong, Daddy?" Libby asked while she threw her arms around him.

"It's Amelia," he said, "I'm terribly afraid that your mother has had a stroke or something."

"Oh no," she cried, "what's happened? I can't bear the thought of anything happening to my sweet Mama. Is she going to be all right?"

"I can't tell. She's mighty weak, I'm afraid."

"Who's with her now? You didn't leave her alone? Please, I need to know," Libby pleaded.

"Dr. Blake is with her at home right now. I just rushed over to tell you. She's asking for you, Libby."

"Let me get dressed! It will only take me a few minutes."

"I'll wait outside in the buggy," James Parker said while he rose from the chair to leave.

"What do you want me to do?" Cole asked Libby.

"You'll have to stay here and take care of Alex until I can get back. I don't know when that will be," she kept thinking. "I know, when Alex wakes up, you can dress him and bring him to Mama's house. Got to go now, my love, see you later this morning."

Rushing outside, feeling somewhat calmer, Libby slid onto the seat beside her father in the buggy. James quickly snapped the reins, and they were off as they headed toward the main road in quite a hurry. Cole stood in the doorway until they were out of sight.

"There goes the trip to Huntsville and my enlistment," he thought while he walked around the side of the cabin and headed to the outhouse.

Minutes now seemed like hours while the two thought they would never get there. Libby held onto her father's arm while he slowed down only slightly to brake for all the curves in the crooked little road while the dust flew from the rear wheels like a storm. James Parker pulled in as close as he could to the porch when they arrived at the house. Libby was down off the buggy and up the front steps before her father had time to completely stop. She never saw the young man, her father's new hire, seated on the edge of the porch while she ran past him. He appeared to be like a silent sentry posted in the shadows while he waited on the boss man to arrive. As James Parker made his approach, the light-skinned lad folded and put away his knife into his front pocket as he stood there attentively in place. The object he had been carving ended up in his shirt pocket while he moved closer to the approaching Mr. Parker.

"I'll take the buggy around back to the carriage house," he said.

"Thank you, Landon, but don't unhitch the rig until I tell you. We may have to use it again. I'm glad you're already here so early this morning. Go to the barn and get started with the milking. I'll be there when I can. I need to get back inside the house right now."

"Yes sir! I hope that Mrs. Parker is going to be all right," Landon said while he passed by the worried husband ascending the front steps.

"We'll see, boy. I don't know," Mr. Parker said while he entered the house and walked into the bedroom.

Dr. Blake stood at the end of the bed while Libby and her father each took their place on either side. Libby fell across her mother in a deep embrace while James placed his rough hands on top of Amelia's. Libby returned upright, almost trembling as she turned and faced the doctor.

"Tell me, Dr. Blake, what's wrong with my mother? She can't even speak to me."

"May we go into the parlor?" he asked. "It will be better to talk in there, I believe."

Libby sat on the green velvet sofa while her father took a seat in his worn leather wingback chair. Dr. Blake stood in front of the fireplace while he continued with their conversation.

"I have examined Mrs. Parker extensively and she may have suffered more than it appears. I have given her laudanum as a sedative and she appears to be resting well as you can see."

"What is her condition? Is it life-threatening?" James asked the doctor.

"Not meaning to be blunt with my answer, but yes to both questions. It is my honest opinion that we may be looking at far more than what presently may appear as a stroke. It certainly can be life-threatening. However, please don't think that I am trying to scare you."

Libby cried. "What can we do? I'm really worried now. Something has to be done to help her."

"I'm sorry, Mrs. McTavish. I don't mean to upset you, but I really can't say right this minute. Most certainly, we need to proceed with a further examination very soon."

"Doctor, what exactly will that involve?" James said while he reached inside his coat for a handkerchief to blot his sweating brow.

"We need to get your wife to the infirmary in Huntsville where Dr. Hiram Levine can examine her and give us a possible diagnosis. I trust this man's opinion, both as a former colleague and personal friend. His former years of medical school and seven years of service in the Huntsville area most certainly give his patients cause to seek his care for their well-being. Also, if a special treatment is found to be needed, he can get that started. Would you both agree to that?"

"Yes, of course," they both answered at once.

"Then I'll begin at once to make the necessary arrangements while you both make plans to have her transported to the Huntsville Infirmary."

"Thank you, Dr. Blake," replied James Parker. "What do we need to do when Amelia wakes up?"

"She will probably sleep well into the afternoon which will be good for her to continue to rest. When she awakens, give her some broth and see to her personal needs. Be sure to watch her closely that she doesn't try to get up by herself and fall. I will return in the morning to check on her. If you should need me before then, send someone to get me."

"I'll see you to the door," Libby said as she walked with the doctor from the parlor.

"Excuse me, Mrs. McTavish, I need to return to the bedroom for another quick check and to also retrieve my bag before I leave."

"Thank you again, Dr. Blake. We will see you in the morning," Libby said as the doctor left and she returned to the bedroom to sit with her mother.

By mid-morning, Cole had managed to arrive at the house with Alex where he found Libby in the kitchen washing the dishes. "We're finally here. I've tried to dress him as best I could, darling."

She laughed when she saw the two of them. "Looks as if you did pretty good by yourself. I must admit that Alex looks a bit better than you, honey. Did you dress in the dark?" Libby took her son from Cole. "Hello, my darling boy! Guess you both are hungry, so I'll prepare a breakfast for us all. While I get started, Cole would you please go check on Daddy? He's in their bedroom with Mother. Thank you, my love."

Libby put Alex down on the floor on a pallet where she could watch her six month old son while she started breakfast. A few minutes later, Cole rejoined Libby in the kitchen.

"Your Pa's just sitting there by the bed and staring out the window. I think I convinced him for us to get to work right after breakfast. The young boy he just hired can't possibly be expected to do everything that needs to be done right away this early in the day."

"That's a good idea for you both. There's nothing either of you can do right now," Libby replied while she began to fire up the stove. "I'll take care of Alex and keep a check on my mother."

"By the way, Lib, I closed up the cabin and brought us all some extra clothes. I figured you'd be wanting to stay here for a few days. What are you going to do about your mother? How is she?"

"She continues to be resting now. Daddy and I will be taking her to the hospital in Huntsville very soon where a Dr. Levine will be seeing her in a few days. That's all I know right now until I talk it over with my father. I hope that he's going to be all right as well. We both are so worried and concerned about her. This has me so upset, not to know exactly what has happened to her and that I could possibly lose her at any moment. Cole, you know you can't leave me now!"

"Yes, darling, I have already ditched that notion for now, and I am planning to stay here at home. Here at the dairy, I will be able to show the new hire exactly how we do things around here. So, don't you worry about that, I'm here. That's a big promise!"

"You are so good to me, Cole McTavish," she said while placing a big kiss on his warm waiting lips. Afterwards, she turned to place a clean skillet on the stove top. "Would you hand me that slab of bacon right in front of you?"

Cole did as he was instructed. "You know, I was just thinking that I, too, could travel to Huntsville with the two of you. We could take Alex over to Lynn where Mama Colleen can look after him while we are gone. She would absolutely love to do that. Once we're settled in Huntsville, I could check out the recruiting office and the new cavalry unit that I hear is beginning to form there. I don't have to join right away, but I could at least go on and register. What do you think about that, Libby?"

"We'll have to talk later. Right now, my bacon is about to burn. When you're finished rubbing around on me, pick up Alex and see if he needs changing."

"From the smell of things, either the bacon is spoiled or he definitely needs to be changed," Cole laughed while he turned his nose aside. He gagged.

"Men," spoke Libby under her breath.

Within the hour, Cole, Libby, and her father sat at the kitchen table to eat the breakfast she had prepared. "We're going to have to do something really soon," James Parker said while he took his last sip of coffee.

"Yes, Daddy, I know. Cole and I are planning to go with you when we take Mother to Huntsville. Mama Colleen will be taking care of little Alex for the time we have to be away. Cole says we could all take the stagecoach. We're guessing that would be the easiest and fastest way, don't you think?"

"When do we need to leave?"

"Daddy, as soon as we know that Dr. Blake has completed all the arrangements, we will be ready to leave."

"Will Dr. Blake be going with us?"

"No, I don't think so. The doctor will have to remain here in Winston County. He has many patients to see every day and look after, you know. I'm sure that Dr. Levine will remain in close contact with him as things continue to evolve. Our major concern right now is to get Mother in a place that will provide her the best possible care."

Shortly before noon the next day, Dr. Blake arrived back at the Parker house. Libby promptly escorted him to the bedroom where she had been sitting all morning with her mother. Alex was napping in the next room and Cole and her father were out tending to the livestock. The doctor walked to the side of the bed and touched the dozing Amelia gently on her hand. A bit startled, her eyes popped open while she tried to fully focus her vision on the man dressed in black standing at her bedside.

"Good day, Mrs. Parker. I hope you are feeling much better today."

Neither did Amelia stir or even attempt to acknowledge his presence, but instead kept staring at the ceiling as if some mesmerizing spectacle was hovering and taking place right above her bed. Her usual bright brown eyes were now darkened and dull.

"I'm sorry she is so unresponsive, Dr. Blake," Libby said while she shook her mother's arm.

"How long has she been like this?" the doctor asked.

"All morning, since daybreak when she first woke up," Libby answered. "I got her up to use the chamber pot and she drank about half a cup of broth and a few sips of black coffee. That's all I could get her to eat. She dozes off at various times, but then her eyes pop open and she just stares at the ceiling."

"Has she talked to you?"

"Once, I thought I heard her say my name. When she opens her mouth to speak, only partial sentences come out in a weakened mumble, mostly words I can't understand. Oh, Dr. Blake, what can we do? She's just pitiful!"

"I have arranged with Dr. Levine and he will be available to see your mother if you could plan to arrive with her at the infirmary within the next three days."

"We can do that. My father has already made arrangements with a neighbor to come and run the dairy along with his two sons. Cole's mother will be keeping our baby for as long as this will take while he also has tickets for our trip already booked. We only have need to talk to our agent and he promises to get the four of us on the next available stage leaving for Huntsville."

"For the rest of the day and tomorrow, try to get your mother to eat some soup or fresh vegetables. If she wants to sit up, that's fine. You may have to assist her. She doesn't need to take a fall. I am leaving a partial bottle of laudanum here for you. Give her a spoonful only if she seems to be growing out of control or she becomes highly agitated. This will calm her down."

"Thank you, Dr. Blake."

"Dr. Levine will be sending me a full report after he sees her, and I will call again to inform you of his findings and any recommendations. Also, at that time, hopefully I can answer any additional questions that you or your father may have."

Dr. Blake felt once more behind Amelia's ears, touching each lobe gently and also re-examining by looking intently up her nose and probing each nostril. He used a cotton ball to retrieve a saliva sample that was taken from a bit of drool that had formed at the corner of her mouth. The doctor wrapped the cotton ball in a piece of sterile bandage and put it into the side pocket of his valise. He picked up his worn black bag, recited his cordial goodbye, and headed to the now familiar front door.

"Have a safe trip on the road, and I will see you again upon your return. Your family will be in my prayers."

Looking back, the next few days proved to be somewhat of a blur for James Parker and Cole, but especially for Libby. Amelia demanded almost constant care while she remained bedridden and unable to do anything for herself. It was up to Libby to provide for each and every need that her mother required over the next days at home, and also for the trip to Huntsville that they would soon be making. At least, Alex was already with her mother-in-law and she didn't have to look after him or have need to worry about her little son. Her main worry now was Mama.

The 10 hour overnight trip to Huntsville for the 85 mile journey was emotionally and physically exhausting for everyone, especially

Amelia. After many stops and starts, the weary travelers finally arrived and checked in to the Huntsville Infirmary. Amelia was immediately taken to a private room and put to bed while the rest of the party was escorted to a waiting area down a long corridor. Since their arrival had been early in the morning, they settled in as best they could to endure the long tiring day ahead.

Hours passed until the door opened and a robust little man with short frizzy gray hair and a long bushy beard and moustache stepped into the room. Libby thought he looked about fifty-five, standing there in his long white cotton coat as he peered at her over his tiny wire-framed spectacles. Cole noticed the writing tablet and big black medical book he held at his side. James Parker was dozing in his chair, so he was completely unaware that the doctor had just made his first appearance.

"Good afternoon, I'm Dr. Levine, and I hope that you have been made as comfortable as possible during what has proven to be a long wait. I apologize for taking so long, but I need my examination of Mrs. Parker to be as thorough as possible. I'm sure that is what you want also, is it not?"

Their affirmation was made by the immediate nodding of the heads to indicate total agreement with the doctor. Dr. Levine forced a slight smile as he bid Cole and Libby to remain seated.

"Folks, I realize how anxious each of you must be at this time, and I apologize again for the delay. It takes extra time in a case like this. I want to be completely honest and accurate in my opinion, so I have to admit that I am somewhat baffled. I have just finished my initial examination of Mrs. Parker, and there is one more thing I need to investigate. I regret that I won't be able to complete it until early tomorrow morning. May I suggest that you secure rooms for overnight at the Fleur-de-Lis on Main Street? It is an inexpensive, quaint, and comfortable inn located two blocks over, sitting next to the Red Lion Tavern. Meet back with me in the morning at 10:00 a.m. and I will do my best to have a complete report of diagnosis for you."

73

"How is my mother at the present?" asked Libby.

"She's very tired, but resting as well as she can. I have given her a sedative, so she will continue to sleep. Please, you all go and get some rest yourselves. I will see you again in the morning. Plan to meet in my office. Nurse Mattie Ryan will show you where I will be. Have a pleasant evening."

The next morning, the three weary travelers arrived promptly on time, and the nurse had them seated in the doctor's office.

"Good morning," Dr. Levine said while he took his seat behind his cluttered massive oak desk. Looking over the lens of his spectacles, the doctor shuffled through a pile of papers until he brought one page to the top of the stack. "I'll get right to the point if you don't mind. I believe Mrs. Parker has somehow contracted *Mycobacterium leprae* caused by an unknown germ or bacteria. In a word, your wife has leprosy, Mr. Parker."

"Leprosy!" Libby gasped while she fell back in her seat. "God forbid, what causes leprosy in this day and time?"

"Leprosy usually causes an infection that affects the skin at first. It can destroy nerves and also cause certain problems in the eyes and nose. Has she experienced any problems recently with her vision, Mrs. McTavish?"

"No, doctor, I don't believe so. If she has, I am unaware of it."

"How can you tell that Amelia really has it?" James asked. "What signs do you see that confirm this diagnosis? Tell me, Dr. Levine."

"Early signs may include spots on the skin that may show up slightly red and will appear darker or even lighter than normal skin color. These spots may also become numb to the touch with even a loss of body hair in that particular area."

"Did you find any such spots when you examined my mother?"

"Yes, I found a small spot on the back of her left arm, and a slight blemish across the forearm. Two major areas on the back of the legs, and also a spot on the ankle of her left foot were the only visible spots I discovered."

"Please continue, Dr. Levine. Tell us all more about what we can expect. I think Libby and Mr. Parker really need to know," replied Cole.

"Sometimes the only sign may be numbness in a finger or toe. If this should eventually happen to Mrs. Parker, let's say her hand goes numb, this could lead to paralysis and the curling of the fingers and thumb."

"You mentioned that you found spots on her leg and ankle, Doctor. Will those spots get worse?" Libby asked while she shifted in her seat.

"We will need to keep watch and observe any changes, but yes, her condition could worsen, and sometimes this will happen rapidly. You see, when leprosy attacks the nerves in the legs, the feet can be severely damaged by untended wounds and infections. However, I did not detect any of these on my initial examination."

"We noticed back home that Dr. Blake examined her nose by probing her nasal passage," Parker said. "Did you find any infection there?"

"No, but let me mention a couple more things that could possibly happen as this disease progresses. If the facial nerves were to become affected, she could lose the blinking reflex of the eye which can eventually lead to blindness. Also, bacteria entering the lining of the nose may cause it actually to collapse. We find that leprosy can cause deformity, crippling, and blindness. I hope this answers your question."

"I have another question," Libby spoke up. "I am really concerned about what is going to continue to happen to her. Do fingers and toes fall off when someone gets leprosy, like in biblical times?"

"No, Mrs. McTavish, not exactly. The bacteria attacks nerve endings and destroys the body's ability to feel pain. Without being able to feel pain, some people injure themselves and these injuries can become infected, resulting in tissue loss. Fingers and toes can become shortened and deformed as the cartilage is absorbed into the body. When this happens, repeated injury and infection of numb areas can cause the bones to shorten. This allows the tissue then to shrink which make the digits of the hands and feet appear extremely short while giving the impression that they have seemingly fallen off. Do I make myself clear?"

"I think so, Dr. Levine," Libby answered, "but how in the world did my mother catch this horrible disease, this leprosy as you say?"

"The leprosy bacteria is known to be transmitted and spread primarily through coughing and sneezing. My medical book states that in most cases, it is spread through long-term contact with a person who has the disease."

She quickly interrupted. "I know of no such person, Dr. Levine."

"Nor I, Mrs. McTavish. I'm sorry, but we in the medical field do not fully understand how modern day leprosy is spread."

"The only long-term contact between my mother and anyone with a disease is completely unknown to me. However, all her married life, she has constantly been around a bunch of cows. My father runs a dairy farm in Winston County. Can cattle be a carrier for the leprosy bacteria?"

"That I can't say. We have no documented evidence on file that livestock could develop the disease or be carriers."

"So, Dr. Levine, what treatment can you prescribe for my dear wife?" Parker asked.

"I regret to inform you, sir, that there is no known medication that will save her, except anything short of a miracle. Do you believe in God, Mr. Parker?"

"I do, but I seldom have time to attend the church. Amelia goes to the Methodist Church sometimes."

"Mr. Parker, the church can't save you, but if you truly believe in God, I suggest you begin to pray in earnest for yourself and your wife. Pray for a miracle!"

"Then, you're saying she..."

"Regretfully, there is nothing that I feel can be done for her. Amelia's condition is terminal."

"Oh no," Libby cried out while Cole, who had remained somewhat silent in the conversation, reached over to try to console his saddened wife. Tears were rolling down her face as Libby sobbed into Cole's chest after he pulled Libby to her feet and wrapped his strong arms around her. James Parker fell back into his chair while he appeared totally stunned with the surprising news.

"I will be releasing Mrs. Parker back to the care of Dr. Blake after you return home. There are drugs available that may be able to keep her comfortable and help relieve any pain she may have that he can provide for you. I suggest you prepare her diet to include as many fresh vegetables as possible, especially the green leafy ones. Also, she needs to be housed into a secluded room with a sterile environment. This is important! You all will need to wear cotton gloves and a mask or handkerchief placed over your nose and mouth whenever you are to have close contact with her. Avoid her coughing and sneezing when in close proximity at all cost. Does anyone have any more questions?"

"May we see her again before we leave this afternoon?" Libby asked while drying her eyes.

"Certainly! Mrs. Parker is down this hallway in the last room on the left. She can be released as early as tomorrow morning if you would like. I will check on her again before I leave for the day. Have a restful night, and I will see you all in the morning."

James Parker, Libby, and Cole's heads were spinning in all directions when they realized the magnitude of the final diagnosis and what would eventually happen to Amelia. They began to pray, feeling that prayer was going to be their only hope. Each of their hearts were heavy as they made plans for the rest of the afternoon. Libby decided that she would remain at the hospital and stay with her mother until morning. James Parker wanted to be alone, so he returned to the Fleur-de-Lis for the rest of the evening and night. Cole decided to take this time as an opportunity to find out all he could about the newly formed Union's First Cavalry Unit of Huntsville. Lucky for him, there was a flyer posted on the bulletin board in the lobby of the infirmary listing practically all the information he needed. Without telling Libby or James, he found his way over to Barlow Street where he met a recruiter and registered. He knew at the time, he couldn't enlist right away, but it would definitely be in his future.

Early the next morning, the stagecoach pulled away from the Huntsville Infirmary for the return trip. After three grueling and tiring days, three weary travelers were taking Amelia Parker home to Winston County.

For the next year and a half, the family watched as Amelia's condition slowly deteriorated. Shortly after they arrived back home, James Parker hired two sisters to take care of his dear wife. Ramona and Randa Jefferson, friends of the Parker family, faithfully stepped in to take care of Amelia. They alternated their time in shifts while Libby made herself available whenever she could. It was a trying and difficult year while James, Cole, and Landon worked the dairy, and Libby had a one year old and husband to care for. The sad part for Libby, being so close to her mother, was watching her as she continued to go down. Word got out and immediately spread throughout the community that Amelia Parker was a leper. Even close friends stopped calling, especially since she had to be kept in isolation. The laundry kept piling up with having to wash the many needed items of clothing, bed sheets, gloves, masks, and night clothes. This was a full-time job in itself.

Dr. Blake returned to the house for a number of weeks, but after a while there wasn't any need for him to continue to do this. He kept the family supplied with any medications needed for pain while the family played the waiting game. Over the next remaining months, and into the new year, the family had to endure the everyday struggles of Amelia. At first, she was able to sit up, stationed by her window to look at each changing season. How she loved the outdoors. The weeks passed, and no longer could she sew her needlepoint as her fingers grew crooked and withdrawn eventually becoming as stubs. Ramona and Randa had to begin to feed her every meal when her arms grew crippled. Following the next month, her legs were also crippled and she could no longer stand or walk. James, Cole, and Landon had the responsibility of lifting her from the bed to her chair and back until she became totally bedfast. After her weight loss, the two sisters were able to lift her with ease whenever necessary.

During the next weeks that passed, Amelia lost the sight in one eye, then the other, leaving her totally blind. Communication was made rather difficult as her speech was slurred to the point of mumbling. It became very frustrating to everyone not to be able to clearly understand what she meant to be saying. Her blindness, most certainly did not help the situation. The most horrible event took place before Thanksgiving that year when Amelia's nose collapsed. This made it more difficult for her to breathe while it also left her once smiling face, now disfigured and ugly to view.

Christmastime and the new year of 1863 was approaching, but there was to be no joyous celebration this time. The week before Christmas, Dr. Blake was summoned for the last time. The family was told they needed to prepare for the now expected departure of their loved one. Although it was sad, especially to James Parker and Libby, God healed Amelia when he mercifully took her home on that cold day 15 January, 1863. She was now walking completely restored in her new body for all eternity.

Following the funeral, after returning to their little cabin, Libby fainted and collapsed across the bed. The sickness she had been feeling over the past mornings soon gave way to the realization of a possible reason. Could she be pregnant?

CHAPTER 7

Huntsville, located primarily in Madison County, is the county seat extending west into Limestone County and south into Morgan. The first white settlers began to populate the area following the Revolutionary War. Veteran John Hunt settled in the land around Big Spring. The 1805 Treaty with the Chickasaws and the Cherokee Treaty of Washington in 1806 ceded all native claims to the United States Government. This great land mass of unknown acreage at the time was subsequently purchased by Mr. LeRoy Pope. Pope named the area Twickenham after the home village of his distant kinsman, Alexander Pope.

Following the plans for the development of his new city, Pope carefully planned that the streets were to be laid out on the northeast to southwest direction based on the flow of Big Spring. During this time, due to anti-British sentiment, the name was changed to Huntsville to honor John Hunt who had been forced to move to other land south of the new city. By 1811, Huntsville had become the first incorporated town in Alabama.

Huntsville quickly grew from wealth generated by the cotton and eventual railroad industry. Finding ideal farming conditions, including both land and climate, many wealthy planters moved into the new area from Virginia, Georgia, and the Carolinas.

In 1819, Huntsville held a constitutional convention in Mr. Walker Allen's large cabinet making shop. The 44 delegates attending the meeting wrote a constitution for the new state of Alabama. In accordance with the new constitution, Huntsville became Alabama's first capital. Later, the capital was moved to more central cities of Cahawba, Tuscaloosa, and finally to Montgomery. In 1855, the Memphis and Charleston Railroad was constructed through Huntsville. This became the first railway to link the Atlantic seacoast with the lower Mississippi River.

Huntsville, along with many other cities and counties, opposed the secession of the state of Alabama in 1861. However, the city provided many men initially activated to serve for the efforts of the Confederacy. The 4th Alabama Infantry Regiment distinguished itself at the Battle of Bull Run/Manassas, which was the first major encounter of the American Civil War between the North and the South. Their commander was Colonel Egbert J. Jones of Huntsville.

On the morning of 11 April, 1862, Union troops under the command of General Ormsby M. Mitchel seized the city of Huntsville. His major objective was to sever the Confederate rail communications while gaining access to the Memphis and Charleston Railroad. Since Huntsville was the control point for the Western Division of the Memphis and Charleston, ultimate control of this railroad meant the Union would have a direct connection to Charleston, South Carolina.

During the first occupation by Mitchel's Regiment, the Union officers occupied many of the grand townhouses and mansions in the city. The soldiers camped in tents on the outskirts of town. The Union troops began their campaign by searching for any Confederate troops hiding in town as well as any stored weapons. Once established into their billet areas, the soldiers did not burn or pillage the city; however, many of the smaller towns around it were sometimes targeted. The general treatment toward the city of Huntsville proved to be rather civil during this particular time.

The Confederates forced the Union troops into retreat a few months later but fought again and returned to Huntsville in the fall 1863. The Union used the city as a base of operations for the remainder of the war. While many homes, farms, and villages in the surrounding countryside were burned in retaliation for the fighting in the area, Huntsville was spared since it housed so many elements of the Union Army.

Three months after the death of Amelia Parker, Libby lost the baby she carried. Another sad event for her, but her loving husband did all he could to help sooth her feelings of depression during this time. Libby took to her bed for three days, but on the fourth day she was back on her feet to resume full care of Alex who was now walking and seemingly into most everything. Most days now, she remembered the wonderful times spent with her mother and the last thing that Cole told her.

"Don't worry, darling! We're still young, and we will have another baby, I promise you that."

Two months later, Cole was packed and ready to leave for Huntsville to join the 1st Alabama Cavalry Regiment. The night before he planned to leave, he and Libby spent a long time with Nate and Marcie Overstreet in their home. Longtime friends, the two couples shared pleasant memories until it was time for their heartfelt goodbyes. Cole was relieved to know they would be there for Libby if she needed them for any reason.

On the day that Cole had planned to leave, Libby put on her brave face, trying to hold it altogether while her husband held 18 month old Alex on his lap. When Cole stood to hand his son back to Libby, she completely lost control and broke down with tears streaming down her face. She fell against him as she held their son between them while Cole's strong arms reached around both of them. They held each other in a fond embrace for the longest time. It was Cole who was the first to finally break away after his farewell kiss had ended.

"Darling, I have to go now, and you know I do. Just keep praying that this war will be ending soon, and I'll be returning home before you even know it."

"I know, my love. This is something that you've felt you had to do and also wanted to do for a long time. I cannot hold you back from it any longer. Promise that you will return to us as soon as you can is all I ask. Kiss me once more, my darling!"

The door to the little cabin closed, and he was gone.

———◆———

The 1st Alabama Cavalry Regiment was made up entirely of Southern volunteers who sided with the Union. By October 1862 while Federal troops still occupied the Huntsville area, plans to form a cavalry unit on the outskirts of the city were put into motion. Construction soon began for a barracks and a stable to be built on the premises to house the men and horses. Presently, the cavalry recruits were living in tents while the horses were held in an old abandoned barn nearby slated to be torn down following the construction of the new livery stables and fencing.

At first, having no established commander, the organization and training exercises became a bit slack until a permanent commander could be assigned to the newly formed cavalry unit. Fortunately, for the cavalry when hope was almost gone, George Spencer came onto the scene to take command on 11 September, 1863.

Colonel George Eliphaz Spencer was a twenty-seven year old attorney from the state of Alabama who enlisted as a captain in the Union Army. While serving on the staff of Brigadier General Grenville M. Dodge, he requested the transfer to the 1st Alabama Cavalry. By the time he took full command of the new unit, Spencer had been promoted to colonel. His future service as commander included the training of his cavalry to work closely with the infantry. During this start up time, the new volunteers began and continued their basic training while each new man learned scouting, raiding, reconnaissance, flank guard, and screening of the infantry while on the march.

Colonel George Spencer had been in command for only six weeks when the new batch of seven recruits arrived at company headquarters in Huntsville. Five men were married and two were single, with ages ranging from twenty-two to thirty-seven. This group would include Cole McTavish, who at twenty-six, was only one year younger than the colonel. Cole's arrival date was 23 October, 1863 at his new post. The first time ever to be away from home, he was both a little nervous and excited. Nervous, at not knowing fully what to expect, but excited and anxious in getting started with his basic training. How Cole wished his buddy Nate was there with him to share in this brand new experience at this very moment.

"All out for Barlow Street," a voice shouted while Cole opened the door and stepped down from the coach. He followed the driver to the rear and watched as he climbed up to retrieve his bag. "This one yours, young man?"

"Yeah, that's it," Cole replied while he jumped backward to dodge his bag as the driver launched it from the stagecoach roof to the street below. Picking up the bag, Cole waited until his driver had climbed back down. "Sir, can you tell me how to get to the 1st Alabama Cavalry Unit?"

"Oh, this here's just the recruiting office building you're standing in front of. The place you're most likely looking for is about two miles out of town down that way." He pointed down the street.

"Can you take me there if it's not too much trouble?"

"No problem, sonny boy, sure can. Just throw your bag inside with you, and we'll leave in five minutes if my other passenger doesn't mind." He waited for a sign from the elderly gentleman seated inside the coach. Seeing the positive response from the man, the driver climbed again to his seat atop, picked up the reins, and they were off once more.

"Thanks for the ride," Cole said while he stepped out and closed the door of the stagecoach.

"Good luck, Yankee boy," the driver spouted off while he pulled away and headed down the dusty road.

84

Cole turned to get his first look at a place the locals called Fort Gallant. It was rather impressive, he thought, but really not all that special. However, for the time being, he would call it home. As he made his approach to the main gate, Cole estimated the frontage ran close to two hundred yards down each side of the double gate that stood at least ten feet tall. Rough textured planks of pine lumber formed the same height fencing that enclosed the entire compound. To the right side of the gate was a guard shack which was presently occupied by a thin little man wrapped in a long blue coat. His chair was propped against the wall until he slid forward to bring it down while rising to his feet to greet another wayfaring recruit.

"Listen up! When I open this here gate, you come in and take a seat on that there bench just inside on the right. Wait there, and someone will be along directly to take you where you need to go. Where you'uns from?"

"Double Springs," Cole answered.

"Ain't never been there myself, but understand it's in that county they call 'the free state of Winston' or something like that, I suppose."

"You're right about that, sir. I was born and raised there and damn proud of it! I'm Cole McTavish. What's your name, if I may ask?"

"Wiley Manfred Butkis Jr., named after my daddy. Around here, I'm known as *Wild Man,* but I know a pervert in barracks *A* that has called me *Kiss Butt,* but not directly to my face. If he ever did that or tried to get too close, you know what I mean? Why, I'd split that sum bitch's skull wide open in a heartbeat. Just be warned, Mac, and let me tell you somethin' right now. You don't ever want to be caught naked in the bath house if he's in there. Enough said about that. Nice to meet you, McTavish, come on through while I open this here gate."

"How long will I have to wait?"

"Not too long, I'm guessing. Usually a lad called Matthew or Matt comes to get all the new recruits. See you around, Mac."

While Cole sat there waiting on the bench, he kept thinking that surely the Wild Man must be from Louisiana, guessing maybe Baton Rouge. Anyway, Mr. Butkis Jr. had a nasty scar running down his left cheek, cut nearly to the ear. Cole thought, put a brightly colored bandana across his forehead, a black patch over one eye, and a gold hoop earring that would peer out from under the long coal black hair and unshaven face, and he would look just like a pirate. Blackbeard's twin, perhaps.

Ten minutes later, nineteen year old Matthew Dunbar walked up, introduced himself, and offered to show Cole to his barracks.

"You have to be McTavish since the other six are already checked in. Good to meet you, sir. Call me Matt. I'm going to show you where to bunk."

Cole noticed the lad walked with a slight limp as they both strode across the huge yard toward barracks B in the distance. Matt's long blonde hair was tied neatly at the back of his neck, and he wore a thin, almost invisible, tiny moustache. He was dressed in a pair of tan trousers, pale blue long-sleeve shirt, and was wearing a pair of dark brown leather boots.

"May I ask what happened to your leg?" Cole remarked while they continued their walk.

"Oh that's nothing and I don't even think about it anymore. I was born that way, I guess. You see, one leg just grew a bit longer than the other."

"You just need a built up shoe for the left leg. Ever thought about that?"

"Naw, doesn't really matter anymore. I'm used to walking like this all the time. Well, here we are. You're lucky, Mr. McTavish, your barracks is practically brand new."

"Call me Cole, Matt."

"Sure thing, Cole. You see A has maxed out at sixty soldiers and B, so far is only half full to capacity. From here you can see up the hill that barracks C is presently under construction. This place is beginning to fill up. We seem to get new recruits every week."

"The new barracks site is going to have a great view sitting up there on the hill," Cole said.

"Yeah, and beyond that ridge over yonder is the new yard and stables. Probably close to a hundred head of horses already here with more to come, they say. That's where I work mainly when I'm not having to help the new recruits."

"I work on a dairy farm in Winston County. I am more familiar with milk cows, but I'm going to like being around all the horses."

"Well, here we are," Matt said while he opened the door for Cole to enter the barracks. "You can have your pick of any vacant bunk you choose. The vacant ones are kept unmade until they become occupied. There's a linen closet over there where the fresh linen, blankets, and pillows are kept. Make yourself at home. Hey, you are home," Matt laughed.

"What happens after I get settled in?' Cole asked.

"I'll be waiting outside to take you to meet Colonel Spencer and the other new recruits when you finish in here. I can get the linen you'll be needing while you unpack your personal items into the chest at the foot of your bed."

Located to the left, approximately 500 yards from the main gate, stood the Gallant mansion built in 1835 by Judge Edward J. Gallant of Huntsville. Following many years of abandonment and neglect, the old plantation home recently had been converted to house the headquarters for the new cavalry unit. Inside, the existing wall separating the two parlors had been removed on the main floor to create one large meeting and assembly room. Across the hall, the former dining room was remodeled to provide the office space needed for Colonel Spencer's business and personal use. The new office was refurnished now to contain a large six drawer oak desk with a matching high back brown leather chair on rollers. The colonel had his desk placed directly in the center of the room. On the right side of the room against the wall was a massive oak sideboard being used presently by the colonel to shelve his books, files, and to store documents that required frequent access. To the right of the sideboard was a beautiful marble fireplace imported from Italy. Over the mantel hung a large rectangular beveled mirror encased in a delicate ornate gold leaf frame. On the left side of the room was a blue velvet sofa and matching side chair separated by a round oak lamp table in between. Over the sofa was placed an early portrait of President Lincoln without his beard in a wooden frame painted gold. On the rear wall below the large window, there was a long oak console table with curved legs that remained original to the house. The table now held a pitcher, water basin, and the colonel's favorite decanters of fine Kentucky bourbon, scotch, and imported wine. Also, there was an array of crystal goblets and wine glasses that he had collected from his travels abroad. The original blue velvet portieres had been removed at his request to provide Colonel Spencer with much better natural light during the day. The freshly painted plaster walls had been brightened by an eggshell colored paint while the flooring retained the original wide plank heart pine floor from 1835. A light coat of varnish had recently been brushed on to give the floor a fresh look. Also, the pocket doors of the room had been faux painted so that now the original pine wood gave the appearance of oak. The large crystal chandelier that formerly hung directly over where the colonel had positioned his desk had been removed and stored in the attic. A long winding staircase led from the foyer to the upper floor where Colonel Spencer maintained the entire upstairs as his personal living quarters.

Viewed from outside, as Cole and Matt entered through the double door of the six Corinthian columned Greek Revival, Cole now had in mind fresh ideas he could use while continuing to build the home already started for Libby when he returned. Once inside the foyer, Cole followed Matt into the assembly room to a corner where the other six recruits were waiting at a small table. At first, there had been no scheduled orientation meeting planned for today while this was simply a time to group up, meet, and get acquainted. Initially, the colonel often preferred to meet his new recruits in a small group setting. Two of the men had grown a bit impatient since they had already been there for a couple of hours. Nicholson and McShan let loose a few more expletives before silencing themselves as Cole and Matt walked through the opened door and into the room.

"For those of you who are already acquainted, this is Cole McTavish," Matt Dunbar announced. "Please introduce yourselves as you welcome him as our last new recruit today. I will be leaving shortly to find out if Colonel Spencer has a change of plans to now address you at this meeting. If so, we will return at that time. Talk among yourselves." Dunbar pulled the doors closed as he made his exit.

"Where you from?" asked the recruit sitting on the end while he motioned to Cole to come take a seat next to him.

"Born and raised in the 'free state of Winston' in Double Springs," Cole answered. "I'm twenty-six, married three years to my beautiful Libby, and a father to my one year old son, Alex. I work for my father-in-law on his dairy farm."

Each recruit continued while they took turns with their initial introductions. The young man who had invited Cole to be seated by him began the conversation.

"Hello, Cole McTavish, nice to meet you. Guess I'll begin since I'm sittin' right beside you. Five of us all came here together from Limestone County with the exception of Callahan, sitting over there on the end, scratching his privates. He's the youngest from Walker County, I believe. Anyway, I'm Garrett."

The recruits spent the next half hour while they provided the small band of future cavalrymen with their personal information. Cole listened intently while every man stood to describe himself. When each recruit had finished speaking, Cole, in his own mind, gave them all a one-word first impression.

"I'm Garrett Niles. You may call me *Gar*. I am twenty-nine, married to Claudine LaPierre Niles from Atlanta. We have been married for four years and presently have no children. We're trying, but none as yet. As you can see, I am 5'11" tall and weigh 175 lbs. with light blonde hair and moustache, and blue eyes. I was born in

89

Limestone County and live in the little town of Elkmont. I work for my father at Niles Livery where I am a blacksmith." *Muscular*

"My name is Patrick Timothy McShan. Friends call me either *Paddy* or *Mac*. At age two, my father moved us from Ireland to North Carolina, and then to Alabama. I have two older brothers who remained in Dublin. I'm presently thirty-one years old, married with two children, and I stand 6'2" tall and weigh 190 lbs. I have long auburn hair, a goatee, and blue eyes. I am a lumberjack. I have worked the past three years at Brindley's Mill. Like Gar, I'm also from Elkmont where we were boyhood classmates in school." *Virile*

"I'm Peter Nicholson, single, age twenty-five from Athens. I'm 6' tall, 180 lbs. with wavy black hair and blue eyes. I was born an only child in Limestone County. I am an undertaker at Lemley's Funeral Home in Athens." *Handsome*

"Guessing I'm probably the oldest in the bunch, my name is Michael Denney and I'm thirty-seven. Jayne Marie Denney and I have been married long enough to increase our family to six children – Elizabeth, Mary, Sarah, Anne, Rosemary, and little Marie. Yes, all are girls and all are married except Marie who remains at home. Our special child, she was born blind and deaf. I am 5'11" tall and weigh about 180 lbs. I have dark brown hair which I usually keep cut rather short and green eyes. In the winter months, I will often let my hair grow longer for obvious reasons. I am an attorney at the law firm of Allison, Crawford, and Denney in Athens." *Intelligent*

"My name is Wade Montgomery, and you may call me *Monty* if you want. I must be the next oldest at age thirty-four. I've been married for twelve years and Missy, and I have three children, a girl and two boys. I stand at an even 6' and weigh around 180 lbs. I have brown hair, a full beard, and brown eyes. I am a cotton farmer from Pettusville." *Honest*

"Guess that leaves me last, fellows. I am Scott Callahan, more often called *Scottie*. I'm still single at age twenty-two. You can hardly miss my curly red hair and green eyes. A lot of people tell me that I could pass for sixteen, but I promise you, I can grow a beard and shave when I want. I love the women, even had a special girl just weeks before I left home to come here; however, she broke up with me. I'm hoping if I survive this war, maybe I can go back home and try to patch things up with her. I'm 5'9" tall and weigh 145 lbs. I was born the only child of sharecroppers in Walker County. We lost my mama two years ago when she caught the pneumonia. I am an orderly at Longtree Infirmary in Jasper." *Pretty*

Scottie was really a pretty boy, beautiful in the face and virginal, if there ever was one. Cole couldn't help thinking this as these words flashed through his mind while he sat there and watched the young lad while he spoke. Cole's first impression of Scottie was that in this growing company of eager men, this seemingly naïve boy would eventually need protection from those who may try to possibly abuse him. Cole began to think again about the man in barracks *A* who "Wild Man" had already warned him about.

What would happen to Scottie now if he suddenly found himself alone with the likes of Big John O'Banyon or someone else just like him?

Cole's thoughts were distracted while the noise of approaching footsteps suddenly halted as the pocket door was pushed back into the wall. Matthew Dunbar limped into the room while Colonel George Spencer shadowed his entrance only two paces behind. The seven men at the table immediately snapped to attention as they rose quickly to their feet and saluted the colonel.

"At ease, gentlemen, be seated," ordered the colonel. "This is not an occasion where a proper hand salute is recognized, nor required." Colonel Spencer moved closer to the table and stopped while Matt set a chair for the colonel behind where he stood. He took his seat, removed his hat, and placed it on the floor. All eyes were on the colonel while the new recruits were silent in anticipation of the colonel's opening remarks.

"We will be quite informal here today. New recruits, at the end of what I have to say, you will be given a chance to ask any questions you may have. Right now, I am battling an extremely sore throat, and the irritation makes it difficult for me to speak very loud. Please listen very carefully to these instructions, along with the rules and regulations for this compound, so I won't have to repeat anything I have to say. You men will soon be sworn in today while you join the 1st Alabama Cavalry as enlisted volunteers to be given the rank of private. Our number of volunteers is on the increase and this cavalry unit is being created as a support for the infantry. Gentlemen, you are not merely soldiers, nor are you part of a company. Men, you will stand alone as the specific unit of military structure for the infantry you will be supporting. As a cavalry unit, you presently will be referred to as troops. When our number reaches three hundred men or more, the reference will be known as squadron instead of battalion which is referenced as such in the regular army. As each of you arrived today, you may have noticed that our first barracks is completely full with sixty men housed in that building. The second one, where you will be is presently only half full. It is hoped, weather permitting, that by the time we fill barracks *B* completely that the much larger barracks you saw on your tour today will be ready for occupancy. The new building on the hill should be large enough to house another one hundred men." The colonel made a distinct pause while he signaled to Matt as he stood nearby.

"Could I get a glass of water, Private Dunbar?"

While Matt excused himself to take leave to get the water, Cole caught a glimpse of the colonel, enough for a quick character study during the pause that lasted only a few seconds. Already knowing that the colonel was only a year older than himself, Cole mentally tried to make a simple comparison between the two of them.

Colonel Spencer appeared to be about the same height, but looking at him now, he had to outweigh Cole at least twenty pounds. He was stout in the mid-section with rounded shoulders, but stood tall and straight in stature. The colonel wore long sideburns which accented his dark brown chin whiskers and hair that he parted on the left side. He had a round face with small brown eyes and a nose which looked as if it may have been broken at one time. Cole wouldn't call his new commander handsome, but thought he was a nice looking man, sitting there immaculate in his dress blues and shiny black boots. Private Dunbar came hobbling back into the room with a glass of water and the meeting was back on.

"Your water, sir," Matt said while he handed the colonel the glass and returned to the place at his side. Colonel Spencer took a big gulp and continued his address.

"One of the older buildings on this property has been converted into a mess hall. This is where you will take all your meals. Following this meeting, Private Dunbar will take you there, and he will also show you the bath house and latrine. Every man is expected to take a job where you will work when not in training sessions or drills. Your sessions and assignments will be posted on the bulletin board in your barracks, and a staff sergeant will be in charge of your every move while you are here. He is your immediate superior, and you will be expected to treat him as such and follow his orders. Failure to do this will result in disciplinary action that may cause loss of privileges or physical pain. Every man is to be respectful of his fellow soldier's person and property. Stealing will get you a dishonorable discharge, and you will be immediately dismissed from this company. You may volunteer for the place in which you choose to work by talking with your sergeant. You will meet him this evening following the supper meal. If you do not choose to volunteer for a specific job, then one will be assigned to you. Are there any questions?"

"What about mail delivery? Where do we post letters and also receive them?" asked Peter Nicholson.

"Your sergeant will have your mail when he calls you together for assembly. You may post any outgoing mail during that time with him. Anyone else?"

"What about laundry and uniforms?" Garrett Niles asked the colonel.

"Laundry and supply rooms are located in the rear of this house. The hours and services are posted on the door of each room. Personal items, including soap, towels, etc. can be obtained during the regular hours of operation. At the conclusion of your tour of the mess hall, bath house, and latrine, I suggest that you go to the supply room to be fitted for your uniforms and pick up any personal items at that time. Does anyone else have a question?" asked the colonel while he gazed at each man sitting at the table. "Seeing that no one has any more questions, the recruits will stand and lift your right hand."

Each man stood at attention and raised his hand to take the oath.

"Repeat after me," the colonel ordered. "I will give honor to the country I serve as a volunteer in the 1st Alabama Cavalry in support of any and all Union infantry assigned to me. I give my loyalty, allegiance, and life, if necessary in defense of the Federal Army of these United States of America, so help me God." The recruits repeated the oath and dropped their hands to the side.

"You are hereby sworn and acknowledged as a private in the 1st Alabama Cavalry Unit in Huntsville, Alabama. This meeting stands adjourned. Private Dunbar, take these men for the remainder of their tour. You men are dismissed."

Following the evening meal, Private Niles, McShan, Nicholson, Denney, Montgomery, Callahan, and McTavish met their new sergeant.

Sgt. William Maxwell Devereaux, age thirty-five, was a former stevedore who worked the docks in New Orleans prior to his present assignment at Fort Gallant. Sgt. Liam was 6'2" tall, 195 pounds, with a tanned muscular physique. He had powerful biceps on his upper body with thighs and calves bulging with solid muscle. Liam's thick medium length hair was black as coal, and he wore a thin moustache. His bright blue eyes accented the rugged complexion of his handsome face. While Sgt. Devereaux led the group from the mess hall, Cole couldn't help but notice the sergeant's most prominent feature while he followed close behind him.

"Damn, he's got a big tight ass," Cole chuckled to himself while trying to act as if he never saw it. "With a butt like that, Sgt. Devereaux could crack open a hickory nut with ease!" Cole quickly drew his attention away from the sergeant while his eyes were now focused on the new area where the recruits were headed.

Upon arrival, Sgt. Devereaux halted the group at the side door which led inside the livery stable. "Step inside, boys," he said while he opened and held the door for the recruits to enter. "Follow me."

Cole immediately caught wind of that all familiar smell as his nostrils re-awakened to the pungent odor of hay mingled with a sudden burst of fresh manure. Not much different from cow patties, he thought. The sergeant continued the tour while he led the men through the stable and yard where they saw at least eighty head of horses in their stalls or outside in the pen. The mounts, consisting of various breeds, appeared healthy and well-groomed while the recruits took notice of the animals in the stable and the men who cared for them every day.

"I have openings for three of you men to volunteer for service in the stable if you want. Any volunteers?" Sgt. Devereaux asked while the group rested against a fence rail. "Call out your names if you wish to volunteer."

"McTavish," Cole yelled almost immediately.

"Niles," Gar spoke up while he raised his hand.

"Callahan," Scottie spoke likewise.

"I see you three and take notice of your volunteering. Hang back with me while you remaining four are dismissed to the barracks," Devereaux ordered. While the others were leaving, the sergeant moved his three volunteers and had them seated on a bench outside the main door of the stable. "Earlier today men, I had an opportunity to look over each of your personnel records. It seems to me that you three should be well suited for work in the stable while I read about your background and experience. Which one of you is Niles?"

"I am, sir, over here," said the man with the blonde hair and blue eyes. "Garrett Niles, but you can call me Gar."

"Very well, Gar. I see you are a blacksmith in your father's livery stable. Not surprising that you volunteered to work here. We can use another good man. You will begin working in a few days with the blacksmith, Big John O'Banyon. Who is Callahan?"

"That's me, sergeant, call me Scottie."

"Scottie, I think you will be best suited to work as a groomsman with Private Matt Dunbar. He will show you how to groom each horse, and you can assist with future new recruits whenever he is unavailable. Guess that leaves you, Private McTavish."

"Cole McTavish, at your service, sir. I work for my father-in-law at Parker Dairy in Winston County. I'd like very much at the chance to work with the horses."

"That's good, Cole. You will also begin working with Private Dunbar and Private Callahan. Any questions?"

"When do we begin work?" asked Scottie.

"I will have your assignments and training sessions posted on the bulletin board in your barracks. You may check your schedules there," said the sergeant. "You may return to your barracks at this time."

Two days later, Niles, Callahan, and McTavish went to work in the stable; Montgomery and Nicholson went to the kitchen mess hall as cooks; Denney went to the supply room; and McShan went to the armory where the weapons were housed. Private McShan entered the armory to begin his training.

"So you are Patrick Timothy McShan, eh private?" asked the young corporal. "You have been assigned to work with me here in the armory. I am Corporal Jeremiah Jensen. Welcome to the place where we keep all the blades shiny and sharpened. Call me Jeremiah. What shall I call you, McShan?"

"Call me Paddy, if you want."

"All right, Paddy. I heard you were a lumberjack, and judging by your physical appearance alone, I don't believe you will have any problem handling all the hardware in this room."

"No sir. Of course, I feel most comfortable with an ax or saw in my hands, but I'm quite interested in learning all I can about the fine precision cutlery I see along these walls. Very impressive, no doubt."

"Paddy, why don't you have a seat on the bench and listen while I tell you all I know about the weapons we have stored here?" said the forty-three year old stocky built corporal with the long brown hair and hazel eyes.

Private McShan moved around and made himself as comfortable as possible on the hard pine bench. "Corporal, before you get started, since we're going to be working together, would you mind telling me a little about yourself?"

"Certainly, son, I can do that. I was assigned and transferred here from Corinth from the 1st Mississippi Cavalry. Along with Sgt. Malcolm McKenzie, we both arrived here about three months ago. The sergeant will be your drill instructor, and you will get to meet him during your first scheduled drill. My unit fought at Antietam in Sharpsburg, Maryland last year where I unfortunately received a severe shoulder wound. At least, I survived that terrible campaign. There were so many of my friends and fellow soldiers who did not. It took a long time for my wounds to heal, and I lost strength in my right arm. I can still handle a sword, but not as good as I once could. My wife died two years ago, and my mother looks after my two young sons while I am away. I miss my boys. You got family?"

"Yes, I'm married, and I also have two sons, ages ten and twelve. I know what you mean when you say you miss them."

"All right, enough about me. Let me tell you about the Model 1860 Light Cavalry Saber." Corporal Jensen turned and took a saber from its mount on the wall, unsheathed it, and placed it into Paddy's hands. "Be careful with the blade, it's extremely sharp," he said.

"Yes, most definitely," replied Paddy as he quickly examined the sword while listening as Corporal Jensen continued his talk.

"The total length of the saber you are holding is 41 inches long with a blade that measures 35 inches with a one inch width. It weighs 2 lbs. 4 oz. alone or 3 lbs. 10 oz. with the iron scabbard. Now, for a little history lesson I will share. Long before the civil war, there was no cavalry in the U. S. Army. Instead, there were units called *Dragoons* that were founded in 1830 followed by *Mounted Riflemen* in 1840. By 1861, these mounted regiments were renamed *Cavalry* and given yellow piping on their uniforms. The original Model 1840 Heavy Cavalry Saber had a brass guard, leather-wrapped grip, and a steel scabbard. The new Model 1860 Light Cavalry Saber received its name to distinguish it from the previous model as it was smaller and easier to handle. The sabers you find here were manufactured by the Ames Company, but there are other factories and firms like Roby, Glaze, Emerson, and Tiffany and Company. M1860 sabers are not only carried by the cavalry, but also by the infantry and staff officers. Regulation Model 1850 is an Army Staff and Field Officer's sword, which is special made and privately purchased by the individual. High-ranking officers often have their swords ornately engraved with gilding and foliage. The 1ˢᵗ Alabama Cavalrymen, along with their sabers, are also issued a sidearm revolver and a Spencer carbine rifle. Naturally, these weapons will be used in event of having to leave the saddle while fighting on foot. Any questions?"

"None at the moment. I believe you have it all covered," Paddy said while he returned the sword to Corporal Jensen.

Several weeks passed while more recruits were processed and filled up barracks *B*. The rush was mounting to finish construction on the new barracks on the hill before the winter months set in. With the additional men, workloads were easing up for Cole and his new buddies. Colonel Spencer had hopes of seeing the housing project completed by early November. He didn't plan for any of his men to have to be housed in tents when the cold weather would eventually arrive. The newest volunteers meant extra provisions in order to keep his camp running smoothly and operational. Spencer ordered two additional staff officers during this time as well as a doctor and dentist.

Sgt. Levon Ferrell McRae, a burly, pre-matured grey haired, thirty-seven year old, arrived from Natchez to become the company quartermaster. In time, he would assume responsibility for the cavalry's operational demands for ammunition, food, transportation, living quarters, clothing, pay, and other vital matters. This proved to be a tremendous undertaking for one man, so McRae asked for the transfer of an associate to come to his aid. Upon approval from Colonel Spencer, the much needed help arrived the next week from New Orleans. Sgt. Raymond Frederick Boshell, age thirty-two, was a brown-eyed blonde with long hair tied at the nape of his neck. He stood 6'1" tall and weighed 175 lbs. with a muscular physique. Boshell was quite experienced in the field of transportation and living quarters which more than anything qualified him for his new assignment.

The two large bedrooms, located on the main floor of the Gallant house, became the clinic and office for the new doctor and dentist upon their arrival that same week. Dr. John Mark Petersen was a fifty-one year old, white haired and bearded general practitioner from Atlanta. He had bright blue eyes and rosy cheeks against his smooth pale skin. He was a retired army captain, having served as a field doctor at Bull Run before taking leave for a severe leg wound he received during the battle. He had returned to private practice back home until he discovered the need for a doctor for the 1st Alabama Cavalry and volunteered his services to rejoin for the cause. A slight limp hampered his normal step, but other than that, Dr. Petersen appeared to be in excellent health.

Later that same week, he was joined by Dr. Joshua T. Abrams, the dentist from Huntsville, who agreed to provide dental services on a part-time basis. Abrams would continue his practice in town, while being able to come to Fort Gallant one day during the week or on call for an extreme emergency anytime. He would share the room across the hall from Dr. Petersen to see his patients. Dr. Abrams had practiced dentistry in Huntsville for nine years and he was a lively, forty-eight year old widower. He was average height and build weighing about 165 lbs. with dark brown hair and eyes.

By December 1863, Fort Gallant was well-established under the capable leadership of Colonel George Spencer while the winter months approached the camp. Recruits continued to fill the new barracks which had been recently completed. The final stages of construction had gone extremely well. Bright, sunny days provided Sgt. Devereaux and Sgt. McKenzie with ample opportunities for drilling and training sessions. Sgt. McRae and Sgt. Boshell had their hands full with living quarters, clothing, and food becoming their main concern while the week before Christmas was fast approaching.

Cole sat on his bunk while the barracks was almost empty as he penned a letter to Libby. The past weeks had seemed so long since they had been apart. He pondered how he was beginning to really miss his family, especially at this very moment.

In the bath house, Big John O'Banyon lay naked, bleeding, and unconscious on the floor.

CHAPTER 8

"**A**lexander Malcolm McTavish, you little scoundrel," Libby scolded her mischievous son while she lightly spanked his hands for nearly destroying her freshly baked fruit cake. "Mama says no!" Libby reached for a cloth to wipe his hands while removing the curious youngster from the table. She returned and tried to repair her cake where his little hands had picked out the fruit pieces now scattered on the table. Libby had less than an hour to finish up and get over to Nate and Marcie's where she had been invited to dinner on Christmas Eve.

Marcie Overstreet opened the door to receive Libby and two year old Alex into the foyer of their home on Poplar Street. "Come in, dear friend, so glad you both could join us for dinner. Have a seat in the parlor while I let Nate know you're here."

"I brought a dessert. Sorry, but you can see what happened to it when I turned my back for just a few minutes," Libby laughed as she uncovered her cake.

"Don't worry about that, Libby. I've baked many cakes that turned out worse than that. How can you hurt a fruit cake? It looks delicious. Thank you for bringing it," Marcie said while she took the plate and left the room. Moments later, Marcie returned to the parlor with her husband.

"You're looking well, Libby," Nate said while he walked over and clasped her hand. "That boy of yours certainly has grown since the last time I saw him. Hello there, Alex."

"I'm afraid he's still a little shy. Alex, say hello to Mr. Nate," Libby said.

Alex ignored his greeting as Nate turned away and took a seat on the sofa beside Marcie. "When have you heard from Cole?" he asked.

"I received a letter from him last week. He's doing well. Right now, they have him working in the stable. He is enjoying being around the horses, riding, and also he says 'wielding a sword' on occasion while he trains."

"Sounds interesting to me," Nate said while producing a slight smile.

"He misses you, Nate. I know he would like for you to be there with him."

"I hate like the dickens that I can't. With Marcie being in the family way, it must be meant for me to stay here."

"He understands that, I'm sure. He would only want you there to be able to share the experience of cavalry life with him as a close friend. He just loves being around you."

"Well, I hope everything continues to go like he expects. Tell him, Marcie and I send our best wishes the next time you write."

"I will, Nate. He always asks about you in every letter I receive."

"You need to write him yourself, darling," Marcie said while giving a little nod. "I have dinner prepared if everyone is ready to eat." She stood from the sofa. "Let's all move to the dining room."

The Christmas Eve dinner was both enjoyable and delicious while the merry friends shared the meal together. Marcie had tried her best to make sure her table was set with her fine china and plenty of food. Her menu consisted of baked ham, sweet potatoes, lima beans, cooked cabbage, and cornbread with a fruit cup of chopped apples and oranges, not to mention the fruit cake. Following dinner, Libby and Marcie cleared the table and washed the dishes while Nate watched Alex in the parlor. After a while, Libby and Marcie rejoined

Nate. The three friends spent the rest of the afternoon talking about plans for Christmas Day.

"Listen, dear friends, I need to get home before dark," Libby said. "Today has been really special getting to be with you in your beautiful home. I appreciate everything you continue to do for me and Alex while Cole is gone."

"Now, Libby, you know you would do the same for Marcie if I happened to be away," Nate replied.

"I would certainly hope so," she answered. "Cole will be so happy when he learns the surprising news about your wonderful new addition. You both have a happy Christmas, and I will see you again soon."

"Wait, don't forget to take your cake," Marcie exclaimed.

"Please, you keep it. I'll get my plate back the next time I see you," Libby said while she prepared to leave the Overstreet home. All the way back to the cabin, Libby could only think how much she was missing Cole.

———◆———

In Lawrence County, Jonah Leviston had been enjoying the pleasure of being a new husband for the past six months. Jonah thought his dreams of romance were finally fulfilled when he married Wanda Jessup that summer on a sudden whim. In heated passion, the two kept the marriage bed frequently occupied while their bodies entwined in ultimate ecstasy every night. Now, Jonah's newlywed status was about to change while he gathered and packed his belongings. He was leaving to join the Confederate forces in Georgia for the next two years.

On a dark rainy night a week later, Wanda Leviston slept with a tall, dark, and handsome man she called Billy. Hopefully, Jonah would never find this out while he sat alone and missing his wife in Atlanta.

———◆———

Back at Fort Gallant, news in the barracks spread like wildfire after those present saw a bloody Scottie Callahan brought in and placed on his bunk. Clad only in his drawers, Scottie lay there motionless while Sgt. Devereaux attempted to question him about his encounter with the wounded man sprawled onto the floor in the bath house. Presently on his way to the infirmary, Big John O'Banyon remained unconscious while two men covered his nakedness with a towel as they lifted him from the floor and made their exit. Cole noticed a large gash on the side of the blacksmith's head as the three passed close by where he stood in the crowd. The silence grew into a muted murmur while the men who had gathered outside the bath house were eager to learn what had just happened there. However, it would take several days until the full story came out.

Sgt. Devereaux ordered everyone out of the barracks while Matt Dunbar brought in a basin of water and bandages to help young Scottie tend to his wounds. While Matt worked alongside to assist, the sergeant continued his questioning of Private Callahan.

"All right, Callahan, let's hear it! What happened in the bath house?"

Scottie raised up and turned to sit on the side of his bunk after Matt finished with the last bandage. He had sustained a busted lip, bloody nose, and a deep cut over his right eye while noticeable bruising began to surface on his cheeks and neck. His upper body was reddened by the apparent blows to his chest. Matt draped a blanket across Scottie's shoulders as he began to answer the questions from Sgt. Devereaux. The sergeant pulled up a stool beside the bunk as he sat to listen to Scottie Callahan.

"I was shaving when I heard him come in. I watched in the mirror as he placed a bar of soap and a towel onto a chair by the tub. I could see clearly, it was Big John. I could feel him staring at me while I continued shaving. At first, he just stood there, not moving and giving me the eye. I could see he was bare chested and wearing only his trousers. At that moment, we were alone with no one else around. I began to feel uncomfortable, so I kept watching in the mirror. He mumbled something to himself. I don't understand what he is saying. Then I watch as he unfastens his britches, and hurriedly slides them down. He steps out of them and also drops his drawers now tangled around his ankles while he nearly loses his balance in the attempt to tear them quickly away. I heard the fabric rip as he fumbles to get them off while he lets out a loud grunt. I can see the man has fire in his eyes. All of a sudden, he made a lunge toward me while I yelled out my warning. *'Don't come any closer! Touch me, and you will live to regret it, I promise.'* Then, he was on my back and I was no longer in control. Clearly upset and defensive, I turned around in a flash and sent my knee right between his legs while at the same time giving a forceful shove to knock him off me. He fell back and landed on the floor while he moaned in agony. He staggered back to his feet, recovering enough to come charging at me with a powerful force. I let into him with all I had while we commenced into a full scale fight. He got a few punches in as I fought to defend myself. The last thing I remember was sending a right upper cut to his jaw as he fell backwards while his head struck against the side of the tub. After that, he just lay there not moving. I thought I had killed him. I'm sorry, but that brute was not going to have his way with me."

Sgt. Devereaux confined Private Callahan to his barracks until he had a chance to question O'Banyon. It took two additional days until the alleged assailant could be stitched up, conscious, and well enough to provide his explanation about the fight in the bath house three days ago. The investigation continued as the sergeant stood at his bedside while John O'Banyon gave his side of the story.

"I entered the bath house while thinking that no one else was in there. I put my soap and towel onto a chair and proceeded to draw the water to take my bath. Then I realized that I was not alone. Private Callahan was standing at the basin. His back was all I could see while I noticed his forearm on the side moving rapidly back and forth. Anyone could see what he was doing. He stopped at once when he saw me in his mirror watching him. An awkward moment, I thought, what to do? I was just trying to be friendly when I walked over to speak to him. Before I knew it, he turned quickly on me and grabbed ahold of my privates. I was shocked! Well, that's all it took before I slapped his hand away and punched him in the face. I may have bloodied his nose or busted his lip, I don't know. Anyway, as I was turning to go back toward the tub, he jumped me from behind. He started the fight that broke out. The boy just went crazy! The son of a bitch was trying his best to kill me, and that you can see from my injuries. Sgt. Liam, he just about succeeded in doing that, wouldn't you agree? He needs to be put away is all I'm saying. Oh yeah, I almost forgot to mention this. After he saw me looking at him, he bent over and pulled down his drawers to show me his rosy pink arse. It was disgusting!"

The following day, Sgt. Devereaux presented his full report to Colonel Spencer. There would be no official court martial; however, this offense would require immediate disciplinary action to be administered by Colonel Spencer. Later that afternoon, the colonel held a separate meeting to question each man in order to establish the truth about the bath house incident. It didn't take long for Colonel Spencer to reach a decision and pass judgment even though there wasn't one single witness. Callahan was given only a verbal warning against fighting while O'Banyon was relieved of his duties and immediately dismissed from the 1st Cavalry on the spot. Sgt. Devereaux watched as O'Banyon packed his belongings and then ushered him through the main gate. Hopefully, that would be the last time anyone had to contend with the likes of Big John O'Banyon.

———◆———

In Winston County, loyal supporters of the Confederacy continued to volunteer for service since it looked as though the war would drag on with no end in sight. Libby's father, James Parker, was among the many concerned residents who sided with the Confederates and attended a recent town hall meeting simply out of curiosity. Trying to suppress the Unionist spirit spreading throughout the county, this group wanted to petition Gov. John Gill Shorter to intervene. These men felt the need to require all of the county's residents to take the Confederate loyalty oath while also providing 250 Confederate soldiers for the war effort. After the petition was received by Governor Shorter, he met with his cabinet for a heated discussion while addressing the main concern. Soon after this meeting, the governor issued writs of arrest for those in the county who remained disloyal to the Confederacy. Also, the demand that any militia commanders who would not take the oath of office were to immediately resign. Needless to say, this proclamation by the governor of Alabama caused quite a stir within the ranks of those who supported the Union.

'Leave us alone!' the Unionists shouted while the governments of the Confederacy and the state of Alabama would not oblige. The conflict begins. Unionists living in the hill country soon faced compulsory enlistment while many fled their homes to seek refuge from the unrelenting conscription agents who remained hot on their trail. Many men left their families to hide out in the rugged forests and canyons in the county. The place the locals called Natural Bridge in western Winston County soon became a major gathering area for Unionists who were avoiding the draft. Also, some men continued to arrive that had simply deserted the Confederate Army. Regardless, the western section of the county was working alive in the camp while many felt compelled to move from the area because of the overcrowding and fear of being caught. Several Unionists eventually made their way north to the Tennessee River to join the Union army while others enlisted in the 1st Alabama Cavalry in Huntsville.

At Looney's Tavern, Bill Looney as the owner and proprietor, served the Union Army by helping to aid Yankee sympathizers escape to the safety of Union lines to the north. During this time, Colonel Abel D. Streight led a detachment of troops into the western area to gather more recruits for the Union Army. The farmers who fled into the woods and those who joined the Union Army to avoid the Confederate draft could no longer work on their farms. Therefore, this caused the county residents considerable difficulty and hardships since it was becoming a real problem. With so many farmers gone, there wasn't enough manpower to plant crops and grow their food, let alone harvest any existing crops. Confederate agents worsened matters by confiscating food and taking livestock from all over the county to feed the Confederate army.

During the various skirmishes that happened in and around Winston County, the citizens soon grew weary, hungry, and afraid while the atrocities continued during the war. Both Unionists and Confederates alike committed acts of robbery, vandalism, and even murder, citing neighbor against neighbor in some instances.

One such incident involved a band of Confederate horsemen against the honorable probate judge Tom Pink Curtis at his residence on S. Main Street in Houston. It was rumored that the judge was known to be secretly hiding and distributing large amounts of rationed salt to the poor. Since he had direct access to the state government agencies, his ties would give him close contact with the agents directing the supply distribution of the salt. The Confederacy soon got wind of this operation and enlisted one of their best men in his field to lead a further investigation into the matter. Posing as a Union cavalryman, Confederate Sgt. Romy Gillette's mission was simply to befriend Judge Curtis in order to find out if the rumors were true and where the salt was being kept.

It was mid-morning while the white-haired, brown-eyed Tom Curtis sat behind his desk in the study of his home. He was busy at work while preparing his upcoming court case for next week. The judge was a short little man with bushy chin whiskers and would be fifty-three years old on his next birthday. His young wife of twenty-four had died in childbirth almost six years ago, and now he was alone in his big house with the exception of her former maid Minerva who stayed in a room near the kitchen. A gentle knock on the door interrupted him while the maid opened the door slightly and waited.

"Yes, Minerva, what is it?" asked the judge while looking over his wire-rimmed spectacles toward the door.

"I's sorry to interrupt sir, but there's someone here to see you," she answered.

"Who is it this time of the morning? I'm not expecting anyone today."

"He say tell you his name is Sgt. Romy Gillette from the 1st Alabama Cavalry in Huntsville."

"I don't know a Gillette from that post. Could it be Devereaux, perhaps?"

"No sir, he say clearly Sgt. Romy Gillette."

"Tell him, I'm busy and cannot be disturbed."

"Yes sir," Minerva replied while she padded back to the parlor to find the waiting sergeant. "The judge say he cannot be disturbed right now."

"You tell the judge it's very important that I speak with him."

Minerva returned to the study with the message as the judge looked up from a document he was reading. "Tell the sergeant to come back in the morning, and I will see him then." Minerva returned once again to the parlor with Judge Curtis' reply.

"Missy, you tell the judge that I will return in the morning. Before I leave, may I trouble you for a cup of water?"

"Certainly sir, follow me to the kitchen."

Sgt. Gillette kept his wandering eyes looking all around the kitchen while sipping on his water. His keen sense of the visual suddenly kicked in while he spotted it across the room. While Minerva had her back turned for a moment, Gillette moved in closer to spy a bundle that set in close proximity to the back door. There to his surprise and utter amazement was a stack of bagged salt just sitting there. He could hardly believe what he was seeing.

"Tell me, why all the salt you have over there?" he asked while pointing toward the pile.

Unknowingly, Minerva was quick to answer the sergeant. "I's not supposed to know, but different men from the Union come to the back door to get the salt."

"So, let me ask you, pretty gal, where is the salt kept? Surely you must know since you are in the house all the time."

"Oh, I can't say anything else 'cause the judge wouldn't like that. I'm afraid he would beat me," Minerva answered while her eyes focused on the door leading down into the basement.

"With all the rationing, I was just curious as to why the judge kept so much salt in the kitchen. I probably need to leave now. I will be back tomorrow," Gillette said while he returned the cup to her. As the sergeant made ready to leave behind Minerva, he had the chance to quickly unlatch the back door as he made his exit.

Just before midnight, Gillette and his band of Confederate horsemen arrived quietly at the rear of the Curtis mansion. The moon was shining brightly among the star-filled sky on this still and silent night while Gillette and his men gathered onto the back porch. He gently pushed up the latch and the door opened with only a slight noise from a rusty hinge. They entered and stood in the darkened kitchen in silence. Gillette halted the three men in darkness with a finger motion at his lips while he alone took the lantern he carried to descend the basement stairs. Holding the light high above his head, he was able to see literally hundreds of salt bags stacked along the basement wall. As Gillette ran back upstairs, he ordered his men to begin loading the salt into the wagon that the horsemen had brought along in anticipation of the sergeant's hunch being right. The loading process was almost complete when one of the men brushed against the kitchen table and toppled a candlestick onto a breaking china plate. The noise immediately awakened Minerva who lay sleeping nearby in the maid's room.

"Who's there? Is that you, Judge Curtis?" shouted the girl as she pulled on her robe and traveled the short distance into the dimly lit kitchen. When she saw the men, she screamed out in alarm at the top of her lungs. One of the men close by suddenly grabbed her and put his big hands around her throat while squeezing until she passed out. He let her fall to the floor and then pulled her arms to drag her out of the way over by the stove.

By this time, the judge had entered the kitchen with his shotgun pointed at the intruders. Without a warning, he fired into the darkness while hitting one of the men in the shoulder. In defense of the action from the judge, and no time to think about the situation, Gillette quickly pulled his revolver and returned fire while he hit the judge directly in the heart, thus killing him instantly. That particular night, Sgt. Romy Gillette, three horsemen including one wounded, and a wagon driver not only got away with over three hundred bags of salt, but murder. Seemingly, no one would ever know who killed Judge Tom Pink Curtis.

Countless other events continued while both Union and Confederate raiders swept through the county. In order to seize deserters and draft-dodgers, Confederate Captain Nelson Fennel led an unsuccessful raid in Winston County in June 1863. Lt. Colonel W.L. Maxwell led another expedition with a similar purpose, but the rugged terrain in the county hampered his efforts.

Union Colonel William J. Palmer, along with Major General James H. Wilson, won a similar skirmish with an encampment of Confederates while liberating a large number of Unionist conscripts, men who had been charged with forceful compulsory enlistment. While the war continued to escalate in several states, it was evident that considerable tensions remained between the soldiers and inhabitants of Winston County leading to occasional violence.

⊷⬧⊶

In Huntsville, Fort Gallant was buzzing with excitement as the news spread among the men. After all their months of training in camp, the 1st Alabama Cavalry was being activated for service. Nobody knew exactly where they were headed, but that only meant more anticipation for the cavalrymen until it was made official. The daily post on the bulletin board in each barracks announced a special meeting to be held in the yard at noon for all personnel. Everyone would be required to attend, at which time Colonel Spencer would be delivering his official address.

Cole McTavish and many others were nervously filled with excitement while they assembled on the yard. The men stood in formation while Colonel Spencer walked from the Gallant house and took his place before the troops. Sgts. Devereaux, McKenzie, McRae, and Boshell stood at his left and right while the colonel began his formal address.

"At ease, men. No doubt many of you have already heard the news I have for you today. I'll try to be brief and not keep you in suspense any longer. I have just received my official orders from Union headquarters that we will be departing here on 1 May 1864 for Whitfield County, Georgia. We will set up an encampment as a designated location nearby the Military Division of the Mississippi where we will assist Major General William T. Sherman, if necessary. We will be providing flank support as our primary source of defense. Gentlemen, should we find ourselves in the fight, we will be going up against General Joseph E. Johnston and the Army of Tennessee. I don't have to tell you that this will be a dangerous mission. Perhaps, it could happen since it is to be our first initial engagement with the enemy. Your sergeants will be directing each of you as we prepare to pack, load, and depart these premises at 0500 hours on the date I have already mentioned. That is all, you are dismissed."

It would become Sgt. Levon McRae and Sgt. Raymond Boshell's responsibility as the joint quartermasters to head up and oversee the next phase of operation. It would be no easy task to begin the departure procedure since this was to be the unit's first activation. It was the hope of each sergeant for everything to run smoothly, but every man would have to be willing to do his fair share.

Each cavalryman would be riding his assigned mount that would carry rider, weapons including the M1860 sabre and Spencer carbine rifle, while some men would have an issued sidearm or revolver, plus a field kit. The wagon team had to load and assume responsibility for the following: feed for the horses, water, firewood, ammunition, cooking utensils, food, and other necessary supplies. Once arriving at the encampment, wranglers and groomsmen would have care and watch over the horses and any additional livestock.

It was now three days until departure on 1 May, and things were coming together as the sergeants had planned. Drills continued as the horses were exercised while the cavalrymen sat astride and practiced wielding their swords at straw dummies. Cole McTavish had proven himself to be one of the best swordsmen in the unit while he rode high in the saddle on his mount, a black stallion named Midnight. If Libby and Nate could only see him now, Mrs. McTavish and Mr. Overstreet would be so proud. His thoughts turned to his feelings for both of them and little Alex while he continued to pack his gear.

The sun was peeking on the horizon at 0500 hours when the 1st Alabama Cavalry passed through the main gate as they headed toward Georgia. It was going to be a long day in the saddle.

CHAPTER 9

Battle of Rocky Face Ridge

Following the two day journey on the march, the 1st Alabama arrived in Whitfield County, Georgia at mid-afternoon where they set up camp toward the west. The Union cavalry remained on standby while General Joseph Johnston moved the Army of Tennessee to entrench them on the long, steep Rocky Face Ridge located eastward across Crow Valley. It was during this time, Major General William Tecumseh Sherman moved his Military Division of the Mississippi toward Johnston's position. He approached this territory with two columns while sending a third through Snake Creek Gap to the south to hit the Western and Atlantic Railroad at Resaca.

The fighting broke out while the first two columns attacked the Confederates at Buzzard Roost near Mill Creek Gap, and also at Dug Gap. The third column, now led by Major General James B. McPherson, passed through Snake Creek Gap while advancing to the outskirts of Resaca on 9 May. It was there that the greatest number of the Confederate force was entrenched along the ridge in wait of the approaching enemy. Sensing their strength, McPherson pulled back his column to Snake Creek Gap and waited. The next morning, Sherman decided to join forces with McPherson in an effort to take Resaca. In addition to these plans, Sherman ordered

Colonel Spencer's 1st Alabama to send his cavalry unit to drive the Confederates from Rocky Face Ridge with a flanking movement. Colonel Spencer ordered Sgt. Devereaux to lead his cavalrymen into action.

"All right, men, this is it," Devereaux gave the order to his band of excited volunteers, "Mount up, and we ride within the hour toward the ridge. Prepare yourselves!"

"Can't believe this is about to happen," Cole said to his buddy standing beside him.

"Believe it!" Callahan replied. "I need some help over here, Cole."

Cole and Scottie Callahan had become friends ever since the bath house incident, and Cole stood by him as a brother to help in any way. In this instance, Scottie called on him to help secure his field kit onto his mount, a Palomino called Blaze.

"Thanks, friend! I believe that will secure it," Scottie said as he swung himself up into the saddle and watched as Cole mounted Midnight positioned beside him.

"Move out!" Devereaux shouted as he gave the command.

The 1st Alabama consisted of nearly three hundred mounted cavalrymen who were about to experience their first encounter with the enemy in support for the Union soldiers who waited nearby Rocky Face Ridge. Colonel Spencer had them divided into both right and left flanks to approach from the east and west to hit the Confederates in a full frontal assault while they lay entrenched along the slope.

A bugle sounded as Devereaux yelled *Attack!* Immediately, three hundred cavalrymen hit the Rebs with swords drawn and blazing in the afternoon sunshine while they rode through the line of fire. Intense fighting broke out everywhere as both sides fought for their lives. Men from bushes and trees burst from the trenches while they fired, wounding and killing several riders and their mounts. The maimed and wounded were heard screaming in agony from their inflicted pain. Those who peered out and stood in the trenches found themselves victims that lost arms, legs, and heads as the cavalrymen wielded their sabers while slashing them to pieces. The bloody fighting continued until dark when the action ceased for the night. By morning, Sherman's army and the 1st Alabama withdrew from the front of Rocky Face Ridge. After discovering Sherman's retreat, Johnston began to move his troops toward Resaca on 12 May.

Casualties and losses for this battle consisted of a count: Union 837 killed – Confederate 600 killed. Officially, this report was primarily given for the regular armies. It was unknown how many casualties existed for the 1st Alabama Cavalry, although Sgt. Devereaux confirmed he had lost at least fourteen men and five horses to the cause. About twenty men received cuts and scrapes with three of them sustaining only non-life threatening wounds. One man had a shoulder wound that required surgery. Fortunately, not one of the six recruits who were present at the time of Cole McTavish's enlistment received any type of wound. Those men counted this as a blessing while they returned to the encampment to await their next orders. Following the aftermath, a small band hurriedly rounded up three stray horses and collected the dead before returning to camp.

The battle of Rocky Face Ridge was counted as a Union victory.

Battle of Resaca

Once again, Sherman and Johnston moved from Whitfield to Gordon County to face each other at the battle of Resaca. Orders from the Confederate headquarters granted Johnston's request for reinforcements to his camp near Dalton, Georgia. While the brigade of Brigadier General James Cantey started their move through the city, Confederate cavalry scouts sounded the alert to General Johnston. At this time, a large number of Union troops were on the move toward Rome along the road that led through the town of

Resaca. At the end of the day, Cantey's brigade had time to dig the trenches to set up their defense positions.

On 9 May, 1864 while moving out of Snake Creek Gap, the Army of Tennessee under the command of General James B. McPherson, ran upon a Confederate cavalry brigade in the area. The day before, this brigade had been ordered to scout the area that was under the command of Colonel Warren Grigsby. Following a fierce battle there, Brigadier General Thomas W. Sweeny formed a defensive line while he drove the Confederates back toward Resaca located several miles to the east.

It was Sherman's plan to hold the railroad and telegraph lines located south of Dalton in an effort to stop Johnston's maneuvers. This would force Johnston to either evacuate his position at Dalton or reduce a section of his army to fight Sherman on a ground more suited to his advantage. If this plan worked, Sherman would move his Army of Tennessee into place while his support armies would join him at the front. The plan was executed as the Army of the Cumberland led by Major General John M. Schofield engaged subsequent attacks on the Confederate front line.

After McPherson's two Corps left the woods, they fought against a Confederate cavalry unit positioned nearby. The cavalry was able to withdraw to a line of fortification on the outer edge of the city. As they continued to move, they were reinforced by the 37th Mississippi, a regiment in James Cantey's brigade.

Later that evening, McPherson sent his 9th Illinois Mounted Infantry toward the northeast. Their mission was to scout out the best route to reach the Western and Atlantic Railroad. Meanwhile, in another direction, Major General Grenville M. Dodge led the XVI Corps in a Union attack against a line of defense along Camp Creek. This combination of forces were composed of the Confederate cavalry, the remainder of Cantey's Division, two batteries which included eight cannons of Confederate manufactured 12-pound Napolean guns, and a fresh brigade of 20,000 men under Brigadier

General Daniel H. Reynolds sent out from Dalton by Joseph Johnston.

Since Johnston had withdrawn his forces from Rocky Face Ridge to the hills around Resaca, Union troops continued to test the Confederate lines to pinpoint their present location. The next day, full-scaled fighting erupted as the blood bath began on site. Seemingly, the Union troops were repulsed except on the Confederate right flank where Sherman did not fully exploit his advantage.

On 15 May, the battle continued with no advantage to either side. Sherman decided to send a force across the Oostanaula River at a point called Lay's Ferry while using newly delivered pontoon bridges to advance toward Johnston's railroad supply line. Johnston was forced to retreat while he was unable to halt this Union turning movement. All that was left for Johnston was to set fire and burn the railroad span and a nearby wagon bridge by early morning the next day. The Union quickly repaired the bridge and afterward transported their men across in pursuit of the fleeing Confederates.

It was later to be reported that among the 98,787 Union and 60,000 Confederate soldiers, the casualties suffered were: 3,500 Union killed and 2,600 Confederate killed. The result from the battle of Resaca proved to be inconclusive at the time.

Fortunately, during this particular battle, the 1st Alabama was only involved while Cole, Callahan, and three others were ordered to the area as scouts for General Sherman. As far as the entire unit was concerned, the 1st Alabama was to remain on standby at their present encampment. Cole and his men brought important messages to the General that proved to be valuable as Sherman assembled his battle plans. Afterward, the men all returned safely to their encampment. Cole and Scottie continued their duties in camp while they fed and helped take care of the horses. That very night, Cole would meet a wounded soldier from Schofield's army who lay hiding in the darkness of the horse pen. It would be through a conversation with this man, Cole would capture in his mind what actually took place at Resaca.

Up until this point in the war, the soldiers on both sides had been ordered to march in a straight line toward the enemy. This naturally proved to be almost certain slaughter for those in harm's way. This was the ultimate horror to the men who stood with their muskets pointed in a line while many faced certain death. Now, something was beginning to happen in the South while Longstreet brought up the idea of trench warfare. This idea was widely dismissed because trenches were determined to be unmanly. For one to hide behind a tree or pile of dirt to fire a weapon while you and fellow soldiers were standing out in the open was simply unheard. You were someone to be ridiculed. At this time, the whole idea of *macho* is very important to the soldiers during the first half of the war. After Gettysburg, there was a profound change in the proposed warfare.

Cole felt the need to go check on Midnight and several other horses before retiring for the night. He grabbed a lantern and headed toward the horse pen. He hadn't been there long when he sensed a strange feeling. Cole turned to move around his mount when he stumbled across the alien soldier laying on the ground in a heap. He could see in the dim light that the man was a Union soldier and he appeared to be hurt in some way. Cole gently kicked him on the bottom of his boot to awaken the sleeping soldier.

"Hey, wake up! Are you hurt?" Cole asked. "Tell me man, are you hurt and in pain?"

The man moaned, "Yes, I've been hit."

Cole bent down and rolled the man to his back while he saw the blood oozing from his mid-section. The man tried to sit up. "No, stay down! Don't try to move. I'll be right back."

In his excitement, Cole ran back to his tent in a flash. He found Callahan sitting outside nearby and instructed him to head for the pen while he ran for the doctor. In a matter of minutes, the three converged upon the scene of the awaiting wounded soldier. Without a word, Cole and Scottie placed the man onto the stretcher they had brought along and followed the doctor to the medical tent.

"Put him on the table," the doctor said. "Let's have a look at you, son."

Cole and Scottie stood by while the doctor tore back the soldier's shirt while slightly lowering his pants. Stuck into his belly, there appeared to be a large piece of shrapnel protruding from his gut.

"This is going to take surgery," the doctor said. "Who is this man?"

"We don't know. I found him only a few minutes ago," Cole answered.

"I'll try to save him," he said while the doctor took charge. "You men stand close in case I need some help."

The soldier lay still and quiet while he drifted into unconsciousness as the doctor immediately went to work on his unknown patient. The doctor quickly spread out his surgical instruments on the table while he reached for the bottle of chloroform. Pouring the liquid onto a piece of gauze, the doctor placed it over the nose of his patient while he watched and waited for a couple of minutes. The sedation took place and the doctor began while he reached for the tongs. It looked as though that there was enough of the shrapnel showing in order to fasten the tongs and pull the fragment out. With one slow movement, the doctor successfully clamped the tongs onto the fragment and gently pulled it out.

"Hold those bandages firmly on the wound," the doctor yelled while Cole quickly grabbed and pressed a bandage over the wounded area. "I will suture him and then we will have to wait and see if he survives after he comes back around. You men may go now if you want. I'll keep a watch over him tonight."

Three days later, Cole found the young soldier recuperating outside the hospital tent as he lay on a pallet in the shade of the Georgia pines.

"Good morning, Corporal. I see you made it back to the land of the living," Cole said while he extended his arm to shake hands.

"I understand that I have you to thank for that, I'm guessing. It was you who found me, wasn't it?" the corporal said while he reached to take Cole's hand.

"Yes, it was fortunate that I went out to check on the horses when I did that night. It's good to see you up today. I'm Cole McTavish, a private in the 1st Alabama Cavalry."

"I'm Corporal Nathan Chappell from Schofield's Army of Ohio. My friends call me Chappy. Guess you already figured that I'm a deserter, huh? I got separated from my division during the battle of Resaca. I'm very grateful to you and Doctor Greenway that I'm even alive today. I appreciate what you both did for me."

"At least, you're not a damn Confederate or you would now be our prisoner," Cole laughed. "Do you plan to find and rejoin your division?"

"Not really, I don't have a clue where they are right now. Figure I could join up with you. This is a cavalry unit, is it not?"

"Yes, we are volunteers out of Huntsville, the 1st Alabama Cavalry."

"Well, I can ride a horse and shoot a carbine rifle. I would have to learn about them swords. When I heal up, I may be able to practice swinging one of those blades. You could teach me, I bet."

"I'll have to talk to my sergeant about that," Cole replied. "You get plenty of rest, Chappy, and I'll see you later this afternoon. I've got to get along to tend the horses now."

Later that evening, Cole was able to secure a field kit for Chappy as well as a spare tent to be placed near him and Scottie. With plans to meet Sgt. Devereaux in the morning, Cole informed his new friend that he would go with him before the sergeant to meet and make the necessary transfer and paperwork. In the meantime, after pitching the tent, Cole sat outside with Chappy while they continued to get more acquainted.

"The 1st Alabama fought at Rocky Face Ridge, but our unit was not activated for the fighting at Resaca," Cole said. "However, Callahan and I did a bit of scouting during that time."

"You were lucky not to have experienced that particular hell, believe me. There was some fierce fighting going on there at Resaca. I had no more stood to reload when that piece of shrapnel exploded from a Parrott shell and hit my belly. I thought I was going to die on the spot until I somehow turned and ran backwards into the woods. I must have passed out soon after that, and when I came to my senses, my unit was gone, and I was lost. Somehow, I stumbled into your camp."

"Well, at least you made it here and got yourself patched up. It was lucky that Dr. Greenway was available to do your surgery. That man stays extremely busy as you can well imagine. What did he say about you the last time you saw him?"

"Naturally, no heavy lifting, and I'm to keep the bandages changed and tightly wound for another week. He told me I should expect to fully recover in time."

"Chappy, it would be interesting to me to learn about everything that happened at Resaca," Cole said. "You wouldn't want to tell me about it, would you?"

"What else is there to talk about?" He paused. "I guess I can tell you a little about what I know. Stop me when you've heard enough."

"Not a problem for me, Chappy. Let me pour us a cup of coffee before you get started," Cole said while he reached for the coffee pot that sat near his campfire.

"Well, it's like this as I recall. That morning, I think General Johnston probably made up his mind to evacuate Dalton. He must have felt like all hell was fixing to break loose as the evidence of a full-scale Federal move continued to mount. Anyway, Johnston ordered the remainder of his army to Resaca across the Oostanaula River to his rear. By sunrise, I don't believe the man could find one single Confederate left there on the northern half of Rocky Face Ridge or even Dalton itself. It must have looked like the whole army had skedaddled, just up and gone. With a day's head start, you would think the Union force should have beaten the main Confederate force to Resaca, wouldn't you? I heard that there were

122

70,000 troops headed through the woods while converging over the narrow, winding roads. Knowing that, any fool could almost figure out the big delay during the Federal march while the troops were moving at a snail's pace. The men were hot, thirsty, and tired. I heard a lot of them just passed out on the roadside. I was having a pretty tough time myself, even back there with my Army of Ohio Division. At this time, we were still camped, but ready to go at any time when the order came. By the time they reached their destination, the sun was too far gone to fight, and it was nearly dark with the exception of a late evening cavalry clash. I heard both sides were trying to stand their ground while a fight broke out between the units of General Judson Kilpatrick and General Joe Wheeler. Would you believe both of those generals were the exact same age at twenty-eight? Hell, I'm almost twenty-four myself, and I don't see young Chappy here anywhere near to being a general. Being a corporal suits this here boy just fine. As the fighting continued, soon Kilpatrick was unhorsed by a stray bullet. Luckily for the Union general, friendly troops managed to lug their fallen leader from the field and out of the war for several months."

"I would like to have been there to see that," Cole interrupted. "Need more coffee?"

"Naw, I'm all right," Chappy answered.

"How do you think Sherman felt about all this?" Cole asked.

"I think Sherman was neither daunted nor discouraged by his loss of the race to Resaca. He knew that Johnston was already there, inviting him to attack as soon as he could get there himself. Sherman knew Johnston had his back to the river, so the fiery general aimed to oblige him and to bring it on, come hell or high water. Informed that Grant had emerged from the wilderness, and was now in pursuit of Lee at Spotsylvania, Sherman was intent to keep the cannon balls rolling. Soon after this happened, my unit was activated, and we were marched to our new encampment while we began to dig trenches. Let me just tell you that some would laugh when the shovels were first handed out to start digging. Later on, they're not laughing anymore because as things kept building, now everyone discovers they can't get enough shovels. To the men on the front line that sees his buddies blown away, over and over again, now hiding in a ditch behind a big pile of dirt suddenly has appeal. We are now realizing that's a very definite change in the way the war is being fought nowadays in 1864. We are no longer going to stand with our asses out in the open while staring blindly into the guns of our enemy and just waiting to get struck down. I know from experience what happened to me, and I felt secure in the trench although I was caught by a stray fragment. It happens, but forming an open line like a row of sitting ducks doesn't make sense anymore."

"What happened next?" Cole asked while he stood briefly to stretch his back.

"As we moved out, McPherson on the right of the Union line, scored what little gain he could by leading his troops to higher ground toward the west of town. Elsewhere, along the Rebel line that ran along a four mile curve, I saw the cannon balls either stopped or were repulsed while our battle began. General Thomas made no headway at the center while we in Schofield's unit began to take a terrible beating on the left. The Confederates were coming at us in full force directly to our front with a sudden attack that drove us back nearly half a mile. Many were wounded and killed on the spot. That's when I was hit. I'm afraid that's all I can remember about the battle at Resaca."

"That's a lot, thank you for telling me what you know about it. Probably very soon now, the 1st Alabama will be moving to another area. Well, we need to think about turning in for the night. I'll see you in the morning, Chappy."

Battle of Dallas

General Joseph Johnston had been in excellent spirit all day while he was seen riding from point to point on his mount along the front lines. It was there a Tennessee private later recalled seeing him at close range. The General was a small man with fluffy white side whiskers, and a wedge-shaped face with a neatly trimmed moustache and a grizzly-looking chin beard while dressed in his daunting grey uniform.

Night brought an end to the fighting, thus preventing General Hood from his intended attack toward the Union right. General Johnston's good mood did not last into the night while a sudden visit from Hood brought about unwelcome reports from his scouts.

First came the report that the Union Corps who remained in Dalton had recently completed a forced march down the rail line to reinforce Schofield. Next, he learned that McPherson had brought his artillery up onto the high ground that General Polk had recently lost during the day. Having an array of weapons which included cannons that could fire long-range shells, McPherson was able to fire upon both the railway and the turnpike bridges closing Johnston's rear. The fire from these guns and artillery endangered Confederate lines of retreat and also limited their means of supplies.

Finally, a third bit of unwelcome news caused an even greater concern to the general. Cavalry scouts reported that the enemy had crossed the Oostanaula River several miles downstream in great strength. By morning, a renewed pressure by the Federal forces was felt all along the line. Johnston was forced to hold his ground until his scouts once again reported the Union troop's location. They were presently across the river and now approaching his escape route in vast numbers. Johnston ordered his forces to break contact and retreat down the turnpike. Sherman pressed after the retiring Confederates hoping to catch up with them before they had time to develop another defensive line.

125

The Union forces pushed onward while they marched in the heat of the day. It was so warm toward the end of May that many soldiers became overheated enough to fall out along the road. Moving slowly, they continued to pursue the Rebs through the woods, mountains, and streams where many places it was thought a northern army would never attempt to venture. One soldier, realizing that his detachment was a bit inferior, had this thought which he felt summed up his situation.

"Our regiment is small now, I fear. We do not have over seventy men who carry a rifle. I hope the damn marching will end soon." – Private A.H. Miller, XV Corps.

At the end of the first day's march, the troops made camp near Calhoun, six miles from Resaca. Johnston continued his withdrawal after not being able to find a favorable defensive position at Calhoun. The Confederates headed toward Adairsville, approximately ten miles farther down the line. Sherman now advanced onto a broad front since the new territory appeared to be more open-spaced in his ongoing race to overtake the Confederate army.

Private A.H. Miller would later recall as he recorded in his diary – 24 May, 1864.

"We had only three day's rations that would have to last for five in order to get us through the countryside we now have to pass. A great many Rebel deserters are coming in and surrendering while saying they are sick of the war. They tell us they get little or no rations, sometimes only a few ounces of cornmeal. The Union rank and file are hopeful at this time and feel confident of success. Some say we don't fight fair by flanking the Rebs and not moving aggressively onto their entrenchments. All in all, our spirits seem to remain high in all three Union Corps. Not only because the Confederates are on the run, but also because the rail repair gangs are keeping the supply lines open for our advancing army. I hear we are heading to Dallas."

Early on the morning of 26 May, Scottie, Cole, and Chappy left camp just before sunrise to scout the area in and around Dallas in Paulding County, Georgia. By mid-morning, they arrived on horseback in sight of the New Hope Church located near Pickett's Mill and hid themselves nearby in the woods. Soon, they were able to locate the Union defense line held by the XV Corps under the command of Major General John A. Logan of the Army of Tennessee. It took some effort while the three men and horses had to maneuver their way toward the line without causing any detection from the Rebs, and also the even greater risk of being mistaken for the enemy and shot on the spot by Logan's sharpshooters. Cole was much relieved when he was able to ride into the encampment and be directed to Major General Logan's tent.

"I've been expecting you," he said while the three scouts were ushered inside the tent where Major General Logan sat beside a makeshift desk. "It's cramped in here, so you men gather round. I have a message for your commander."

"Sir, we are Private Callahan, Chappell, and McTavish at your service," Cole announced while the three completed a rapid hand salute.

"At ease," Logan replied. "So, I see you are the scouts for the 1ˢᵗ Alabama. You are to inform Colonel Spencer that I may have need of him by tomorrow afternoon. We are presently digging our line of defense, so we are still a bit uncertain."

"How's that?" Cole asked.

"The Confederate line is about three miles north of New Hope Church. You may have passed the church on your way here."

"We did, sir. I remember it well," Cole said while his two companions gave their similar nods of affirmation.

"I'm thinking, if I could have Spencer's cavalry come from behind the Confederate line, the 1ˢᵗ Alabama should be able to drive them toward us where we'll be in position to launch a frontal surprise attack. We can catch them in between us, and they won't know what hit them until it's too late," Logan said.

"I believe that just might work, sir," Callahan spoke up.

"All right," said Logan. "Here's what we need to do to make this happen. Shortly, I will have my aide draft my exact plan. One of you should return to your camp to deliver the order to Colonel Spencer. Two of you will remain here to be on hand to lead the flank movement where I tell you. Who's going and who is staying?"

"I can go, I'll deliver the orders," said Callahan.

"Very well, private. That will leave you two here with us overnight. Don't worry, I will have my sergeant take you both to the places you will lead the cavalry flank movement. One flank to the left, and one to the right to join up, close in behind, and begin the attack. I will announce the exact time tomorrow morning. Please wait outside while I call for my aide. Get yourselves something to eat and drink at the mess tent over yonder. I'll call for you when I have completed my orders."

It took at least two more hours for Logan to finish devising his plans while he met with his officers. While the Major General sat on a stool in the doorway of his tent, the men all gathered around to listen as the plan was finalized. The three scouts watched from where they stood about fifty paces away while they nibbled on hardtack and drank black coffee. Cole, Scottie, and Chappy sat around and talked among themselves while they patiently waited.

"Chappy, how did you come by joining up with Schofield's Army?" Cole asked the tall, lean private who lay resting in the shade. Rolling onto his side, Chappy brushed the long brown hair from around his face while he rose to sit cross-legged on the ground.

"My brother, Charles and I fought together at Antietam where I watched him die while standing right beside me. It must have been a minie ball that tore through his skull and took off the top of his head. The good thing was that he probably never knew what hit him. After that battle, I went back home to Ohio with the news of his death to my family. Our mother and father were grief-stricken over that tragedy for a long, long time. He was their baby boy. Later, they tried desperately to stop me from re-enlisting in the Army of Ohio. Against their frantic pleas for me not to join, being the stubborn man I can sometimes be, I did it anyway. Major General John Schofield happened to be a family friend, so his acquaintance made it a bit easier for my folks to accept after they finally gave me their consent. I made a solemn promise that I would return after the war."

"Guess we both know that you were the lucky one after I found you that night in the horse pen," Cole replied.

"You're mighty right on that account. I owe you my life, Cole."

"Think nothing of it, Chappy. I would hope you'd do the same for me."

"You married?" asked Scottie.

"I was for almost three years to a sweet little gal named Mandy. Mandy was my true love, crystal blue eyes and long black hair with a body that most men could only dream about. We kept trying to start a family, but that all stopped when I left home to go to Antietam with my brother. While I was away, one day I got a letter with news that she had run off with my best friend Shane and was pregnant. I was devastated over the news, heart-broken, and then angry to the point of being, well, just crazy mad, you know. I thought about killing him. Hell, I even thought about killing her, but then I thought about the baby. What if that baby was mine?"

"Surely, you didn't," Cole said while he grew more attentive to the conversation.

"Well, I almost did. I had it all planned out while I waited on the chance to strike. All the time I was gone, day and night, my wheels kept on spinning almost out of control. This is awful to say, but I kept on fantasizing what I would do. You see, I wanted to catch them both together in bed. Of course, I would have to track them down first since I had no clue where they had gone. She left me and took practically everything I owned. I imagined myself at last finding them together. I could see them both naked as the day they were born while my best friend Shane lay on top of her as he pounded Mandy with all he had. I could even hear them. They were moaning in ecstasy while I stood at the end of the bed, my anger building and ready to explode."

Cole and Scottie sat there on the ground, spellbound while they listened intently.

"I waited for the climax, then made my silent move closer to the bed. At the last moment, when I saw Shane's butt cheeks finally stop to relax, the only sound was a creak from the floor while I moved in closer to surprise the unsuspecting lovers. Then came the moment I had waited for a long time. I simply pushed the barrel of my shotgun into his rectum, and pulled the trigger."

"Damn! And this was your fantasy?" asked Cole. "Heaven help us!"

"Oh yes, I couldn't really do that. It never happened. I loved her then, guess I still do in a way. Later, we divorced, she married Shane, and moved to Missouri where I heard they had four or five kids now. What about you two Romeo's?"

"Oh, I'm still single," Scottie said.

"I'm married to my beautiful wife Libby and we have a two year old son named Alex in Winston County, Alabama," Cole answered.

"You looking to get married, Scottie?" Chappy asked.

"One of these days, I suppose. Heck, I'm too young right now."

"Naw, you ain't too young. My pappy always told me that when the big head finally took control over the little one, then it was time to get married. Pappy was nearly thirty by the time it happened to him," Chappy laughed.

"Hey, Logan's aide is motioning for us to come over there," Cole said. "We'd better get going."

After meeting briefly with Major General Logan, the three scouts said their goodbyes to one another. Scottie saddled up as he tucked the orders for Colonel Spencer into his coat pocket, and headed to the road that would take him back to his camp. Logan's aide led Cole and Chappy to meet the sergeant who would take them to the place where the cavalry would start their moves tomorrow

130

afternoon. Following this, they were taken to a tent where they would spend the night.

Before Cole turned out the lantern, he had to ask Chappy one more question.

"Chappy, you never told us if you ever found out whether or not the baby was yours?"

"Well, to answer your question, I didn't know for a long time afterward. The last time I ever saw her, Mandy told me that I was the father. I have a son who's probably close to nine years old by now. His name is Rhett, and although I have never seen him, I hope to find him one day."

"You need to, Chappy. You really do. Thank you for sharing that. I didn't mean to get so personal. Good night!"

"Good night, Cole."

General Joseph Johnston had initially formed his defensive line along the south side of Pumpkinvine Creek in the Cassville-Kingston area. Following several smaller skirmishes at that location, Johnston's army fell back first to Allatoona Pass and then to the Dallas area where they dug out their trenches. Sherman's army continued to test the Rebel line while they themselves did the same.

On the afternoon of 28 May, the battle of Dallas occurred when the Confederates soon found themselves caught between the 1st Alabama Cavalry's flanking movement, and Hardee's Corps, along with the rest of Logan's Army of Tennessee. The mass of nearly 80,000 Union and 40,000 Confederate, plus 300 soldiers from the cavalry commenced into a gruesome, bloody battle. The Rebels were crushed while both sides suffered heavy losses and casualties, some 2,400 Union and nearly 3,000 Confederate. The 1st Alabama lost thirteen men including one of Cole's first friends at Fort Gallant. Sadly, Cole viewed the retrieved bullet-ridden body of the fallen Private Peter Nicholson from Limestone County. The single, twenty-four year old undertaker would never return to Athens while his buddies hastily buried him in Dallas. Sgt. Devereaux escaped with a slight gash on his right leg while Cole, Scottie, and Chappy remained unharmed.

By the first week in June, the 1st Alabama helped Sherman capture Allatoona Pass which had a railroad and now would allow supplies and additional men to arrive by rail transport. This strategic movement forced Johnston to remove the remainder of his troops completely from the area. The battle of Dallas in Paulding County, Georgia was yet another Union victory.

CHAPTER 10

The baby was born dead.

In the next few moments, the mother followed her little angel through the portals of Heaven while a warm gentle breeze blew through the bedroom window curtains on that tragic morning in July.

Nate Overstreet is probably one of the nicest young men that you would ever want to meet. At least, that's what Greta Hassendorfer would tell you because she took a certain pride in knowing about most everything in Winston County. Things like a person's age, their health, their wealth, and of course, who was seeing whom, kept her mind filled with the latest information. Naturally, Greta was also very quick to share that information, and including most times, a person didn't even have to ask. In fact, her closest friends were quick to tell you, if Greta didn't know, it hadn't happened yet.

Since her school days, Greta had a crush on handsome Nathaniel Overstreet, but when Marcie Merriwether snatched him away, she had to settle for Jacob the Jeweler. Sometimes, having a rich Jewish husband who happened to own Hassendorfer Jewelers didn't seem so bad after all. Her three-carat diamond ring sparkled almost as much as the gleam in Jacob's eye whenever Greta allowed him to leave the lamp on whenever he went for the missionary position. This made Jacob a happy little Jew while his big grin displayed the gold fillings in two of his front teeth.

Nate's muscular physique and natural good looks in his overall appearance drew him to almost everyone he came into contact with in town. Most men wanted to be like him while there were several women who just wanted him, regardless. Marcie realized that observation early on in her marriage. She considered herself the lucky lady who ended up with the man of her dreams. Her faithful husband of nearly three years now, Marcie had no complaints about his treatment of her. Nate was an honest, caring, and hardworking man that provided all she had come to expect in his love and support for her well-being. That was quite evident in the way he always demonstrated himself at his job down at the lumber mill and anywhere he happened to be seen in public. His attitude and performance at work after nearly five years had earned him the respect of his employer, Thaddeus D. McCorkle, owner of the lumber yard simply called The Mill. Following a recent vacancy, the position of General Manager had been offered by Mr. McCorkle to Nate Overstreet. In his newly found excitement, this was the news he couldn't hardly wait to get home to share and discuss with Marcie. Now, with a baby on the way, this new promotion couldn't have come at a better time for Nate and his family.

The Mill closed for the day, and Nate was anxious to be leaving for home. He usually came in from work through the back door into the kitchen where sometimes he would find Marcie waiting. Today she wasn't there, and the house was still and quiet. This was kind of unusual. Most days, upon his arrival, there always seemed to be some type of noise coming from somewhere in the house. Familiar sounds like company conversing in the parlor, house cleaning, washing dishes, churning, and the clatter of pots and pans were typical sounds that Nate was used to hearing on any given day. Perhaps his beautiful wife was sitting in the parlor this afternoon. Whenever she was reading, Marcie rather enjoyed a quiet, peaceful setting. The dark hallway led him past the staircase in the foyer while Nate paused at the doorway to the parlor. A quick glance inside told him that she also wasn't there. He saw her book on the table by her chair in the same place it had been whenever she left the room last night. *Where was she?*

"Marcie!" he called out from the foot of the stairs. "Marcie, darling, I'm home. Where are you, sweetheart?"

There was no answer.

Thinking that she was probably off somewhere with Libby, Nate bounded up the staircase to change clothes, pull off his work boots, and freshen up before Marcie arrived back home. *That's odd, the bedroom door is still closed. We both know that the last to leave the room always leaves the door open.* Without another thought, Nate reached for the knob, turned it to the right, and with a gentle push, he opened the door. From the dimly-lit bedroom belched a smell like no other as Nate gazed toward the bed while he reached into his back pocket for his handkerchief. His eyes began to water while he covered his nose, and fell down on his knees. It was the smell of *death.*

Laying there on the bed in quiet repose was his beautiful Marcie. Not breathing, not moving, how could this possibly be? Nate slowly picked himself up from the floor while he moved a bit closer to the bed. For a moment, he just stared at her while trying to take it all in as he could sense the look of agony on her face. *What horrendous pain she must have had to go through this entire day while left all alone with no one to help her in any way.* Nate quickly broke down with tears of grief. The fingertips on his right hand reached down upon her eyelids while he gently closed her once bright blue eyes. Her body was cold to touch while Nate fell prostrate across her breast when he kissed her on the lips. Her long brown hair was completely disheveled while it lay pushed back from her face and matted to her head. Nate couldn't help but see the large spot of blood as it had soaked through the bed cover and dried on top in a rust-colored hue. With one fell swoop, Nate reached down and snatched the coverlet back while he saw the saturated bed sheet filled with partially dried blood. The sheet clung to her somewhat like a mummified cocoon while it encased her body. He gently loosened and pulled the bedsheet downward to now reveal the baby boy she had carried for almost seven months that now lay dead between her legs. Marcie's arms seemed to be at her side and stretched as far down as she could reach as if trying to touch her baby. Nate had only time to throw the covers back over his wife and son before he fell in a pitiful heap onto the floor.

As the time passed, Nate could not remember how long he lay passed out. He was suddenly awakened by a loud knocking downstairs at the front door. He crawled over to the bed and pulled himself to his feet. With a look of total desperation, he looked down once again at Marcie before he turned to leave the bedroom. Nate closed the door, and headed down the stairs to answer and open the door. To his surprise, it was his parents, Elvin and Sharlett Overstreet, who had just happened to stop by for a surprise visit.

"Daddy, I need some help," the massive strong man said while the son fell sobbing into his father's arms. Sharlett Overstreet was speechless.

The next few hours proved to be quite busy at the Overstreet home on Poplar Street. Elvin Overstreet returned downstairs after he had briefly went alone to view the body of his precious daughter-in-law. He rejoined his wife in the parlor as Sharlett sat beside their grieving son on the sofa.

"I'm going for the sheriff," he said. "Sharlett, you stay here with Nate."

After quite a while, Elvin Overstreet returned to the house with Sheriff Thomas Kincaid, his deputy Joe Williams, and the county coroner, John Milton Loxley. The four men went immediately upstairs to the bedroom. Only several minutes had passed until Mr. Overstreet returned to the parlor where he found his wife seated in a chair while Nate lay sprawled on the sofa while he stared blankly across the room. After half an hour had passed, Sheriff Kincaid returned downstairs while leaving the coroner to make his examination and report.

"Nate, I need to ask you some questions. May we talk outside, perhaps?" asked the sheriff.

Nate got up from the sofa in silence while he motioned the sheriff to follow him to the front porch. Once there, the two sat close together in the rocking chairs, side by side. After a moment, Sheriff Kincaid cleared his throat to begin his interrogation.

"Son, I know this is tough for you, but I have to ask you these questions. Please answer me as best you can, understand?" Nate remained silent, staring straight ahead while looking across the street. "Nate, when did you arrive home this afternoon?"

"Guess it was about 4:30 P.M."

"Were you at work all day?"

"Yes, I have to be at work by seven o'clock. I usually get off at 4:00 P.M."

"When you arrived home, what did you do?"

"I always come in through the kitchen door. Sometimes, Marcie is there in the kitchen. Today, she wasn't. The house was all dark and quiet."

"What did you do next?"

"I went to look for her in the parlor, but she wasn't there. I thought she might be with Libby. Libby McTavish, she's the wife of my buddy Cole."

"So, you weren't able to find her until you went upstairs?"

"Yes, I went up there to change my clothes."

"How long did all this take after you entered the residence?"

"Four or five minutes, not long."

"Did you notice anything out of the ordinary when you reached upstairs?"

"Yes, the bedroom door was closed."

"Closed, what do you mean?"

"It's this thing both of us do every day. Whoever is the last one to leave the room, that person usually leaves the bedroom door open."

"I see. So, you open the door, what did you first notice?"

"I saw Marcie on the bed, and the *smell*. The smell in the dimly-lit room was so strong."

"How strong was this smell?"

"Even with the window opened, it was over-powering enough that I had to put a handkerchief over my nose at first."

"What did you do next?"

"Tears came into my eyes as I walked closer to the bed. I could see that Marcie wasn't moving, and it appeared to me that she also wasn't breathing. I knew she was dead. I fell onto the floor."

"How long were you on the floor?"

"That's what I don't know. I have no idea how long I lay there."

"When you came back around, what next?"

"I walked over to the bed and reached down to close her eyes. Those once beautiful eyes, now so dull when I looked upon her face. I leaned over to kiss her while her body was cold to the touch."

"Is that all?"

"No, I saw all the blood that had soaked through the cover, so I pulled it down toward the end of the bed."

"What did you see after that?"

"I saw the baby. He was there, crumpled between her legs with the cord wrapped around his little neck. It was quite pitiful to see. All I can think about now is that there wasn't anybody here to help her. I threw the covers back over them and left to answer the knock I heard at the front door. That's all I can remember, sheriff."

"All right, son, that's all for now. You may go back inside to join your folks if you want."

"What about the coroner? I assume that he's still up there."

"Yes, I believe so. Nate, I'm going to wait out here on the porch until he and my deputy come down. Are you going back inside?"

"Yes, I'll be waiting in the parlor with my folks."

"Would you tell Joe and Mr. Loxley that I am waiting for them out here?"

"Certainly, sir."

Within the hour, the coroner had made his report while he and the deputy returned downstairs to the parlor. Nate directed them to the front door to rejoin the sheriff on the porch. Deputy Williams remained on the porch while the coroner walked with Sheriff

Kincaid down the front steps into the yard. They both stopped at the end of the walkway for a brief conversation. Their meeting ended momentarily, and the coroner left for town in his buggy. The sheriff returned to the parlor to inform the Overstreet family about what needed to happen next while the night time drew near.

"The coroner wants to conduct an autopsy. Do I have the family's verbal consent to order the autopsy?" asked the sheriff.

"Why is that necessary?" Elvin Overstreet spoke up immediately. "You can clearly see what happened to our Marcie."

"Yes sir, but the circumstances concerning this death at home, alone, with no witnesses will help convey and establish a time frame and cause of death, please understand."

"That decision will be up to my son, Nate."

The sheriff looked at Nate and waited for his answer. Nate affirmed the request by a simple nod of his head and the wave of his hand.

"Very well. Folks, after I return to town, we will be sending a hospital wagon here tonight to transport Mrs. Overstreet to the morgue. Following the autopsy, the body will be released to the family where you may make plans for the burial arrangements. I am deeply sorry for your loss, and I will be in touch with you in the next several days. May you all have a restful night," said the sheriff while he turned to leave. Motioning to his deputy while crossing the porch, Kincaid and Williams mounted their waiting horses and rode back to town.

Sheriff Kincaid returned to the Overstreet home after three days in late afternoon. The findings from the autopsy were in, and the sheriff felt it was his duty to immediately share the results with the grieving widower. It was almost supper time when Sheriff Kincaid arrived at the house. Nate left the kitchen where he was preparing his supper meal to answer the knock at the front door. He opened the door to see the serious looking Thomas Kincaid standing before him on the porch.

"Good evening, sheriff. Won't you please come in?"

"Hello, Nate. I hope I'm not interrupting anything."

"I was about to have my supper, but that can wait. Let's move into the parlor."

"I'm sorry to barge in on you like this, but I have just received the findings from the autopsy. I felt that you would probably want to know the results as soon as possible."

"Certainly. Have a seat on the sofa, sheriff, and let's get to it," Nate said while he took a seat into his chair.

"Instead of reading the entire report, Nate, allow me to give it to you in simple laymen's terms. It is the opinion of the coroner that the time of death for the seven month old male infant was nearly one hour prior before the passing of his mother. As the result of a hard labor through the birth canal, he was strangled when the umbilical cord became wound around his neck during the birthing process. The baby was born very much alive, but when he came out in delivery, the cord had tightened enough to restrict the oxygen to the brain. This resulted in his death by strangulation/asphyxiation, thus causing him to suffocate. For an undetermined reason, Mrs. Overstreet went into early labor due to stress, physical strain, or any other ailment that would somehow trigger the onset of the labor process. She probably went into labor the night before, not even realizing it by the time she went to sleep. Regardless, she endured a hard labor that resulted in her actually bleeding to death. The baby weighed only three pounds, but he literally tore through her uterine wall while he struggled and came out a breached birth. She would have seen the baby born, but grew helpless in her weakness and the tremendous loss of blood before she quickly ebbed away. At this point, she felt no pain while she bled out and drifted into semi-consciousness until her heart finally stopped. One final notation, there was an obvious amount of bruising to her neck, particularly around the throat area. It was determined that death occurred around 5:00 A.M. that morning."

Sheriff Kincaid passed the written report to Nate as he drew himself forward to take the paper. He looked down while his eyes focused on the final statement at the bottom of the page.

It stated: Cause of death – Undetermined.

(signed) John Milton Loxley, Coroner, Winston County, Alabama – 21 July 1864.

"One last question for you, Nate. Was she ---?"

"She was awake when I left for work," Nate quickly interrupted. "It was just after seven when I kissed her goodbye and left the bedroom. Her last words were *I love you, and you're going to be late again.*"

"So, she was awake and talking that morning?"

"Most definitely, I can assure you."

With that, the sheriff excused himself and left. Nate returned to the kitchen, sat down at the table, and picked at his plate of cold food.

Needless to say, the days following the news of the death of Marcie Overstreet and her baby was received by an outpouring of sympathy which suddenly spread like wildfire through the little town of Double Springs. For the first three days, the Overstreet house was open while countless friends and neighbors called to pay their respect. Many of the visitors came bringing tributes of food and flowers while sharing their kindly worded testimonies of condolence. Libby McTavish was one of the first to arrive to see Nate after learning the news from her friend Greta. She was totally shocked and dreaded the letter she knew that she was going to have to write to her husband, Cole. Those two women alone were responsible for planning all the meals that were brought in for the family for several days. Although Marcie's parents, Huel and Dalinda Merriwether, were both deceased, she did have one older sister living in Massachusetts. Rachel Merriwether was now an invalid, and quite unable to make the trip to Alabama for her sister's funeral.

After her body was released, the funeral for Marcella Diane Merriwether Overstreet was held on 25 July at the Mt. Calvary Methodist Church in Double Springs with burial in the adjoining cemetery. It was to be a closed casket service at the request of Sharlett Overstreet to help prevent any further grief from the initial viewing for sake of the family and close friends. In death, Marcie was made up to look like the bride she was on her wedding day. Veiled in her wedding gown of ivory, and laid out beautifully in a pine box, Marcie held her son, wrapped in a baby blue blanket, cradled in her arms. Nate was heard to tell several of the mourners that Marcie had wanted to name a boy, Michael Channing Overstreet, and call him Chan. She had never mentioned the name for a daughter. That was her wish.

As the graveside part of the service ended, the friends began to depart: church friends, men from the mill, numerous townspeople including Jacob and Greta Hassendorfer, Libby McTavish, Elvin and Sharlett Overstreet who were among the last to leave the cemetery with Nate. Under the shade of a big oak tree not too far away, Sheriff Kincaid remained while he watched everyone as they left. After he was certain that Nate Overstreet had seen him standing there, he turned and walked away.

That evening in the Overstreet house, those who had gathered there began to leave the premises. Jacob and Greta left. Soon after, Libby and Alex left. The last to leave were Elvin and Sharlett as Nate bid them all a good night and closed the door. Now, Nate was alone. It was the first time ever that he was truly alone. That reality began to set in while he walked from room to room in the big house. All of a sudden, he became completely overwhelmed in grief with all that had transpired over the past week. With his wife and baby gone, he began to sink rapidly into a deep depression. He was so sorry, not only for them, but also for himself.

Nate went upstairs to change out of his dark blue suit that he wore to the funeral. How he hated that suit, even though it was the suit he wore at his wedding. He stripped it off, along with the shirt and necktie, and threw the clothes across the bed. His shoes and stockings had already been removed the moment he walked into the bedroom and kicked them underneath the bed where he now sat. Clad only in his drawers, he reached down into the flap to scratch an itch before standing to leave the room.

Upon entering the kitchen, he padded toward the massive oak sideboard against the wall. It had taken him almost six months to design and build it for Marcie. After opening the cabinet door, he pulled out a crystal goblet and a decanter of his favorite Kentucky bourbon before heading to the parlor. He lay back, propped against the sofa arm to make himself more comfortable. He poured himself a drink and placed the bottle on the floor beside him. Putting the glass to his lips, he swallowed its contents in one gulp. Then he poured himself another, and another, and another. He was getting quite drunk, but that was his intent to begin with. He wanted to get totally wasted, and then maybe he would wake up and realize that all this had been just a bad dream after all. Marcie would have two more months before the baby was due, and she would be so happy to learn about his promotion to General Manager. Thaddeus McCorkle had already told him to take off for as long as he needed, so he would do just that. The mill would just have to run without him right now.

At some point, before Nate completely passed out, his body became hot and sweaty. He was restless. He began to move his hips with a thrusting motion until he eventually put a hand into his drawers. The next morning, he had no recollection of how he had ended up in the parlor and laying naked on the sofa.

The next days and weeks saw Nate heading into a downward spiral. He turned down the job of general manager at the mill while he continued either coming in late to work or not at all. His noted tardiness and absences could no longer be tolerated, and he was eventually fired from his job. This was the cause for even more drinking. He no longer wanted the company of Jacob and Greta, Libby, and even his parents. After several arguments, Elvin and Sharlett Overstreet were told by their son that he no longer wished to see them. This nearly broke his mother's heart. After their last confrontation, Nate left the house, slamming the door in a fit of rage. He thought he could cool down at Looney's Tavern. All he needed was another drink.

During the next several days and nights, Looney's would be the place that Nate Overstreet could be found. On the nights he was too drunk to go home, Bill Looney would see that he was taken upstairs to one of the rooms and put to bed. On the days he was more sober, Nate would try to find his way back home. Presently, he still concealed a large amount of cash in his bureau drawer, but his frivolous spending was beginning to reduce that amount quickly.

The next day found Nate back at Looney's. He depended on the cook at the tavern to provide him with each meal he took whenever he stayed there overnight. Nowadays, he was scarcely eating while his drinking continued to consume him. He was losing weight while Bill Looney, the proprietor, could tell at a glance that Nate had lost at least twenty pounds. Also, his personality and entire demeanor seemed to be changing, and not for his own good. Some of the local patrons and others who knew him, no longer wanted to be in his company. He's pathetic, they'd say behind his back, a born loser.

Nate was sitting at a table near the back one afternoon when a young girl named Lucy suddenly appeared, gave him a wink, and dropped herself onto his lap. With one arm around his neck and a hand underneath her placed on his crotch, Lucy smiled and giggled at his delight. Dropping the arm around his neck, she allowed him to caress her to the point of guiding his hand under her skirt and making her moist. By nightfall, she led him out back to the alley where for the price of two dollars, Nate pushed her forward against the wall, lifted her skirt, tore open his fly, and took her from behind. Then, the two of them went back inside for a round of drinks. The next morning, Nate woke up in the bed they shared upstairs to find Lucy already gone from their night of pleasure, along with all his money. He called her a few choice names while he dressed and left to go back home for more money. He kept thinking about what he would do to her if he ever found her again.

The next night, Nate returned to the tavern where he met a much older woman named Abigail. Abby, a married lady herself, took him to bed where she showed him all the things he had always imagined that Marcie would never do, not in a million years. Nate liked Abby very much. In fact, she became almost a regular partner while they spent several nights together whenever her husband was out of town on a business trip. She was a woman who could hold not only her liquor, but his manhood between her soft fingers with a warm gentle touch. Aside from that, Nate liked drinking and talking to her. Abby was quite experienced, and was really a nice lady even though he had never met her or her husband before. One night, Abby confessed to Nate that on one occasion she had seen him at the bank several weeks ago. She hoped one day to have a chance to actually see what he was packing below the Mason-Dixon Line as she put it bluntly. Nate took that as a compliment, so neither of them seemed the least bit disappointed. Then one day, Abby was gone, and he neither saw nor heard from her again. This was a good excuse to keep on drinking.

A week after Abby had left on a stagecoach to Macon, a very drunken Nate was seen by Bill Looney attempting to escort another young girl upstairs to his room. This one was a light-skinned black gal who looked about sixteen. Bill was quick to confront Nate at the bottom of the stairs while advising him that he was not allowed to take any more women up to the room. Otherwise, his sorry ass would be put out on the street for good. Looney's Tavern was simply an Inn, not a whorehouse.

This scene naturally brought about some loud cursing that ended in a fist fight. Nate sent the first blow, a right uppercut, to Bill's chin which landed him on the floor as he fell over a chair. The other bartender on duty rushed to pull Nate away, throw him into a chair, and threaten him not to get up until the sheriff could get there. Fortunately, a regular patron sitting nearby volunteered to go get Sheriff Kincaid. After that last incident at Looney's, Nate was taken to jail by the sheriff and locked up overnight to sleep it off.

The next morning, Nate awoke to the smell of freshly-brewed coffee while the sheriff stood at his cell and offered him a cup.

"Before I let you out, Nate, I still have something that continues to bother me quite a lot," said the sheriff.

"What's that?" Nate asked while he took the coffee cup from the sheriff between the bars and sat back on the bunk.

"I believe you already know what I intend to ask you, son. You killed Marcie, didn't you?"

"Sheriff, I can't believe you could think that! I most certainly did not! Why I've known Marcie over five years when her and her sister Rachel lived over on Cotton Avenue. I could never even begin to think about hurting her in any way, and for me to be accused of killing her and my unborn son, there's no way. Sir, you're crazy if you think that!"

"All right, calm down. I just needed to see your reaction, that's all. Tell you what, Nate, if I let you out of here today, will you promise to try and get some help, and straighten out your life before it's too late? Just the other day, I ran into McCorkle in town and he told me that he had to fire you. As a father myself, son, you need to straighten up your ass, get back in church, and go back to work or try to do something constructive for a change."

Nate took this all in, but could hardly believe the sheriff thought he was a cold-blooded killer, the man who could murder his family.

"You're free to go now," said Sheriff Kincaid.

On his way home, Nate began to think about what he really wanted to do now. He would sleep on it overnight, and hopefully make up his mind in the morning. After a restless night, Nate was up early. He packed a few clothes into a large leather bag and brought it downstairs, and placed it in the foyer by the front door. He turned to make a final walk throughout the house while he went from room to room while visions of past memories flooded his mind. Having secured all his remaining money and the house key in his pocket, he picked up the bag and was out the door on his way to see his parents. Upon arrival, Nate gave Elvin and Sharlett Overstreet his most sincere apology, and the key to the house on Poplar Street. He shook his father's hand and kissed his mother goodbye as he turned to leave.

"Where are you going, son?" they asked.

"I'm headed to Georgia," he replied.

While Alex slept, Libby sat at the table in her little cabin to begin writing that dreaded letter to Cole. It all still seemed like a bad dream. How will we be able to get over this and move on?

CHAPTER 11

The morning after Nate Overstreet left Double Springs for parts unknown, the sleepy little town awakened to a sensation that would hold the attention of the residents for the next several months. It was 3 August, 1864 at two o'clock in the morning when neighbors along Cotton Avenue were awakened by a loud cry for help. Some women were heard screaming and crying while other voices yelled *murder.*

The shouting was coming from the direction of the Methodist parsonage occupied by Rev. Walter J. Goodhue, 32, and his plain looking wife, Agatha, 29. Pastor Goodhue had recently delivered the very eloquent eulogy for Marcie Overstreet while Agatha sang one of Mrs. Overstreet's favorite hymns. It was misting a light shower, but residents up and down the street hardly took time to dress while many bounded out of their homes to answer the call of distress. Before several neighbors reached the parsonage, the minister was found lying face down by the roadside. He was moaning in pain, and clad only in his nightshirt. A couple of men who had discovered the unfortunate victim tried to pick him up when they saw he was covered in blood from head to foot. They carried him up to his house while noticing that the side door to the kitchen stood open and decided to take him there rather than trying to enter by the front door. The two men nearly dropped him when they came to the threshold in frightful surprise as they came upon the body of

Mrs. Goodhue lying face down with her head near the bottom of the stairs. Agatha Goodhue was quite dead with a bullet hole through her head.

Rev. Goodhue told those who had gathered inside the house that he and his wife Agatha were attacked in their home by two armed masked men who immediately fled the scene after trying to rob them. In the process, his wife was shot dead, and he was shot in the right side and received numerous stab wounds throughout different places on his body. Those men who were first on the scene took note and recognized what the Reverend was telling them as they stood to listen and give witness to the facts while Rev. Goodhue tried to speak.

Mrs. Lancaster, the next door neighbor, ran back to her house to gather some towels and bandages to attempt to stop the bleeding and dress the wounds of the minister. While Mrs. Lancaster continued to work with him by making him as comfortable as possible, she and those who stood close by, listened intently while the reverend continued to speak.

"I was awakened from a sound sleep by a gunshot close to my head. Standing over me was a brute of a man, a bandana covering his face, who had just reached across me and fired a bullet through my wife's head. I immediately sprang from the bed and began to try to fight him off. I was no match for him in strength, but continued to grapple with him to dislodge the weapon from his hand. We struggled all over the bedroom and then fell through the doorway into the darkness of the parlor. Once there, I discovered another man in the shadows that I now had to contend with. His accomplice was a wiry little man, also masked, who was armed with a straight razor. He slashed at me again and again to try to force me to release my hold on the big man. By this time, we moved to the dining room where the big man broke free from where I had him around the neck. Suddenly, a white-robed figure of Agatha rushed into the room while calling for me. Then, both men jumped me and our fight continued into the kitchen, out the side door, through the gate, and into the street. It was there that the big man shot me in the side while both of the murderous villains fled the scene."

Long before the sun was up that morning, countless inhabitants gathered onto the lawn of the little parsonage in an uproar. They were demanding to know what dastardly villains had used the cover of darkness to creep into their peaceful little town to invade the home of their beloved pastor by killing his wife and attempting to murder him with such a gruesome act of violence. Telegraph operators and the newspaper spread the news while various newspaper correspondents headed to Winston County. A reward for the identity and capture of the two alleged murderers soon reached $2500 while many private detectives started to work on the pending case.

Two weeks after the murder, two of the leading merchants from Double Springs called on homicide detective Lanthus Oneal Hagelmeyer to take up the case. Lanny Hagelmeyer refused, stating that he did not work on reward cases. Calvin Whitmire, owner of Whitmire Mercantile, pleaded in earnest with Hagelmeyer.

"Lanny, this entire affair has been a disgrace to our town. It's terrible, and so tragic that something like this could ever happen here, and in this particular neighborhood. I am begging you to work on solving this case. Just name your price, and the merchants will pay for your salary and expenses out of our own pockets. Let it be understood that this matter will remain a secret between us. If you solve the case, and even end up with the reward, well and good for you. If not, we will still pay for your time and expenses."

On these particular terms, Hagelmeyer could not decline while he went to work the very next day. Lanny Hagelmeyer moved to town and took a room at the Duvall Boarding House on Main Street. He devoted his first few hours in town while listening to current gossip on the street.

At first, there was only one theory concerning the murder. Hagelmeyer wrote into a little black book he kept inside his coat pocket:

Most people seem to think that the two robbers entered the house to commit a simple robbery. They went into the bedroom to search for valuables when Mrs. Goodhue suddenly awakened. The intruder nearest the bed turned in his desperation with the intention of killing them both until Walter Goodhue surprised him as he rose quickly from the bed in his defense. A fight ensued while the struggle saved Goodhue's life, but it was too late to save his dear wife. The whole town is praising the good reverend for his actions. The Rev. Walter Goodhue is a nice looking man, caring and compassionate for his congregation at all times. He is reported to be very popular with his flock, but now he is seemingly idolized.

After learning about public opinion, Hagelmeyer turned to his examination of the exterior of the parsonage of the Mt. Calvary Methodist Church. He knew that the robbers could not make a forcible entrance into the house without leaving some form of evidence to indicate the break-in. He found nothing to show how the house had been entered in the first place.

The minister's brother, David, learned that Detective Hagelmeyer was in town and went to Duvall's to meet him there. David soon volunteered to show him the scene of the crime without any further thought about Sheriff Kincaid and his investigation. After all, the crime scene had already been secured, and gone over with a fine tooth comb, as they say, while Rev. Goodhue was recuperating in the house. David insisted that the detective come to the house and personally talk with his brother. Hagelmeyer at first declined by saying he did not wish to disturb his brother since he was still suffering with his wounds. However, older brother David kept persisting until Hagelmeyer finally accompanied him to Goodhue's bedroom. Hagelmeyer took out his little book and began to write as he made his observation:

When I entered the bedroom of Rev. Goodhue, I expected to see a victim suffering from a pistol shot in his side and seventeen razor slashes. Also, I was expecting a gentleman who looked like a refined reverend in appearance and having a clerical and holy countenance. Instead, to

151

my surprise, there was nothing that reminded me of a young minister at first glance. His face could match the look of a chiseled prize fighter while his virile body would show a greater advantage in the ring rather than the pulpit.

Brother David introduced the two men while he and Hagelmeyer stood at the bedside as Rev. Goodhue gave his account. For the next ten minutes, the detective asked no questions, but kept his sight on the face of the injured man while he listened to the whole story. The calm look of the detective spooked Goodhue while it unnerved him as he grew confused. His face grew pale and flushed as he tried to continue until finally he seemed to go blank. Hagelmeyer turned and left the room with David without having spoken a dozen words to either of them. His initial thought was that this man is not who these people think he is.

During the next few days, Det. Hagelmeyer went into seclusion at the boarding house while he continued to work on various theories that had never occurred to others. A short time later, he went to the court house and appeared at the office of James Franklin Hammond, prosecuting attorney at Double Springs. He presented Mr. Hammond with an outline of the facts while surprising the prosecuting attorney when he told him that he was ready to charge Rev. Goodhue with the murder of his wife.

Two weeks after the tragedy, Goodhue had recovered from his wounds enough that he was seen lifting fallen limbs and debris in his back yard that were strewn across the yard following a recent storm. The detective, accompanied by Sheriff Thomas Kincaid, went at once to the Goodhue residence on Cotton Avenue and arrested the young minister. Rev. Goodhue had to testify before a coroner's jury the very next day. The arrest of Rev. Goodhue was the sensation of the year. Many people in the county declared the arrest an outrage, and denounced Hagelmeyer as an opportunistic reward seeker who should be run out of town after being tarred and feathered.

The following morning, an inquest was held without incident while according to the detective's original agreement with the prosecuting attorney, Goodhue was released from custody. It was Hagelmeyer's plan to have all the evidence submitted to the grand jury to have the reverend indicted in the regular way.

Behind the scenes, Hagelmeyer secured the county coroner, John Milton Loxley, to conduct an autopsy on Mrs. Agatha Goodhue whose remains had been placed in the Goodhue family vault. The coroner reported upon his examination that the bullet passing through Mrs. Goodhue's brain at the point that it did, proved that it had killed her instantly. Therefore, Goodhue's story about her coming into the parlor during the alleged struggle and speaking to him was a lie. It was also proven that if Mrs. Goodhue had fallen on the spot she was found on the doorsteps, the force of the fall itself would have propelled her out the doorway and into the yard. The position of her body indicated that she had been dragged there. This was evident upon further examination of her nightgown.

After the autopsy, results were made public while popular opinion began to change as many now sided with the detective. Mr. Hagelmeyer might have made his case after all. In addition, the detective had discovered the motive. Rev. Goodhue had a lover. Miss Lula Crenshaw was a beautiful blonde, almost forty years old who looked twenty-five; and had captured the heart of the Methodist minister. Rev. Goodhue frequently conducted revivals in other nearby towns and would travel there alone while leaving his wife in the care of a good sister in the congregation. He would soon return back home always citing some excuse or feigning a sudden illness. Since Miss Crenshaw's house was only a few houses away, it was quite easy for her to slip out of her house to Goodhue's and back home again without attracting any particular notice. That is, except the one time Mrs. Lancaster saw her leaving by the back door just before daylight, while showing that she had indeed spent the night with her lover.

Three days later, the grand jury was in session. The called witnesses were being examined while the good reverend stood outside the door. He was quite busy instructing his friends on what to say when they were called to testify before the jury. On a late Thursday afternoon, the Grand Jury indicted Rev. Walter Joseph Goodhue for the murder of his wife. The judge refused his bail while he was placed in the Winston County jail to await his speedy trial in a couple of months.

While preparations got underway to go to trial, the family of the murdered wife believed the Rev. Goodhue was innocent, with one exception, while they used their wealth for his defense. With a combined effort, family members bought the highest-price defense attorney in the State at the time, Alfred Winslow McDermott from Montgomery. During this time, the outspoken mother of the murdered woman believed with all her heart that her son-in-law would never do such a thing. However, Agatha's father was the only one in the family who totally disagreed. He was convinced that Walt Goodhue had indeed killed his only daughter in cold blood. Zachary and Sarah Penrod had shared almost thirty-five years of marital bliss together, now to become so embittered against each other. Their differences of opinion over this matter could never be resolved, so they eventually separated and were later divorced.

The brief trial lasted only one week while it began on a cool day during the last week in September. Several witnesses were called on to testify on behalf of Rev. Goodhue in his defense. The most convincing testimony came from Detective Hagelmeyer while his account greatly influenced members of the jury. Hagelmeyer was called to take the stand while he began his testimony.

Rev. Walter Goodhue's wounds were self-inflicted. The gunshot to his side merely grazed the flesh. The angle that the bullet traveled across his mid-section showed the pistol had been held in his own right hand. The seventeen razor cuts on his upper chest were scarcely more than skin deep. Their obvious direction showed how he held the razor while he carefully drew it across his muscular body. There was not a vein found to be severed. It would be almost impossible for anyone to receive seventeen long slashes with a sharp razor, especially in the dark while the razor marked the flesh at each stroke. Some of the longer cuts appeared to be just scratches.

No such struggle could have taken place in the house as Goodhue described. It is a known fact that those who entered the house immediately following the tragedy, saw everything completely undisturbed in each of the rooms. In the dark parlor, there had been a round mahogany table with a large floral arrangement and a silver candlestick placed in full view in the center of the room. The placement of the table was directly in the path of the three men who had wrestled their way into the room. In the dining room, the table was set with fine china and crystal which was also in the way. Other furnishings and assorted pieces of furniture in each room were not disturbed in the desperate struggle taking place within the house. Outside, the Reverend falling in the rain by the roadside was only a staged scene by Goodhue to create the illusion that this tragic event was absolutely real. However, his wounds were not enough to cause him to fall, either from pain or loss of blood.

Goodhue described to a number of residents that the robbers stole his pistol and razor from the top drawer of the kitchen sideboard, and tried to kill him with his own weapons. One of the men took his trousers from a chair, and after taking thirty dollars from the pockets, he threw them into the back yard.

It was Goodhue who actually went out to his woodshed located at the back of the property to dispose of the items. He leaned out of the window, and threw the bloody trousers into the weeds in one direction, and the razor in another. Later that morning, both were eventually discovered as they were found lying in the wet grass where they had been thrown. When Goodhue leaned out the window, his blood-stained nightshirt had left a smear of blood on the window sill. Unknown to anybody, the investigators had this section of wood dismantled and taken in to be analyzed by a chemist. He found the blood stains on the exhibit to be the same as were on the nightshirt of the minister. Its appearance at the trial created an unexpected sensation for the jurors.

Goodhue's pistol was found on the side of the road located about as far as he could throw the weapon after shooting himself at the spot where the neighbors found him. Sheriff Kincaid checked the revolver that night and discovered two chambers were empty. One witness, assumed to have been greatly influenced by the defendant, claimed to have seen two men in a buggy. He described them as wearing masks and hurriedly driving away from the parsonage precisely at the time that Rev. Goodhue was calling for help. Other witnesses were brought in that stated they had seen this same buggy on the road leading out of town, some three or four miles away. However, there were no buggy tracks found in the mud in front of the house after the heavy rain that fell around midnight. It was quite remarkable that all of Goodhue's tracks were clearly visible there on the roadside, while footprints of the two robbers were not to be found anywhere.

On the afternoon of 6 October, 1864, the jury delivered their verdict.

Walter Joseph Goodhue was found guilty of murder in the second degree as charged in the indictment and sentenced for thirty years to life imprisonment in the State Prison of South Alabama. The disgraced, defrocked, and defiant Rev. Goodhue always denied what he had done.

Lanny Hagelmeyer collected the $2500 reward money; however, he didn't keep it for himself. Instead, he donated it to the Confederacy for the war effort. The divorced father of three grown children from Huntsville chose to stay awhile longer in Double Springs. He now had a specific reason in mind. A few days after the trial had ended, while finishing his supper at a local restaurant on Main, he met the now available Miss Lula Crenshaw. She joined him at his table for an after dinner drink and conversation. An hour later, the beautiful blonde accompanied Hagelmeyer to his room at the boarding house where she quickly undressed the detective and allowed him to sample all her charms. The poor man was instantly bewitched, bothered, and bewildered while he moved into her stately home on Cotton Avenue. Once there, he took up residence in the house that the neighbors simply called the "Love Nest" while rumors of an upcoming wedding began to circulate. In the springtime, a private wedding ceremony took place at the Winston County Courthouse. Two weeks later, Mrs. Lula Hagelmeyer gave birth to a healthy baby boy that the couple named Neal.

CHAPTER 12

Battle of Atlanta

27 July 1864

Dearest Cole,

My Darling, I have just finished reading your last letter, and I feel so over-joyed in knowing that you are both well and safe. Those particular battle scenes that you described about all the fighting were horrendous. I was quite shaken and disturbed over the fact that so many were wounded, maimed, and killed on both sides. War is a terrible thing! I can hardly wait until you return home. However, it pleases me to know that you found a new friend in Nathan Chappell, the man at Resaca you called "Chappy." Hopefully, he will remain a good friend much like Nate and Scottie Callahan as you always mention in your letters. Alas, my dear, lest we not forget Sgt. Devereaux. With your precise description of him and his manly attributes, what gossip would Greta now begin to spread about him? If she only knew, but I shall never tell her about him. As for me, I don't have to worry since I have you, even though I miss you so much right now.

I was deeply saddened to learn that Private Peter Nicholson was killed during the battle of Dallas. If I am not mistaken, I believe my father knew his father Jeremiah from Athens in Limestone County.

You asked about your son, and I have to tell you that Alex is growing up fast as you can well imagine. I sit here watching him sleep while I write this letter. Just the other day, I was dressing him for church and realized he had already outgrown his Sunday clothes. I am busy now trying to make him a new outfit. How I also miss Mama, she was always the seamstress.

Cole, my precious husband, I have some rather bad news I must share before I close. I have dreaded this moment in writing for quite some time. It grieves me to have to end my letter this way, but I must, my darling. It's about Nate and Marcie, and it's not good news.

It's been several weeks now, and Nate came home from work to find Marcie and her baby boy both dead. We all were so shocked! Let me try to explain as best I can. While she was at home alone that day, her labor began. The baby came out and was strangled by its cord wrapped around his little neck. Following the delivery, after everything was over, the coroner ruled that Marcie had slowly bled to death.

After he found them that evening, Nate was so upset I thought he was losing his mind. He went on a rampage, cursing and blaming himself for not being there. Marcie was only seven months along and no one was expecting this. After all the birth pains with the baby, the coroner told us that Marcie felt no pain in the end while her life just ebbed away until her heart finally stopped. Darling, I am crying now, and I still cannot believe that she is really gone.

After the funeral, Nate seemed to lose all control. I heard he went on a drinking binge and was fired from his job because he wouldn't go back to work at the mill. The last anyone heard about him was two weeks ago when he supposedly took a room at Looney's Tavern for a while. After that, I learned that he had an argument with his parents, gave them the key to his house, and simply left.

Cole, we are all so very worried, and feel so helpless. Nobody knows where he went. I pray for Nate every day. I know he is truly in God's hands.

Darling, I have to go now while I send you all my love.

Your loving wife,
Libby

Cole sat there alone outside his tent, while the letter fell from his shaking hand onto the ground. He could hardly believe what he had just read while he slowly reached down into the dirt to retrieve Libby's letter. He didn't seem to hear Scottie as he came running up shouting the news.

"Pack up, we're moving closer to Atlanta. Devereaux just ordered it," he said.

"What's that you say?" Cole asked while he folded and returned the letter to his shirt pocket while he got to his feet.

"What's wrong?" Scottie asked.

"I'll have to tell you later. I can't talk about it now," Cole replied.

While Cole pondered in his heart and mind about the letter he had just read, this tragic event had already happened almost a month and a half ago. It was now September as the battle in Atlanta continued. Union General William Tecumseh Sherman's main objective was to seize the highly important rail and supply center of Atlanta that was presently being defended by Confederate General

John Bell Hood. At this time, the 1st Alabama Cavalry was ordered to move to the outskirts where they would remain on standby alert. This was a major ordeal to relocate almost three hundred horses and cavalrymen, but as a support unit, it was entirely necessary amidst all the cursing and discontent from several of the soldiers. Cole always chose to do as he was ordered, never complaining.

For the Atlanta Campaign, the Union force came from a division of the Army of Tennessee who was commanded by Major General James B. McPherson. He was a very lively man, quick and aggressive, and was well-liked by Sherman and Grant. Sherman knew very well that McPherson was a man that could get things done. Within Sherman's army, there was the XV Corps commanded by Major General John A. Logan; the XVI Corps under Major General Grenville M. Dodge; and Major General Frank P. Blair commanded the XVII Corps. Commanders of the Confederate forces were General John Bell Hood and Lt. General William J. Hardee of the other division of the Army of Tennessee. The first clash began on 22 July 1864 in Fulton County.

During the months leading up to this battle, Confederate General Joseph E. Johnston repeatedly had to retreat from the superior force of Sherman's army. Spread along the Western and Atlantic Railroad line from Chattanooga, Tennessee to Marietta, Georgia, various skirmishes broke out while Johnston took up a defensive position. Over and over, he was forced to retreat while Sherman marched to outflank him. After Johnston's final retreat following the battle of Resaca, the two armies clashed again at the battle of Kennesaw Mountain. By this time, Confederate headquarters in Richmond was unhappy with Johnston's seemingly reluctance to fight the Union army, even though he probably had little chance of winning. As a result, on 17 July 1864 as he was preparing for the battle of Peachtree Creek, Johnston was relieved of his command and replaced by Lt. General John Bell Hood. Hood, who was known for taking risks, lashed out at Sherman's army at Peachtree Creek where he lost 2500 casualties in the attack.

It was extremely important to defend the city of Atlanta. Hood knew this locale was the rail hub and industrial center of the Confederacy, but his army was small in comparison to those that Sherman commanded. What could he do? He decided to withdraw to entice the Union troops to come forward, not realizing that now McPherson's army was rapidly closing in from Decatur, Georgia to the east side of Atlanta.

Meanwhile, General Hood issued three immediate orders: First, Lt. General William J. Hardee's troops were ordered to march around the Union left flank; Second, Major General Joseph Wheeler's cavalry would ride and locate near Sherman's supply line; Third, Major General Benjamin Cheatham's Corps would attack the Union front almost as a last resort, while definitely needing to complete the plan, Hood sent Spencer's 1st Alabama Cavalry toward the Union right flank. However, the Confederacy encountered a major problem when it took longer than expected for Hardee's troops to get into position. During this time, McPherson immediately suspected a possible attack to his left flank and sent his XVI Corps to help strengthen it. At this point, Hardee's troops met this reserve force, and the battle began. While the first Confederate attack was repulsed, the Union left flank began their retreat. It was during this time, an unidentified Union corporal witnessed General James B. McPherson as he rode to the front line to observe the battle. This would prove to be the last ride for the General. The corporal saw McPherson as he was shot by a Confederate infantryman while he instantly fell dead to the ground from his horse. Several nearby soldiers were able to get to their commander, but it was too late.

Cole, Scottie, and Chappy were three of the 1st Alabama who followed Sgt. Devereaux while they led the charge that day. Sabers were gleaming in the sunlight while the blood splattered onto the right side of the field where its participants were covered in a blood bath of gory suffering as many lie maimed and killed on both sides. The attack couldn't have lasted more than an hour when the cavalry was driven back from the thunderous gunfire into retreat to prevent further loss of life.

In late afternoon, the three buddies were on the detail to help retrieve the bodies of their fallen comrades and bury the dead. The 1st Alabama lost at least thirty men including four of the original recruits at Cole's induction into the cavalry. Among those dead were: Private Michael Denney, 37, the attorney from Athens; Private Wade "Monty" Montgomery, 34, the cotton farmer from Pettusville; Private Patrick Timothy "Paddy" McShan, 31, the lumberjack from Elkmont; and Private Garrett "Gar" Niles, 29, the blacksmith, also from Elkmont. It was a sad day for Cole as he threw his last shovel of dirt onto the small mass grave while his thoughts turned to Marcie and Nate.

"Snap out of it, Mule! There's nothing more we can do for them," Scottie said.

"Yeah, I know. What about you? Your arm is bleeding."

"Aw, that's just a scratch," he answered. "It will take more than that to take down Scottie Callahan."

"Sorry, I just keep thinking about Michael, Monty, Paddy, and Gar. Just doesn't seem fair to me. They're all young family men, except Gar who had no children. I remember Garrett telling me that he had only been married for four years, and his wife Claudine's family was from here in Atlanta. How are they ever going to know that he died here today?"

"Where's Dunbar? We can find him and report that we buried these men. Matt will take care of it," Scottie said.

"Guess you're right. Where's Chappy? He was here just a minute ago," Cole replied.

"I see him over there in the trees. Must be taking a piss."

In a few minutes, Chappy rejoined Cole and Scottie where they were resting on the ground.

"I'm hungry," Chappy said. "Wonder where we're going to find something to eat?"

"No time to eat right now," Cole said. "We've got to see about the horses now, and round up the strays. Any animals found wounded badly or nearly dead will have to be shot."

"We can eat some horse meat, you know. Speaking of horses, what about your stallion Midnight? Have you seen him recently?" Chappy asked.

"He's all right, but I need to check on him," Cole replied.

"I hear Sgt. Devereaux calling for us to assemble over there," Scottie said while pointing to a clearing. "Let's go!"

"Listen up," Devereaux said in a loud voice while a large group gathered around the sergeant. "Men, pass the word. You will begin to pack up immediately and prepare to leave the area. We have only few rations now, but while we are on the march, Sgt. McRae should have us something to eat when we make camp for the night. In case you are wondering exactly where we're headed, I can tell you we are moving south toward a little town called Jonesboro. On my order, we will ride out in one hour. That is all, gentlemen."

The next day, fighting continued while Hood planned to attack the Union forces from both east and west. The battle line now formed an "L" shape while Hardee attacked the point forming the lower part of the "L", and Cheatham on the Union front on the vertical line. The main fighting centered on Bald Hill located east of the city. Union troops had already arrived two days earlier as they began the shelling while several civilians were killed as a result. Fierce fighting continued around the hill while hand to hand struggles broke out until dark. After a tremendous loss of life, the Union held the hill while the Confederates retreated to the south.

During this same time, located two miles to the north, Cheatham's troops broke through the Union line in close proximity to the Georgia railroad. It was there near Sherman's headquarters at Copen Hill where twenty artillery pieces were positioned and shelled the Confederates. Along with General Logan's XV Corps also in position, the Southern troops were finally defeated. This was a devastating loss for the reduced number of Confederate soldiers, but they tried their best to hold on to the city with the sacrifice of many lives.

CHAPTER 13

Battle of Jonesboro

Nate Overstreet woke up at the Oakleigh Inn on the Jonesboro Road. It had been raining there all night. He pushed the hair back from his face as he sat on the side of the bed while placing his feet onto the bare wide-plank floor. He watched the rain as it hit upon the window and ran down the window panes. A vision of Marcie and baby Chan flashed before his eyes while a burst of lightning suddenly lit the tiny room. Nate jumped up from the bed. He walked over and closed the curtains as if that would shield him from the rain and visions he kept having. As he stood beside the dresser to relieve himself into the chamber pot, the mirror reflected the image of the naked woman who lay sleeping in his bed. Quickly, Nate dressed himself, gathered his belongings, and went downstairs.

"What time is it?" he asked the short, bearded man behind the counter.

"Almost half past eleven," the innkeeper replied.

"Is this rain ever going to stop?" Nate asked.

"Eventually, I'm guessing," the man laughed. "Going somewhere, I gather?"

"Yes, when this rain lets up, I'll be leaving here to get back on the road."

"While you're waiting, may I suggest the Magnolia dining room? Have yourself something to eat. We will begin serving at noon."

"Is it all right to leave my satchel by the door?" Nate asked.

"Give it to me, and I'll hold it here for you behind the counter until you are ready to leave."

Nate placed his worn satchel on the counter top and walked the short distance into the dining room. As he entered through the double doors, Nate spied a place to sit near the table where two local gentlemen were seated. Across the room, a young couple sat at a cozy table by the window. They were talking softly while they waited for their meal to be served. Nate walked to his table and took a seat next to the two men.

"Excuse me, gentlemen. May I have a word with either of you?"

"Certainly, young man. What is it?" asked the older of the two.

"Just wondering if by chance you knew where the 1st Alabama Cavalry was camped."

"Don't believe I've heard of that particular unit," he responded and looked across the table. "Thom, you ever heard of them?"

"Don't reckon I have either, son."

"Thanks. Hopefully, I'll be able to find someone who will know. It's really important to me."

Nate ordered a country ham biscuit and a cup of black coffee as the dark-skinned servant girl took his order. He sat there quietly waiting while glancing out the large dining room window. At least, the rain had finally stopped. In a few minutes, the server was back with the food she placed before him on the table.

"Will there be anything else, sir," she said.

"No, thank you. Everything looks fine."

As Nate was finishing his small meal, he was joined by a well-dressed and attractive lady. The woman who had shared his bed suddenly appeared at his table and took a seat across from him.

"Good afternoon, Nate. I was hoping that you would still be here," she said.

It took a moment for him to realize who she was while he tried his best to remember her.

"Oh, it's you, Mrs. Grayson. Hope you weren't too disappointed last night."

"On the contrary, sweetheart. A doctor's wife should always be open to any emergency situation. I must say, you completely satisfied and fulfilled my every expectation in bed. I was hoping to see you again tonight."

"I'm afraid that's going to have to be it for now, darling. You see, I'm leaving here soon, now that the rain has stopped. How much for your services?"

"Please, do not insult me by offering me money. If anything, I should have to pay you, honey. You took me to a place that my husband hasn't been able since his medical school days. Where are you heading, darling?"

"I'm trying to find where the 1st Alabama Cavalry is camped to find an old friend of mine."

"Why I believe the doctor might know if you could wait until I can ask him this afternoon. Wait here and spend another night with me, and I'll get you that information."

Nate looked into her big brown eyes and smiled while he agreed to her proposition. Melinda Grayson left Nate sitting there in the dining room while she went to find the good doctor.

The next morning, Nate arose from bed, and dressed himself while the early morning sunshine peeked through the window. Once again, he packed up his belongings, kissed the doctor's wife goodbye, and walked downstairs for breakfast.

With a vague sense of direction in his mind, Nate caught a ride in a supply wagon headed north out of town. He hoped that the information from the doctor would prove to be accurate while Nate began his search for Spencer's Cavalry. If Cole was still alive, hopefully he would find him there in the camp. All Nate could do now was to keep looking for his buddy Cole.

Deep in the woods south of Jonesboro, the 1ˢᵗ Alabama settled in for the night. Sgt. Liam Devereaux found Cole as he sat alone outside his tent while he made his approach.

"Just passing through the area," he said. "How goes it, McTavish?"

"I'm doing well, Sergeant. Sit down and take a load off."

"Don't mind if I do," Liam said while he sat cross-legged on the ground beside Cole. "I'm about ready to turn in, aren't you?"

"In a bit, I guess. I'm just sitting here thinking about my family. You got family, Sergeant?"

"Not really, not anymore, I'd have to say. My parents and baby sister died in an accidental fire incident in New Orleans several years ago."

"Sorry to hear that, sir."

"You don't have to call me that when we're just talking like this. Call me, Liam."

"All right then, Liam. I'll try to remember that the next time we're alone."

"I do have a younger brother named Kyle. He's off somewhere in France near Paris, I believe. I haven't heard from him in several years."

"So, you're not married, Liam?"

"No, son, I'm not married. Came close a few years back, but now at thirty-five with my career as a soldier, I'm not really looking."

"Sometimes, you don't have to be. It just happens. With your good looks, I'm guessing you're no virgin, and you've … I believe you know what I'm saying."

"I did have one extraordinary affair when I was twenty-three that nearly cost me my life, but you wouldn't want to hear about that, I'm afraid."

"Why not, Liam? What else do we have to talk about? I'm not sleepy, so tell me about it."

'Well, Cole, make yourself comfortable. Just remember you asked for this," Sgt. Devereaux replied while he stood to his feet. The sergeant did a walkabout to ease a cramp in his leg while he moved closer to Cole and took a seat by his side. Liam took his long black hair and pulled it back over his shoulder while he began to speak.

The year before I became a stevedore on the New Orleans docks, I was employed as a groomsman on the Hamilton Plantation in Baton Rouge. Myself, along with two other young lads, had charge of the stables where Master Karl David Hamilton kept his three prized horses, two black mares and an elegant white stallion named Cristobel. I soon learned that Master Karl thought more of his stallion, with its long-flowing mane and tail, than most humans. Cristobel had a beautiful black leather saddle, trimmed in sterling silver and imported from Great Britain. It was the youngest lad named Michael whose primary task it was to keep that saddle polished and ready for use at all times. I got along well with Michael and James, the other boy. I do remember walking in and seeing Hamilton in a bit of a rage while he struck Michael with a blow to the side of his face on one occasion. He was upset over a small smudge on the leather which Michael had obviously overlooked.

Two months after I came to work on the plantation, Mrs. Hamilton died suddenly in her sleep one night. She was an elegant looking lady who was always dressed in the finest silk with her silver-grey hair piled on top of her head and pinned with an ivory comb. Her personal maid, Gertie, was grief-stricken at the loss since it was she who discovered Angela Hamilton's body that morning. Gertie entered Mrs. Hamilton's bedchamber each morning to draw back the curtains and open the shutters on the two windows in her room. Her death seemed no great surprise to Karl Hamilton, at least to me it didn't, while everyone rarely saw the man as he moved through all the rooms of the big house. He was a strange bird all right. All this was told to me by the cook since I had only been in the house on two or three previous occasions, and that was in his study soon after I hired on. Once, I caught a glimpse into the parlor while I walked from the foyer and into the study after Hamilton had summoned me there to meet him. I knew the bedrooms had to be upstairs since I first met Mrs. Hamilton on my initial visit when she descended the green carpeted staircase. Angela Hamilton introduced herself while extending her hand in the absence of her husband.

Karl Hamilton, on the other hand, seemed to me like a complete mismatch while I understood that Angela Hamilton was actually his second wife of three years. Master Hamilton maintained a very private life as I myself knew very little about the man. He looked to be about fifty-three years old with dark black hair and a beard. He had dull black eyes with a rather large nose and a ruddy complexion. Karl had a medium build on his tall six foot frame, and whenever I saw him, he was usually dressed in dark clothing with polished black leather boots. Belinda, the cook, told me that he had inherited his fortune from his father, Master David J. Hamilton, a rich cotton farmer upon his death almost ten years ago. Karl Hamilton was usually away from home for weeks at a time. Following Mrs. Hamilton's funeral and burial in the family plot located in the rear of the big house, it was several months before anyone ever saw him again.

When he finally returned home, Karl Hamilton had married the most beautiful girl I had ever seen. He came riding in that day on Cristobel with Cassie holding on for dear life while her arms were locked around his waist. I soon learned that the former Mrs. Hamilton's maid, whom she called Gertie, was overly fond of Michael, the stable boy. Sometimes, after talking to him on occasion, Gertie would share with him many things that had occurred recently in the house. Idle gossip, perhaps, but it was Gertie who always knew what was happening at Hamilton Manor. That is precisely how I found out what happened on Cassandra Hamilton's first night with her husband.

Cassie, a virgin at twenty, sat on the side of the bed in her white long-sleeved silk nightgown while she awaited the arrival of her husband into the bedchamber. Her long dark brown hair draped across her shoulder while her hands rested in stillness upon her lap and her bare feet touched down onto the hardwood floor. The soft glow from the lantern on the bedside table projected her shadow onto the back wall while she continued to sit in the unfamiliar bedroom and wait.

The sound of footsteps approaching outside the door signaled his entrance. A click and turn of the doorknob, the door opened while the master of the house now stood silently in the doorway. He gazed momentarily at his young bride and then stepped into the room while closing the door behind him. He spoke not a word, but walked to his chair near the fireplace and took a seat. He sat there for a few minutes and simply stared at the girl from across the room. Out in the hall, Gertie knelt silently at the door while she positioned one eye to look through the keyhole. Her eye was clearly fixed upon the scene that was about to play out while she kept staring straight ahead.

"Stand up, and turn this way," he said. Cassie obeyed his command while she rose from the bed and turned her petite body toward her husband. "Take off your nightgown," he ordered.

With only a slight hesitation, she reached for the ribbon on the neckline, unfastened the tie, and opened the front of her gown. Pulling her arms from the sleeves, and allowing it to fall, the gown slid from her body to the floor around her ankles where it came to rest. She stood naked before him, frozen like a statue.

"Walk over to the wall by the window," he pointed as he spoke sternly to her. Cassie walked to the window, turned, and faced him with her arms folded across her breast. "Drop your arms, turn around and face the wall," he said while uttering his last command.

Cassie stood there looking out the window while she endured listening to the sounds coming from the chair where he lay slouched. When he had finished, Karl Hamilton stood, fastened his trousers, and left the room. He passed by Gertie who was now coming down the hallway while never turning his head to acknowledge her presence. These similar nocturnal events continued for several nights as I understood until I saddled Cristobel for him and watched as Karl Hamilton rode away on a sunny afternoon that July.

Over the next weeks and months following the return of the Master, it was assumed that the marriage had finally been consummated. During this time, the new Mrs. Hamilton seemed to move more freely around the house and grounds. She took up horseback riding on the two year old dapple grey mare named Daisy that her husband had recently bought for her. I was privileged to go riding with her on several occasions during his absence while I soon found myself falling in love with her. Her beautiful *smiling face and bright blue eyes completely captivated me although I never attempted to show or tell her how much I really cared for her.*

One day when we were alone in the stable, she took my hand and led me into one of the vacant stalls. She moved my hand onto her breast while pressing her body close to mine.

"Make love to me," she whispered while her gentle hands began to unfasten my britches. From that moment on, I was smitten. We soon seized every opportunity to be together at every turn while we risked getting caught in the very act to suffer the unknown consequences for our infidelity.

At first, Karl Hamilton would take Cassie horseback riding into the dense woods, just the two of them. Then, one day out of the blue, he asked me to saddle up and accompany them. I would follow along behind while they rode ahead in the distance. On this particular day, I watched as they stopped suddenly in the clearing, a place seemingly familiar to them. Master Hamilton dismounted and tied Cristobel to a small tree nearby while he kept his gaze fixed upon Cassie. He walked around to where she was stopped while she remained seated upon Daisy. Karl Hamilton took the reins from Cassie and led her mare next to his stallion and tied Daisy beside Cristobel. In a flash, without a word spoken, Karl pulled Cassie from the saddle and carried her in his arms over to the place where part of an old oak tree had fallen. He set her down while turning her body facedown to bend over the log. Lifting her skirt while he pressed himself against her motionless body, he ravished her from behind until he was quickly finished. I saw him briefly as he looked my way to seemingly make sure that I saw what he was doing. At that point, I felt like I wanted to kill the bastard. Fortunately for me, that was the only time I ever saw them together. She later confessed to me that Karl told her that if she ever tried to leave him, he would kill her.

The climax to my story came almost three months later on a clear summer evening. Cassie and I were laying together in the upstairs bedroom when we both heard the familiar sound of Cristobel's hooves on the pavement as the Master arrived home unexpectedly. Cassie threw on her robe while she motioned me toward the closet. I quickly grabbed for my clothes and hid there while I managed to pull on my pants in a hurry. Karl Hamilton made his way immediately into the bedroom where he found Cassie seated at the dressing table as she brushed her hair. He told her to strip naked and climb onto the bed on all fours while he began to undress himself. About the time he was unfastening his britches, I bolted from the closet, sprang toward him, and landed an upper cut to his jaw knocking him down against the side of the bed. He fell back onto the floor in a heap while he fumbled at his pocket. I stood back and motioned Cassie from the bed while I watched as Karl took aim at me. He drew a small derringer and fired while the bullet whizzed by my left shoulder and hit the wall. We commenced into a blow by blow fist fight as we tore into each other for the next few minutes. My last hit sent Karl Hamilton stumbling back onto the fireplace hearth where his body fell and finally came to rest. No movement now while he lay there motionless. As quickly as it seemed to happen, Master Hamilton was dead.

I buried his body in an undisclosed location in the woods and remained only two more nights with Cassie. Although it was self-defense, I never meant to kill Karl Hamilton. I just couldn't stand how he mistreated Cassie. In the end, only Cassie, Gertie, and Michael ever knew whatever happened to Master Karl Hamilton. I rode out the next day on Cristobel, never to see the beautiful Cassie again while leaving her to explain her husband's failure to return home following one of his many unknown trips. Many years later, I heard that Cassandra Hamilton eventually married the governor of Louisiana and was the mother to three of his children. No, I never married and that's my story, my friend.

"I need to get going, Cole. We have to be up early in the morning. I bid you a good night."

Night settled in while the 1st Alabama bedded down in hopes of getting a little shut eye before the expected early sunrise. Several men positioned near Cole remained awake while they gathered personal effects and packed their gear in preparation of the early morning call. Cole lay bare-chested on his back with his face pressed near the open flap of his tent while he gazed up at the starry sky. The full moon seemed extra bright tonight while he thought of Libby and Alex moments before he fell asleep.

"Halt! Who goes there?"

With his weapon drawn, the sleepy private snapped his body into full alert from its previous dozing position while he halted the approaching night intruder.

"Whoa! It is I, Nathaniel Overstreet. I come into your camp seeking Private Cole McTavish. Would you happen to know him and where I might find my friend?"

"Approach near the lantern where I can see you, Overstreet," replied the sentry.

Nate complied immediately with the young private's instruction while he stepped into the light.

"Place your satchel on the ground and step away with your hands open in front where I can see them."

Once again, Nate did as he was instructed while he stepped aside as ordered by the guard on night duty.

"I'm tired, hungry, and sleepy now in my quest to meet up finally with the First Cavalry. It's been days since I began my journey," Nate said.

"What is your business with Private McTavish?" asked the young sentry while he slowly relaxed and drew the rifle he held to his side.

"I wish only to meet up with my friend and volunteer to join the cavalry," Nate answered.

"Very well, Overstreet. You can bed down over there by the fire until morning. I can get you some coffee and something to eat right away if you like."

"Yes, anything. That will be good. Thank you, Private."

"After daylight, I will return and we'll get you signed up as a new recruit and I'll help find your friend."

The dawning of the new day made its entrance while the morning sun cast its rays through the trees where the cavalry lie camped. What had passed as a relatively quiet night suddenly began to change while the men were waking up and making ready for the new day. Cole McTavish was unknowingly about to get a big surprise while he suddenly received an order to report to the headquarters tent.

As Cole made his way through the camp, he was stopped dead in his tracks when he caught the first sight of headquarters following his brief early morning trip. He could hardly believe what he was seeing. Seated outside the tent on the ground was his buddy Nate Overstreet, smiling at him with a big grin while he jumped to his feet. Cole broke into a run as the two men met in a big bear hug while they embraced as long lost friends.

"Can't believe it is really you!" Cole exclaimed, while he released his hold on Nate and stood back just to look at him. "You've lost a lot of weight, my friend."

"You're not any better looking," Nate laughed.

"I've just joined as a new recruit about an hour ago. You'll have to help me pull my supplies and get settled in this morning."

"Gladly, come with me. We're expecting to be on the move again shortly. Just stay close to me, and I'll help you as much as I can. At least, you are already a good shot and can ride a horse. Wielding a sword from horseback may prove to be a challenge; however, when your life is depending on it, quite amazing what you feel you can do naturally."

"So true, Mule. I just hope I'm ready for this. At this point in my life, I feel I have nothing else to lose."

"Libby wrote me about Marcie. I am so sorry for the loss of your precious wife and baby."

"Yeah, it's been hell for me. If it's all right with you, can we just talk about it later?"

"Certainly, Nate! Come on and I'll take you to see Sgt. Boshell and he will get you fixed up with everything you'll be needing. After that, I can pick out a good mount for you. I'm still riding Midnight, and we have already been through two battles together and survived."

"Amazing! You'll have to tell me all about it. Gosh, it's so good to see you again Cole. I really mean it!"

※

During the many raids of the Atlanta campaign, Sherman had temporarily cut off Confederate General John Bell Hood's supply line. His success came from using small detachments, but the Confederates always seemed to repair the damage quickly. It was Sherman's belief that if he could completely sever the railway system lines of the Macon and Western, along with the Atlanta and West Point Railroads, the Confederate general would be forced to evacuate Atlanta.

Following his intended plan, General Sherman decided to move out six of his seven infantry corps against the Confederate supply lines to hit the railroad between the towns of Rough and Ready, Georgia and Jonesboro. Learning of the plan and to counter the move, Lt. General William J. Hardee, along with two other Confederate corps led by General S.D. Lee, were sent south to Lovejoy Station to halt the Union troops. At this point, General Hood was completely unaware and failed to realize that most of Sherman's army was rapidly approaching the area, thus causing Hardee's troops to be highly outnumbered.

The order finally came that Spencer's Cavalry was to embark immediately and take their position by the morning of 31 August, 1864 in Jonesboro. Sgt. Devereaux prepared his troops and the 1st Alabama moved into place and waited.

Union Major General Oliver Howard had two corps positioned in trenches on the east side of the Flint River. John A. Logan's XV Corps were dug in, positioned on high ground facing east toward the Macon and Western Railroad. The XVI Corps, led by Thomas Ransom, formed a right angle connected to Logan's right flank and faced toward the south. The XVII Corps, under the guidance of Frank Blair, were holding a reserve position west of the Flint River.

Confederate Lt. General William Hardee left Patrick Cleburne in command of his troops while he directed the two-corps assault. Moving from the left at Lovejoy Station, Cleburne's men headed north to attack the Federal line held by Ransom while Stephen D. Lee planned the second attack on the right against Logan's line. Mark Lowrey led Cleburne's Division from the northwest, and while it was turning toward the Federal lines, Lowrey was unexpectedly hit by H. Judson Kilpatrick's dismounted Union Cavalry. Armed with Spencer repeating rifles, his men were concealed behind fence rails and trees while they set up to surprise the Rebs. Kilpatrick's fire power was so effective that Lowrey broke his attack against Ransom's main line while heading his entire division toward the west against the 1st Alabama Cavalry. Only a brief encounter happened during this movement since their mounts hindered the mounted cavalry from fighting in and around a rather dense pine forest. Only minor injuries were sustained by the cavalry while Lowrey succeeded in driving them into the woods and back across the Flint River.

Stephen D. Lee mistook the firing between Lowrey and Kilpatrick as the main assault and attacked long before Cleburne's troops had engaged into the action with Ransom. Lee ordered a frontal assault, but his action was repulsed with heavy casualties. Soon after Lee's troops had been defeated, Hardee wanted to renew the attack once again. Lee responded back by informing him that his troops were in no condition to do so. At the end of the day, Lee suffered a loss of 1,300 casualties, and Cleburne's 400 to the Union total of 179. As a result of Hardee's inability to defeat the Union forces at Jonesboro, and fearing a direct attack on Atlanta, Hood withdrew Lee's Corps from Hardee's force that night and into the city's defenses. This move would prove to have great consequences the following morning when the fighting resumed.

The next day, September 1, Sherman led an attack on the Confederate lines north of Jonesboro. Despite the overwhelming force of the Federal attack, Hardee managed to push forward three reserve brigades in a last ditch effort to try and stop the Union penetration of the Confederate line and destruction of the entire Corps. Historians continue to debate whether it was the exceptional leadership ability of Lt. General William Hardee or the onset of darkness that saved the Confederate Corps. As a result, the remains of Hardee's Corps managed to retreat south in good order to Lovejoy Station.

That night, Hood ordered the evacuation of Atlanta and the final act of destroying 81 rail cars filled with ammunition and other military supplies. The resulting fire and multiple explosions were heard for miles that night. The Battle of Jonesboro was the final battle of the Atlanta Campaign that put the besieged city of Atlanta into Union hands.

History records that the capture of Atlanta greatly aided the re-election of Abraham Lincoln in November while it hastened the end of the war. Hood was forced to move his defeated army away from Atlanta toward the west while opening the way for Sherman's March to the Sea.

CHAPTER 14

In Winston County, signs of an early fall began to appear while a gentle breeze moved through the trees that surrounded Cole and Libby's new house that September morning. Libby wiped away a bead of sweat from her forehead while she stopped to pull her hair back and clip it. Since Ramona, one of the Jefferson sisters, now helped take care of Alex, Libby was on the front portico attempting to whitewash all four columns. The actual painting wasn't all that difficult for her while she whisked away with a large horse hair brush. The hardest part was mixing the whitewash in the tool shed and then having to carry the bucket up the steps and onto the front portico. While Cole was away, this was her way of keeping busy while attending to things she could do to help out. One less thing for Cole to have to do was always her main focus nowadays.

For a while now, it was just her, Alex, and Ramona together every day except on the days she would go to check on her father. Cole was gone. Her Mama was gone. Marcie was gone, and most recently, Nate had suddenly disappeared. Libby was determined that she wasn't going to let all this get her down, so she countered it by staying as busy as she possibly could. She knew Cole would be so proud of her when he returned to see everything she was doing while the actual construction was still on hold.

The framework of the house was almost complete at the time Cole had to leave, and all construction had come to a halt. Door and window casings were cut in and framed, but no glass was available at present to put in the windows. Floor joists were installed, but no flooring. Rafters in place, but no roof. It would take a lot more money and labor to finish up, but at least, the major construction was already this far along. So each day, weather permitting, Libby would look for little projects she could do herself in and around her skeleton of a house.

A sudden scream, along with a baby's loud crying, sent a jolt through Libby as she jumped from the ladder and ran toward the open door of the little cabin. Just stay calm she told herself, while she stopped at the doorway to look in to see a terrified Ramona and a toddler screaming his lungs out. They were huddled together on the floor in front of the fireplace.

Libby ran in and threw herself down while she pulled Alex from Ramona's arms and into her own. At the same moment, she realized the cause for alarm. Looking down, she saw the burns across Alex's upper body, arms, and both of his little hands. He appeared to have been scalded by the contents of the black pot that was presently extended outward from the fire.

"What happened, Mona?"

"I had just stirred the soup and left to get the poker to push the pot back over the flames when I was distracted by a fly that kept buzzing around my head," Ramona answered. "When I turned around, the baby had taken both hands and pulled on the pot enough to have the hot soup spill out on him. I'm so sorry. What can I do?"

"Get me some fresh linen towels and wet them in cold water while I try to get his clothes off."

Libby laid Alex on the floor away from the hearth while she carefully began to remove his clothes. At first glance, his hands seemed to be the worse, but the splatter of hot liquid on his tender skin had to be equally as painful.

"It's going to be all right, little man. Mama is here to take care of you," Libby said while his crying eventually turned to whimpering as she began to apply the cool, wet cloth to his hands and body. Judging from everything that had happened, she thought this situation could have been extremely worse. She thanked God for this blessing. Fortunately, Libby happened to have an aloe vera plant blooming on her window sill. It would provide a helpful remedy to use for burns that her sweet mama had taught her about many years ago.

It was well into the afternoon until Libby would finish everything she could do for her son while she placed him on his bed to sleep. Ramona took over the watch care while she continued to apply aloe vera to sooth Alex's little body at various intervals. Libby returned to finish her painting by late afternoon.

It was early afternoon on the day Libby's friend Greta came to visit her at the little cabin. Ramona had Alex down for a nap while Libby sat on the porch as she was sewing on a feed sack apron for herself. Greta pulled up in her buggy, climbed down, and fastened Orion to a small tree that visitors often used as a hitching post.

"Well, hello there Mrs. H! It's so good to have you stop by. Come on up and sit a spell," Libby said while she put her sewing aside.

"I see from the looks of the new portico that someone has recently been quite busy," Greta said while she greeted Libby with a hug before taking a seat across from her. "The place is looking really good. Let me tell you, our porch needs to be white washed, but can I get anyone to do it? Heavens no! With Jacob and so many men folk gone, it seems we women have to do it all ourselves."

"I really don't mind, Greta. Right now, it helps me to keep my mind occupied as I find there are little things I can do around here to help us out. When did you last hear from Jacob?"

Probably a couple of months ago, I reckon. His last letter was from somewhere in Georgia. He said he was doing fine at the time."

"Cole is in Georgia as well. You'll remember me telling you that he joined the 1st Alabama, Spencer's Cavalry. Who's in command of Jacob's outfit?"

"Jacob is a private in Lt. General William Hardee's Infantry."

"Oh my, Dear Jesus, the last I heard from Cole, they were about to head out to possibly do battle against Hardee."

"Oh no, now that worries me! How would those two ever know that they could be going up against each other?"

"Greta, I pray that will never happen!"

"Also in his letter, Jacob told me he had witnessed several men in his company who had recently been shot and killed close to him. He told me that he was lucky to be alive."

"Cole has written me almost the same while stating that four of the young men he met on his first day as a new recruit were now dead, and he helped bury them."

"Oh Libby, that is so sad. Just try to imagine how all those families must feel. What if that were to happen with us?"

"War is a terrible thing! Our town, county, and state will all suffer for it, I'm afraid."

"Even with the differences and loyalties that each of our husbands are fighting for right now, it seems all they can do is try to tolerate each other."

"I remember Cole saying to me how he could never understand how Jacob, of his own free will, could join the Confederate Army."

"My Jacob probably felt the same way about Cole. Just like all the many folks in Winston County, everyone has their own individual opinion."

"Greta, please let's talk about something else if you don't mind. Most days I don't even try to think about the war that's going on." She paused. "I've always wanted to know, but have never asked you this very personal question, do you mind?"

"What's that, Libby?"

"Was Jacob your first and only true love?"

"Now Libby, you know that I had a crush on Nate Overstreet as a young girl, but Marcie snatched him away. I don't guess he ever knew that I really loved him and longed to be his wife after we finished school."

"I vaguely remember, now that you mentioned it. Who wasn't in love with Nate back then?"

"Well, to be perfectly honest, I have never known a man other than Jacob Hassendorfer. Does that answer your question?"

"Yes, but I remember a particular young man back in school. What was his name? Tall, blond, with a bulge, you know who I'm talking about Missy, remember?"

"You don't mean Clint? Clint Norstrum, the Norwegian they called 'Socks.'"

"Yes, that's him. Didn't you go out with him once or twice?"

"Only once, and that's when I found out how he got his nickname," Greta laughed.

"How's that?"

"Clint asked me to the spring dance that year, and after it was over, he took me home. We sat together on the front porch for a while. We talked a bit, cuddled, and then he asked me if he could kiss me. I said yes, and moved in closer while he put his arm around me. We kissed and he suddenly put his hand underneath my blouse. Not to be outdone, I quickly thrust my hand down the front of his pants and grabbed it. After I realized in my excitement what I thought I was holding onto, I yanked my hand back out and with it come a pair of rolled up woolen socks. I burst out laughing, and he was so embarrassed and begged me not to tell. So, I promised him I wouldn't ever tell and I never have. He moved on, and I quickly forgot him. In a few weeks, I met Jacob, and you know the rest."

"Yes, I do, Greta. You know how much I like Jacob. You two make a wonderful couple, and it's a joy to be friends with you both."

"I'm on my way to town to do some shopping. Would love for you to come with me on this beautiful afternoon. What about it?"

"As much as I would like it, I had best stay here today, but thanks for asking. I would love to go with you next time."

"Before I leave, would you let me look in on Alex? Don't remember how long it's been since I have seen him."

"Certainly, come with me. It should be time for him to be waking up from his nap."

Libby held the door while Greta stepped into the cabin to view the sleeping child. Ramona was dozing in a nearby chair until Greta's presence quickly awakened her. She slid from her chair and quickly moved away in order for Greta to get a good look.

"My how he has grown. Look at all that hair. So sweet!"

"Thank you. He's a good boy. I've been debating this week about cutting his hair. He was three years old this past July and now the long curly hair makes him look like a girl. I may just have to cut it after a while. What do you think?"

"I believe I would. A simple hair cut will make him look like a little man, so much like his daddy."

After Greta left, Libby sat alone for quite some time while her thoughts as always turned to her missing husband. How she missed his loving touch and warm caress as he held her in his arms.

During this same time, support for the Confederacy in Winston County kept growing while many men continued to volunteer for service in the Confederate Army. With great fervor, they petitioned the Governor of Alabama, John Gill Shorter, in an effort to suppress the Unionist spirit pervading the county. They were demanding an order that would require all of the county residents to take the Confederate loyalty oath while also providing 250 Confederate soldiers. As a result, Gov. Shorter responded by declaring that writs of arrest be issued for those in Winston County who remained disloyal to the Confederacy. In addition, the demand of any militia commanders who would not take the oath of office were to resign immediately.

Union sympathizers in the county simply wanted to be left alone while those siding with the Confederacy would not oblige. The demand that Unionists face an act of compulsory enlistment caused many hill-country residents to flee their homes and farms in complete abandonment. Seeking refuge from the conscription agents, many Unionists scattered into the county's rugged forests and canyons. Many took refuge at Natural Bridge in western Winston County becoming a major gathering place for those men avoiding the draft or who had deserted the Confederate Army. Many of the Unionists eventually made their way north to the Tennessee River valley and joined the Union Army with most commonly enlisting in the First Alabama Cavalry USA. Several county residents, including Bill Looney, also found ways to help serve the Union Army by helping Unionists escape to the safety behind Union lines in the north.

In July, 1862, long before Cole McTavish even thought about enlistment, Colonel Abel D. Streight led a detachment of Union troops through the county to gather more recruits for the Union Army. There were many Unionist farmers who fled into the woods to hide while others joined the Union Army to avoid the Confederate draft. Their farms were left unworked in complete and total abandonment. As a result, county residents had difficulty in planting, working the fields, and harvesting enough crops for food. Confederate agents would worsen matters by confiscating food and livestock to feed the Confederate Army. This led to a number of acts of robbery, vandalism, and even murder against former neighbors during this time. These atrocities were committed by both Unionists and Confederates.

Union occupation of several counties in north Alabama gave Union Colonel Abel Streight a base which enabled his troops to carry out raids on the railroad between Chattanooga and Atlanta. The railway system provided the needed transport for supplies to the Army of Tennessee at this time. Streight's 1,700 troops left Tuscumbia in April 1863 to make a hit on the railroad. Four days into the raid, Confederate cavalrymen led by General Nathan Bedford Forrest, met them on Sand Mountain while they began to harass the Union raiders. A local girl, Emma Sansom, led Forrest's men across Black Creek after the raiders had burned the bridge while the Confederates continued their pursuit. A few days later, near Rome, Georgia, the exhausted forces of Colonel Streight surrendered and were sent to Libby Prison in Richmond, Virginia. Although this raid wasn't considered as a complete success, it would not be the last raid into Alabama. The Union strategy was to put a squeeze upon the state from north to south with one main objective. They would try to destroy Alabama's ability to feed the armies and supply the troops with additional weapons.

Throughout the war, Alabama escaped much of the terrible devastation that other Confederate states did not. There was one significant raid that caused wide-scale destruction that crippled the state. Union General James H. Wilson launched a raid from Lauderdale County that destroyed parts of the University of Alabama, iron furnaces in Jefferson and Bibb counties, and the main industrial area in Selma. In the end, war created widows, orphans, heroes, a different economy, politics, and varying identities. Yet, for many Alabamians little changed, if anything.

CHAPTER 15

C happy relayed his good night motion with a simple wave as he left to go to his tent while leaving Cole and Nate seated around the campfire. Most of the men had already settled down for the night. The First Alabama had completed their current mission and were camped just outside Jonesboro while awaiting further orders. Cole and his team, which now included his buddy Nate, had finished checking on the horses and getting them settled for the night when they sat down to talk. Cole threw another few sticks onto the fire and then sat cross-legged next to Nate.

"So, tell me Nate, how have you really been? What's it like? You've held back long enough, and we both know that Marcie is not coming back. I hate to see you seemingly down all the time."

"I miss my wife terribly! Marcie was a wonderful girl, so vibrant, so full of life. The day I found her dead and the baby...well, that was the worst day of my life. I felt so helpless!"

"What do you think must have happened to her?"

"The autopsy concluded that during the onset of her labor, the baby came out breach, entangled in its cord and suffocated. Marcie, in pain and so weak, couldn't do anything herself, so she eventually just bled to death. No one was there to help her...oh God, I should have been there!"

"Were there any signs that she could be going into an early labor?"

"If there was, I certainly wasn't aware of anything. When I left for work that morning, the last thing she said to me 'You're going to be late!' I just chuckled and walked out the door."

"Nate, it's just going to take time to get over this. You know Marcie wouldn't want you to take all this out on yourself."

"Yeah, but then to be accused of killing her myself!"

"What? Who would accuse you of such a thing?"

"The sheriff did. Sheriff Kincaid came right out and said to me up in my face, 'You killed her, didn't you?' I swear I didn't. Cole, you know me like a brother. Am I a killer? He seems to be out to get me."

"No, you are not a killer. Why would the sheriff ever think otherwise? He knows you better than that."

"It still bothers me though. Makes me feel deep resentment for the man."

"Don't let it continue to bother you. Forget it, forget him. Formal charges would have to be brought against you, along with an arrest warrant. I don't believe that will ever happen, do you?"

"Who knows? That didn't stop the sheriff and that private investigator Hagelmeyer who seemed to be hell bent on convicting the righteous Reverend Goodhue for the murder of his wife. Last I heard, that misfortunate bastard got sentenced to rot in the pen down in south Alabama."

"Yes, but the difference is that he really did do it. At least, that's what the jury thought when they rendered their guilty verdict."

"Again, there is absolutely no way that I would ever harm my beautiful Marcie." Nate shifted and pushed back from the fire. "Tell me, Cole, any news recently from Libby?"

"In her last letter, Libby told me that Alex was three, and she finally cut his hair; Greta wants a baby when Jacob gets back home, and her father is seeing the widow Bailey. It appears to be getting rather serious."

"You don't say… Mrs. Charles Bailey? Good for you and Libby!"

"Why is that good for me, Nate?"

"Most likely, you will have a wonderful new mother-in-law and Libby's father will have a live-in companion, someone to take care of him. I believe Mrs. Irene will be a good wife for Mr. Parker."

"For me, I feel that I will be in the same situation like Jacob Hassendorfer when I get home. Libby has already informed me that she wants a girl."

"Well, old friend, I can't help you there. You both will do quite well with another kid. Why stop at two? Have a house full of young'uns."

"Don't think so, Nate." They both let out a laugh while Nate shifted their conversation.

"Hey Mule, why don't you tell me about everything you've experienced in the cavalry so far? Was the training hard? What is it like to kill someone in battle?"

"Well, you got to experience a little of that yourself in Jonesboro. First, why don't you start by telling me exactly how you felt before I try to answer you?'

Nate stood to stretch a bit before returning to his seat on the ground.

"I was bringing up the rear, so the front took on the heaviest fighting. Pushing through the trees toward the Rebs was somewhat difficult for me to maneuver my mount until I reached a small clearing. It was there a young boy appeared out of nowhere in a flash. He couldn't have been more than eighteen. He made his sudden approach to my right, grabbed onto my leg, and tried to pull me off my horse. Instantly, I swung my sabre downward while it slashed through his collar bone in one solid blow. He yelled out in pain as he fell back onto the ground. I don't know if I killed him since I was already in motion while I kept riding forward. All I can remember is seeing that brief look of surprise in his eyes on that boyish face while hearing his cry of agony as he fell back. That still haunts me!"

"It's tough to have to kill, Nate, but the war dictates 'kill or be killed.' Men, young and old, just like you and me, are forced to face this same dilemma. The only difference is that now, they are the enemy. I'm hoping this is our last campaign. I'm ready to go home."

"Me, as well, Cole. I'm only here because I wanted to find you. I couldn't care less about this war. I just want to be left alone like so many others in Winston County."

"Guess we need to think about turning in, Nate. Morning will be here before we know it."

"You're right about that, so I'll bid you a pleasant good night, my friend. See you tomorrow."

"Good night, Nate."

Miles away, located south of Jonesboro, a lone Confederate soldier lay near death in a private home. His condition remained highly critical during the past two weeks following the departure of Hardee's Company from Lovejoy Station. Not fit for transport, he was taken into the home of Carolina Stevenson and her husband, Matthew, at their insistence to provide watch care over him. The soldier had been brought into the little country church, which was presently being used as a field hospital where Carolina was serving as a volunteer nurse. At first sight, she felt so much compassion for the man that she convinced her husband to move him into their modest home to continue care for him. After the first day, it seemed doubtful that he would make it through the night, but that was nearly two weeks ago. Matthew and Carolina felt it was a miracle that he was still alive.

The doctor had done all he could for this particular young man, including the amputation of the left leg below the knee without chloroform; removal of shrapnel fragments from the chest and belly; and most critically, a gaping wound to the left eye socket where the eyeball had been blown out. It had been a nasty wound, and the doctor couldn't tell if there were any small fragments still embedded in the socket. Now, Carolina observed his breathing was becoming more labored while she feared pneumonia was setting into the lungs. Both she and her husband took turns around the clock while they cared for the man who appeared to be around the same age as their dead son. For several days, they referred to their patient as Private Johnny Reb while they didn't know his name.

On the day he was brought into the church, Carolina noticed the two men who carried him on a stretcher and left him just inside the front door. In a moment, they were gone as quickly as they first appeared. Carolina ran toward the door, looked out, but to no avail. Whoever the two men were, they had suddenly disappeared. Concerned about what appeared to be a critical situation, she had two men serving as orderlies to move him to a place on the back pew where the doctor could see what he could do for him. At the time, his name wasn't as important as trying to save his life. It was days later when Carolina went through the pockets of the man's discarded jacket that she found his identification papers. Now, she knew his name and where he was from. After she folded the papers and returned them to the pocket, she wondered how his family could possibly be notified. Carolina knew in her heart that one particular wife in Winston County would most definitely be anxious to hear about her severely wounded husband – Jacob Hassendorfer.

Carolina continued to pray in earnest that Jacob would survive his ordeal and live while she cared for him as her own son. Matthew felt the same as the couple worked together each day while they sought to make Jacob as comfortable as possible. Suddenly, Jacob's breathing seemed to improve while his one eye would open and close at various times. Carolina felt that he was trying to communicate with her, but he only muttered at times since he was unable to speak. This went on for days while fresh dressings and bandages were applied and changed daily by the caregivers. Carolina realized that her work at the church, although unattended by herself, was being taken over by others who were as concerned as she. She couldn't explain it, but somehow she felt her devotion must lie with the healing process of Private Hassendorfer. Her personal involvement came from knowing that an unknown Christian lady from Chancellorsville had cared for her son during the days before his death. She felt now this was the least she could do for another human being.

Each day, Jacob continued to improve until the time finally came when he regained total consciousness. Matthew and Carolina worked with him daily while explaining how it came about that he was presently staying with them. At first, Jacob was unaware that he had suffered the loss of an eye and leg until Matthew was able to sit him up on the bed. It was then that reality set in, and he realized what actually happened to him. His eye began to water, but he couldn't produce a tear. His lip slightly trembled, but he didn't cry out. He suddenly knew that he was lucky to be alive. He called out for Greta in his loudest voice, but she wouldn't answer.

"Jacob, we have sent a letter to your wife telling her that we have you here with us at Lovejoy Station. That is all I can tell you right now," Carolina said as she stood beside the bed.

"Thank you," Jacob replied in a muffled whisper.

"Could you eat some soup? It will help give you strength if you could take some right away."

He nodded in the affirmative while Carolina left to pour him a bowl of creamy potato soup. After he finished with all he could get down, he rested for a couple of hours. Later that afternoon Jacob shared his survival story with Matthew and Carolina as best he could remember. After hearing it, they all had to agree that he was indeed a very lucky man to be alive.

My company, led by Lt. General William J. Hardee, along with another Confederate company under the leadership of General S.D. Lee, moved south to join together at Lovejoy Station. Our task was to defend the Confederate supply line along the Macon and Western Railroad. We sheltered down into a ravine along the railroad track among the trees. The place where I was positioned provided the least amount of protection since there were fewer trees in my concealed location. There we waited, and for how long, I cannot remember. It seemed like hours though. I whiled away the time by talking to my buddies to my right and left after making sure that my rifle was ready to fire. Young Private Charles Crenshaw, a lad of twenty-one from Florence, sat on the ground to my right. Charlie had become my best friend, and we had been through a lot of fighting since our first meeting. He had a severe shoulder wound that was almost healed now. I don't know what happened to him. I believe he was still standing by me at the time I was hit.

Then it started, like a tremendous thunder bolt, they were on top of us! All of a sudden, the 1ˢᵗ Alabama Cavalry came at us through the trees to our rear. Trampling the underbrush and hearing the breaking of tree limbs, the force of a hundred horseback riders rode toward us while they slashed their way among the many unfortunates who lay in their path and were caught in the surprise attack. I only caught a quick glimpse as the blood bath commenced. It was then, we were hit in a frontal assault by General John A. Logan's XV Corps while all hell broke loose. Mortar fire and cannons suddenly filled the air while we were bombarded with Union firepower at first from across the tracks. After the first wave of mortar and cannon fire had ceased, from out of nowhere came hundreds at us with fixed bayonets. From my crouched position, I must have jumped to my feet. All I can remember is that I stood to reload and must have taken a direct hit from mortar fire before it finally stopped and the charge began. That's about all I can remember until waking up here in your house. All I want to do now is find out what happened to Charlie and see my sweet Greta once more.

Ten days later, Matthew and Carolina Stevenson received a special delivery letter from the secretary of Lt. General Hardee that contained an important message. It read:

Mr. and Mrs. Matthew Stevenson
194 West Bloomington Street
Lovejoy Station, Georgia

14 October 1864

Greetings Mr. and Mrs. Stevenson:

It has come to my attention that you, sir and madam, along with the possibility of several other families, are caring for our wounded soldiers in various homes in your town. To relieve you of your current responsibility and return our men to their families, there will be a military squadron arriving in Lovejoy Station in one week to gather and transport each man to his respective home by wagon train. My source tells me that you are presently housing Private Jacob Hassendorfer from Winston County, Alabama. You will need to have him at the Lovejoy Station Depot on October 21 at 11:00 a.m. ready for transport.

Sincerely yours,
Staff Sgt. Willard D. Cronier, Secretary
Lt. General William J. Hardee,
Corps of the Army of Tennessee, CSA

Greta was home alone in the parlor when she heard several footsteps, along with men's voices, coming from outside on her porch. Anxiously, she rushed to the front door, quickly unbolted it, and threw open the door. She wasn't prepared for what she saw when the door flew back to reveal all the men gathered before her. She felt faint, but immediately she knew she had to remain calm and strong at all cost. There, standing in the center of three other soldiers, was her returning husband who had been away fighting for almost a year. Jacob said nothing at first while a tear formed in his eye while Greta rushed to him and threw herself into his arms.

"Oh, my darling, you're finally home and I am so happy to see you. Come into the house, you men, too, and I'll get us something to drink."

Jacob stood erect and walked in hobbling on a crutch while allowing the help of two fellow soldiers to accompany him while they guided him to the sofa in the parlor.

"Oh, Greta, I'm so sorry to have you see me like this. I…"

"Hush, hush, don't say another word, you hear? Your condition doesn't matter to me, only know that that I am so glad to see you and have you back home. You are still the wonderful man I married. That will never change. I thank God for the doctor and the Stevenson's who I've learned took you into their home and cared for you so you could come back to me. That's what I'm most grateful for, in addition for the love you have for me."

"Yes, my darling, Matthew and Carolina Stevenson were a Godsend to me. They both sacrificed so much to keep me alive, and now I'm here and so grateful for their kind, loving mercy."

"I will have to send them a letter of thanks, won't I?"

"Yes, that's the least we can do! Also, we are grateful to you men here with us who helped to get me home," Jacob said while he looked into the face of each man present.

The three soldiers shared a cup of apple cider with the Hassendorfer's and then excused themselves to leave. After Greta closed the door, she rejoined Jacob in the parlor and gently placed herself onto his lap.

"I'm not hurting you, am I?" she asked.

"Not in the least, my darling. It feels rather good having you sit on my lap," he said.

Greta cuddled up against him, and leaning onto his chest, she planted a passionate kiss on his waiting lips.

He sighed with a grin.

She sighed with a grin.

Jacob began to wiggle slightly underneath her.

"I think it's time to try for a boy, don't you?"

CHAPTER 16

The morning dew covered his tent while Cole took it down to fold and pack in preparation to leave the area. He gathered the top in both hands in an effort to shake the tent dry as possible before folding it enough to pack it away. He, along with Nate and Chappy, were happy to receive the news that they had orders to return to Huntsville. At last, after three brutal battles, they were all going home.

Just before dawn, Colonel Spencer and his aide, Matthew Dunbar, along with Corporal Jeremiah Jensen and Sgt. Malcolm McKenzie, left the camp as they headed northwest toward Huntsville. They were closely followed by a small squad of horsemen that completed their entourage. Sgt. McRae and Sgt. Boshell headed up the supply wagons that were set to move out at noon under the command of Sgt. Liam Devereaux. While the camp continued to break up, several cavalrymen began to group together for the ride home. Cole, Nate, and Chappy were about finished loading their gear when they were joined by Private Wiley Butkis and Private Scottie Callahan.

At the same time, unknown to the 1st Alabama moving caravan, a division of Hardee's troops still remained camped in their path near the Alabama state line. They were waiting on orders to relocate while gaining a brief rest from fighting while receiving fresh supplies. Confederate scouts patrolling the area soon discovered the approaching cavalry and sent word immediately back to Lt. General

Hardee of their movement located five miles east of them. In haste, Hardee ordered a trap to be set along the road in hope to ambush the remnant of Spencer's Cavalry who would soon be traveling on the same road toward them. It would be a grandstand surprise attack, and the cavalry wouldn't know what hit them until it was too late. Infantrymen lined the roadside among the trees and ditches while cannons were moved into place as quickly as possible. Precise timing was of the essence while the Confederate line was now in place with less than twenty minutes to spare. They waited.

Fortunately, for Colonel Spencer and his small band, he had chosen an alternate route that morning by moving southwest on a less traveled road, thus avoiding the upcoming attack. It was almost dusk by the time Sgt. Devereaux led his men down the winding road and into the trap set for them. A bugle sounded, along with a thunder of rebel yells, as it signaled the outburst as the attack commenced upon the 1st Alabama. Cannons roared, rifles fired through the trees as billows of grey smoke filled the air as the sudden blast bombarded the unsuspecting victims. A loud cry went up as Sgt. Devereaux yelled out to his men.

"Dismount, take cover, and defend yourselves!"

Cavalrymen hit the ground while frightened horses scattered up and down the road. Several of them were killed on the spot while the fire power rained down among them. Revolvers and rifles were quickly drawn and fired from the men who were fortunate to have them. Some men with their sabers drawn, headed into the woods in an attempt to kill those who were positioned near the road. Devereaux was laying on the ground when he ordered the supply wagons to advance and make a run for it since they were in position at the head of the caravan. Both Sgt. McRae and Sgt. Boshell whipped the horses into their fastest speed as they galloped away to make their escape while losing several pots and utensils that flew from the wagons and spilled onto the road.

Others in Spencer's Cavalry were not so fortunate. Private Wiley "Wild Man" Butkis took a bullet to the head and was killed instantly. Pretty boy Private Scottie Callahan took a hit in the leg, followed by a blast to his right shoulder. Chappy received a blow to the side of his face where a piece of shrapnel had barely missed his head. The fighting continued.

"Retreat! Make a run for it, men" Sgt. Devereaux sounded the command while he was felled where he stood by a blast into his side. He hit the ground in agony.

Nate and Cole took advantage of nearby strays while each grabbed onto a horse near the place where they had been returning rifle fire while laying side by side. Swinging up into the saddle, both Cole and Nate headed away from the road in an attempt to retreat. Nate had only gotten about a hundred yards away when a shrill blast brought down his horse and he took a hit in the back as he was going down. Cole, who was riding ahead, turned around to see what had happened to Nate when he was shot from his saddle. Cole hit the ground with a thud. He was grazed in the left arm, but was knocked semi-conscious as he fell from his horse.

The skirmish continued until dark when it was difficult to determine who was fighting whom. During the night, many made their escape to safety while the dead and wounded lay where they had fallen. At first light, Hardee's troops began rounding up their dead and wounded as well as taking a small amount of Union prisoners who had survived. Among those were: Sgt. William Devereaux; Private Scottie Callahan; Corporal Nathan Chappell; Private Cole McTavish; and Nathaniel Overstreet.

Since this encounter had been a one day skirmish, and not a full-scale battle, it was listed as unknown in recorded history along with the total casualties suffered by both the Union and Confederates. Although each of the five men were unaware, enough time had passed back at regiment headquarters in Huntsville, they had already been given their unofficial promotions. The new ranking listed them as follows: Lieutenant William Devereaux; Corporal Scottie Callahan; Sergeant Nathan Chappell; Corporal Cole McTavish; and Corporal Nathaniel Overstreet.

Following their initial capture, each man was shown mercy by allowing them to receive medical treatment depending on available supplies. Devereaux had a piece of shrapnel removed from his side with the wound dressed and bandaged. Chappy had the left side of his faced cleaned and bandaged where he had a gash from a shrapnel fragment. Nate had a bullet removed from his back, stitched up, and bandaged. Cole had a bandaged upper left arm where a bullet had grazed him. Callahan's injuries were a little more severe while having a bullet wound in the leg that now appeared to be infected along with a slow healing wound to his right shoulder. The prisoners were taken by wagon to Lt. General Hardee's headquarters near Nashville during the next week to await transfer by rail to the Confederate prison in Richmond, Virginia. The First Alabama five were loaded into a boxcar, along with fifteen other prisoners. It was soon to be learned that this particular prison was reserved mainly for Union officers. Any others were usually sent down south to Sumter County, Georgia to Andersonville.

The almost three day journey to Richmond in a boxcar with no windows was deemed so degrading, humiliating, and just plain unhealthy to several of the higher ranking officers. With only straw on the floor, one water container, and three pots to use for piss and shit, the stench alone was almost unbearable after a three day trip having little or no air circulation. On the first day, the five huddled together as one group while the remaining fifteen mixed and mingled in groups of two and three. The second day, following a very uncomfortable first night, the 1st Alabama men reached out to become acquainted with some of the other officers. In total, there were four captains, two lieutenants, six sergeants, and three corporals whose home states ranged from Georgia all the way to New York.

Cole took a particular interest in each of the new men that he presently viewed as strangers while he noted their every move, gesture, and conversation during each waking hour. After a day, he pretty much had all the men figured out in his mind. He soon determined who seemed to be the most intellectual, talkative, boastful, optimistic, pessimistic, funny, angry, timid, dim-witted, and just plain stupid. One specific young officer he took special note of was Lt. Byron Cathcart who most of the men called "Red" simply because of his very noticeable hair color. By far, Cole thought him to be an exceptional man of intelligence and leadership ability. Red couldn't be more than twenty-six with broad shoulders on his six foot frame, and the brightest blue eyes he had ever seen. Well almost, he had to think again about that. Nothing could ever compare to Libby's clear blue eyes as he suddenly flashed back to his memory of her at that very moment. Cole had observed Red from the first day he saw him and knew that he needed to get acquainted with him when the opportunity presented itself; however, this was not the time.

The train stopped, and it was time for another feeding which consisted of hardtack, salt pork, and a cup of cold black coffee. The water container was checked and refilled as needed while the piss pots were emptied on the ground and returned without rinsing. At the end of the second day, everyone learned that if the train didn't stop, there would be no food, no water, and the pots would go unemptied. Two of the men had already reached the point of not being able to take this treatment any longer. One banged his head against the door at times while the other continually ranted and cursed out loud and often. As one of the guards closed the door for the night, most of the men heard him say, "Sleep well, you bastards, tomorrow you will arrive at your new home!"

Libby Prison

The original building was built prior to the civil war as a food distribution warehouse. It was structured as a three-story brick warehouse on two levels located on Tobacco Row on the waterfront of the James River. Before it was modified to become a Confederate prison to house mainly Union officers, the warehouse was leased by

Captain Luther Libby and his son, George to operate their grocery business.

In 1861, the Confederate government took over the facility and began to use it as a hospital, and by 1862 it was converted into a prison due to the influx of prisoners who were mainly Union officers. The main structure contained eight low-ceiling rooms with each one measuring 103 feet in length and a width of 42 feet. Prisoners were housed on the second and third floors. The windows were barred and open to any current weather conditions. The elements most certainly increased the discomfort of each prisoner. Also, the lack of sanitation and eventual overcrowding caused disease to spread among all the inmates. With the prison's beginning in 1862 with 700 men, the number grew to 1,000 by 1863. From that time until the next year, mortality rates began to increase at a fast pace. By the time the 1st Alabama prisoners arrived in 1864, prison conditions were aggravated by shortages of food and supplies, disease, and death.

Prior to Cole's arrival with the others back in March 1864, there were certain worries over the safety of the capital of Richmond and the security of the prison. Added to that concern was the limitations for food and supplies. During this month, most prisoners of war at Libby were evacuated from Richmond to Macon, Georgia. The enlisted men were sent to Andersonville while many officers were transferred to the new prison in Macon. For those who remained, Libby continued to be used mostly as a place for the temporary confinement of Union officers and a small number of Confederate military criminals. On 18 September, 1864, only a month before Cole's arrival, it was reported that approximately 230 prisoners remained in Libby Prison.

Following a brief check-in, with only the clothes on their back, the Alabama five were searched and separated. Devereaux was placed into one room, Callahan in another, while Chappy, Nate, and Cole were ushered into what Cole could only describe as a "dungeon from hell." The three of them moved together across the crowded floor until they found a place to sit against the cold brick wall. A slight chill blew through the barred open windows that October day while Cole and his two buddies caught a glimpse of what day one was beginning to be like. Each of them began to look around the large room that they now shared with approximately 85 other pitiful-looking inmates.

"Would you look at that?" Chappy pointed across the room. Standing over by one of the windows, a skeletal-looking man about thirty-five, clad only in a pair of worn out drawers, held onto the bars while he coughed and struggled to breathe. His pee ran down his leg and puddled around his feet. Close by, next to him, lay rows of men side by side. Some rested on tattered blankets on the filthy wood floor in their own piss and feces. The smell alone in the room was something hard to get used to, so very bad. A few men were seen with dirty handkerchiefs and rags tied around their faces. Some inmates were singing, some shouting and cursing while some talked low to one another.

"Laughter is most certainly the one thing that's missing here," Nate said while he closed his eyes to escape the horrible sight.

Cole witnessed during the day that some men were able to take things from those who were asleep by simply stealing. Some robbers would openly snatch items, mainly food, from those who were too weak to defend themselves. At varied times during the day, guards would come into the room and carry out those near death or who were already dead. Some were taken downstairs to the hospital; others to the morgue. Able-bodied men could be seen sometimes moving a deceased inmate to a place near the door. It was never completely quiet and peaceful in the room while there was the constant sound of noise, either moaning, grunting, crying, and coughing. The greatest amount of movement occurred as the room became in a frenzy whenever the guards came in to distribute the food. Usually they carried shoulder bags containing cornbread and sweet potatoes that they handed out individually. Each guard would reach into his bag, grab a potato and piece of cornbread, and place them into the hands of those men who were able to stand. For those who could not, their portion was simply thrown down close to them where they lay. For those who no longer could eat, either from sickness or for any other reason, their food was quickly snatched away and confiscated by their nearest neighbor. It was common to see fighting break out over an extra piece of bread or potato. Meat was no longer furnished to any class except to a few officers who were in the Libby hospital located on the first floor.

"Well, dammit, we have almost survived our first day. Don't know how much more of this shit hole I can stand," Nate said while he stood to go to the latrine which was nothing more than several buckets located in the far back corner of the room. Drinking water was brought in periodically and put into a large container with two dippers by the door. Sometimes it would take hours before it could be refilled after going empty. In desperation, some inmates would drink from the large tub of water put there for general use and bathing.

Following a supper meal of the same, most activity in the room would begin to settle down by nightfall. Several men were able to gain extra blankets or clothing whenever a nearby inmate was carried out of the room or found dead where they slept. For their first night, Chappy, Nate, and Cole had no access for any extra essentials, so they used their boots as pillows and slept on the cold, bare floor. Each night would provide the same scene of men so crowded, nearly touching head to feet, it looked like they were packed together like a can of sardines.

There was even an article printed in the *Daily Richmond Enquirer* that vividly described the conditions at Libby Prison. One news reporter had this to write about it in his column:

Libby Prison on Tobacco Row takes in the captured Federals in vast numbers, but doesn't let them out. The men are huddled up and jammed into every nook and corner; at the bathing troughs, around the stoves, and everywhere there is a wrangling, jostling crowd. At night, the floor of every room they occupy in the building is covered, every square foot of it, by sickly men, lying side by side and heel to head, as tightly packed as if the prison were a huge box of nocturnal sardines.

So, now it was to be the same for every long tedious day that all prisoners would have to endure this inhuman treatment until their day of release, either physically or by death alone. As the weeks passed into months, Cole couldn't help wonder about Scottie Callahan, Liam Devereaux, and Lt. Byron Cathcart whom he never got to meet. He often thought about whatever happened to the young lieutenant.

As conditions in the room worsened, the three of them would try to help or assist those who could no longer care for themselves. Fevers, dysentery, and diarrhea were running rampart throughout the overcrowded population while it seemed that death took the weakest body almost every day. While the weeks progressed, Cole befriended one of the guards who sometimes would supply him with leftover food to share with others. Also, this same little guy, only known to him as Jeb, kept him informed about certain things going on inside and outside the walls of Libby Prison. That is precisely how he was able to find out about Devereaux, Callahan, Cathcart, and the great escape that took place only months before he and his buddies arrived at Libby.

Liam Devereaux was housed up on the third floor in a room with 53 other high ranking officers who seemingly remained more healthy than most. His daily routine ran much the same as his fellow Alabamians, although he would never know whatever happened to them or at least, not for a long time. In this prison, an inmate never saw anyone else other than those in his assigned room. Devereaux tried to avoid contact with those in his surrounding area who seemed feverish or infectious in any way. The wound in his side had completely healed, but it left an unsightly scar as a reminder of what happened to him on the day of the ambush. He, like Cole, spent his time trying to assist and help those men who were weakening day by day. The lack of food was beginning to show on him while his weight began to drop very rapidly.

Scottie Callahan, on the other hand, wasn't doing well at all. The last few days had been almost unbearable for him while he was taken from his room and moved to the hospital on the first floor. The wound to his right shoulder still would not heal, while his leg was so infected that pus would continue to ooze from his leg in an open bleeding wound that the doctor determined was gangrene. The leg was going to have to come off and there was no chloroform, nor any sterilization for the one and only hacksaw with the jagged teeth that was used in every amputation. Added to Scottie's present condition was a high fever that would not go down.

The doctor came into the room and stopped at the side of the table where Scottie lay outstretched and motionless before him. Looking somewhat like the angel of death, the doctor was wearing a blood-soaked long white coat with a pair of wire-rimmed spectacles peeking from its top pocket. He picked up the saw and began to wipe the blade with a cloth that happened to be lying nearby on the edge of the table.

"Put that leather strap into his mouth and hold it firmly," the doctor instructed his assistant. "This is going to have to happen quickly."

The doctor applied a makeshift tourniquet to Scottie's upper thigh while he glanced over to where two other men waited across the table. He nodded at them while one man positioned his body over Scottie's torso as the other grabbed onto and held his leg in place. The doctor put his glasses on, wiped his brow, tore back the rotted fabric of the trouser, and held the saw just above the knee. With his left hand on Scottie's thigh, his right came down with the saw while its jagged edge ground into the meat and bone, splattering blood all over the place, while it quickly severed the leg that dropped from the table onto the floor. Scottie gave one loud outcry as his body felt the pain while he convulsed into unconsciousness. Every effort was made by the doctor and his team to control and stop the blood flow that continued to spill out from the stump, but it grew hopeless. Scottie Callahan lay dead on the table.

It was weeks later until Jeb informed Cole the sad news about the pretty young boy from Alabama who died on the operating table.

"What happens to the dead here at Libby? What about Scottie?" Cole asked Jeb after receiving this surprising notification.

"In some instances here at first, arrangements could be made to have bodies shipped back home for burial. Nowadays, graves are dug behind the prison near the waterfront and the dead are buried there. Your friend will most likely be given a number and placed into a grave with all the unknowns. I'm afraid that's all I can tell you."

"If you have a minute, could you tell us about the prison escape that happened earlier this year?" asked Cole.

"I have to go make some more rounds now, but I'll come back later and I can tell you what I know," said Jeb.

As he promised, Jeb came back after a while and sat down close to Cole, Nate, and Chappy who were huddled close together. He reached into his pocket and brought out three small crabapples that he slipped to Cole. While mouthing a silent thank you, Cole hid the apples in his jacket pocket.

"Jeb, before you begin, would you happen to know the whereabouts of Lt. Byron Cathcart, a young officer known as Red?"

"Oh yeah, I've seen him. Best I remember he's up on third floor in the same room as your friend, Dev..."

"Devereaux?"

"Yes, that's it. That's him, I do believe. The man's doing all right, I guess, but looks like he's losing a lot of weight."

"Thanks for letting me know. I've been wondering about him for weeks."

"Listen, if I'm going to tell you about the escape, I need to get on with it. I don't have all day, you know."

"Yes, please tell us. We all want to know." said Cole while Nate and Chappy drew in closer while Jeb began his story.

Best I can recall, what is now referred to as the Libby Prison Escape actually took place during the second week of February this year. Captain Martin Tower of Company B, 13ᵗʰ Massachusetts Infantry, along with 109 Union officers planned and executed their escape at that time. It all began on the night of February 9ᵗʰ under the cover of darkness. The tunnel that had been dug for so long was finally complete. Along with Captain Tower, Major Hamilton, and Colonel Rose, among several others, were among the first to pass through in total darkness. Colonel Davis and others from the 4ᵗʰ Maine passed through to the yard just as the clocks of Richmond were striking midnight. It was nearly daybreak when all the escapees reached a thicket in the woods where they all stopped to rest. Only Captain Tower and Colonel Davis avoided re-capture while they soon joined 57 other escapees who made it to the safety of Union lines.

Afterward, the tunnel was discovered at the base of the east wall about twenty feet from the front on Cary Street. The entrance had been hidden by a large rock which fit the opening in a very precise and exact formation. With the stone rolled away from the mouth, it revealed the small avenue which led to the outside. The passageway lay directly beneath the feet of three sentinels who walked the length of the east end of the prison, across a paved alley way, in a distance of more than fifty feet. Its end broke up inside the enclosure in the rear of the Carr warehouse. The tunnel was gauged to almost perfection that when opened the prisoners were able to worm themselves through the tunnel, one by one, and emerge at least sixty feet distant from the sentinel post, through an arched gateway, to freedom. In order to reach the entrance to the tunnel, it was necessary for the prisoners to cut through the hospital room and the closed stairway leading into the basement.

It was determined that all the labor that had gone into the dig had been performed always at night. Any trace of the work accomplished at night was either closed up or cleared away before each morning. The tunnel itself was a work of genius engineering for several months by an unknown number of men. In the end, it measured about three feet in diameter and at least sixty feet in length. Also, it had to be dug around any rocks that lay in the path of the curving tunnel. Over time, three tunnels were built. The first one ran into water and was abandoned. The second hit the building's giant log foundation. The third reached a small carriage shed about fifty feet away, and it was at that point where the Libby prison escape actually happened.

"That's all I know, fellas! Now, don't you get any ideas about trying to escape 'cause that tunnel has long been closed and sealed up. Besides, all the inmates here couldn't leave if they wanted too since they are barely able to move around in the first place."

"Thanks Jeb, for telling us about it anyway. We can always dream about it, can't we?" Cole laughed while Jeb got up to leave.

Meanwhile, Lt. Cathcart had already met Devereaux on the first day they arrived and were placed into their third floor room at the top. Their room looked out across the James River over to the Belle Isle encampment. Smells from the waterfront and all the other rooms would waft their pungent odors through the many barred opened windows. The view was quite nice, but not so, from the smell of the river mixed with odors of puke, vomit, piss, and shit. With no available green leafy vegetables and no pork, beef, fish, or poultry, most prisoners were contracting rickets, scurvy, extreme diarrhea, while facing complete starvation. There were cases of new inmates that were so sick when they came into the prison that they died there on the same day.

Lt. Cathcart became one of the misfortunates who came in the first day as the picture of health, a robust, virile young man, but now he was plagued with scurvy, massive bouts of diarrhea, and fever. After weeks, he continued to waste away until he began to look like a living skeleton just barely alive. He was eventually carried to the hospital and isolated on a cot along the back wall where he lay completely naked and uncovered. For days, he drifted in and out of consciousness until he was ready to go. It was early morning on Christmas Eve with a light dusting of snow falling over Richmond that Lt. Byron "Red" Cathcart started his journey toward his heavenly home. That same evening, he was there.

When Jeb finally alerted Cole of his passing, all Cole could feel was a deep sorrow for an outstanding young man that he never got to meet.

Several more months of extreme hardship and starvation would continue in the new year at Libby Prison until finally there was news that Lee had surrendered at Appomattox on 9 April, 1865 and the civil war was over. Libby Prison closed down shortly thereafter while arrangements were being made for the release of all prisoners. Although they had battled fevers, sickness, and near starvation, Cole, Nate, Chappy, and Devereaux had survived. All that was left to be done now was to complete their discharge papers, get them some proper food, and put four skinny Yanks on a train in Richmond that was heading south to Huntsville, Alabama.

Lt. William Devereaux, Sgt. Nathan Chappell, Corporal Cole McTavish, and Private Nathaniel Overstreet all received honorable service medals after they soon rejoined the 1st Alabama Cavalry Regiment. The regiment was mustered out of service at Huntsville, Alabama on 20 October 1865 with 397 men present. Out of all the men who served in the unit during the course of the war, 345 were killed in action, died in prison or from disease, 88 were captured, and 279 deserted with no accurate record count of the number of wounded.

Cole McTavish began to make plans for his homecoming after saying goodbye to Chappy and Devereaux. In the morning, Cole and Nate would be heading home to Double Springs. What could he expect had happened in Winston County during his absence?

CHAPTER 17

Libby sat by her dressing table in the cabin while she re-folded and put away the letter she had already read three times. Her husband was alive and well, and he would be coming back home shortly. She could hardly believe it, but there it was in black and white and written in his own handwriting. He had been gone from home since 23 October, 1863 when Alex was only 18 months old, and now it was October 1865. It had been a long two years, but just to know that he was safe and sound meant everything to Libby right now. She had wanted to go to him as soon as she learned that he was back in Huntsville, but Alex had been sick during that time, and she would not leave him. She felt she had waited for two years already, so a few more weeks didn't really matter.

Jacob had come home to Greta. Cole was coming home to her. Nate, he was...

Libby felt so sorry for him. Cole had also mentioned in his letter that the two of them were alive and well, but that Nate would not be coming back home with him. He was staying in Huntsville for a while to sort things out before moving on. That's all that Cole had mentioned in the letter.

Libby wished that Nate would have at least come back long enough to see his elderly mother and father. They were still faithfully keeping his house as best they could, but their health was failing and presently they had no one to take care of them. She couldn't understand why Nate was being so difficult and uncaring.

Two weeks later, Greta halted Orion near the porch of the little cabin where she was dropping off her passengers, Libby, Alex, and Mona from an afternoon shopping trip to town.

"Won't you come in?" Libby asked while she stepped down from the buggy.

"I would love too, Sweetie, but I best get home to Jacob and Natasha right now. Maybe we can all come back next week sometime to see you," Greta said.

"Mona, why don't you take Alex and gather the eggs in the hen house before you come in?" Libby mentioned to her while she reached into the buggy for her bag of groceries.

"Need some help?" Greta asked.

"No, I can manage," Libby said while she waved goodbye to Greta as she left. Libby reached down into the bag, pulled a grape from the bunch on the top, and plopped it into her mouth before picking up the parcel and walking up the front steps. She opened the door, stepped inside, and kicked the door shut with the swift motion of her foot. In a moment, she froze in her tracks while almost dropping her groceries and choking on the grape. She gulped, and it went down. *What is this?*

There on the table was a lit white taper in the candleholder that had belonged to her maternal great-grandmother. Libby knew she normally kept it wrapped in a black velvet cloth in the second drawer of her dressing table. Also, on the table beside the candle was a medal of some kind, bronze with a royal blue ribbon attached. Before she could think about even trying to move, the floor creaked while a secluded figure stepped out from the shadow against the back wall and started toward her. The groceries she held in her now trembling arms dropped to the floor as she fell into the outstretched arms of her loving husband, Cole.

What a joyous reunion as she screamed out his name so loud that it brought Mona and little Alex running from the hen house to the doorway in a panic. Alex ran to his father's side as Cole reached down and lifted him into his arms with a tight squeeze. The three of them held onto each other for the longest time while they kissed, caressed, and hugged. There was joy and happiness that day in the little cabin in the woods. Cole McTavish felt extremely fortunate to return to the family he loved, and to the place he loved equally as much in the "Free State of Winston."

9:24 a.m.
April 1, 2020
Trussville, Alabama

ACKNOWLEDGMENTS

A special thanks to everyone at iUniverse who worked with me during the preparation and publication of *A Place Called Winston*. It has been a fun ride!

Also, I am grateful to my editor, Steve Collins, for all his work to help me correct my errors and polish the manuscript in order to present my work in its finest form. Thank you, Steve!

Just so you know, all persons and places from actual history, along with each major battle, were taken from historical notes I read about online from various Wikipedia accounts. All other characters and events were created from my own imagination. In certain places, I took liberties by adding additional events to help dramatize particular scenes that I felt necessary to the story.

As always, a very special thank you to all family, friends, and fans everywhere in the world who continue to provide me with love and support. It is greatly appreciated!

God bless the U.S.A.

Jon Howard Hall

Printed in the United States
by Baker & Taylor Publisher Services

Printed in the United States
by Baker & Taylor Publisher Services